THE CHAIN

Thom Wolf

Zipper Books

This book is dedicated
to Liam
with love

First published 2003 by Zipper Books,
part of Millivres Prowler Limited,
Unit M, Spectrum House, 32-34 Gordon House Road, London NW5 1LP
www.zipper.co.uk

A catalogue record for this book is available from the British Library

ISBN 1-873741-88-X

Distributed in the UK and Europe by Airlift Book Company,
8 The Arena, Mollison Avenue, Enfield, Middlesex EN3 7NJ
Telephone: 020 8804 0400
Distributed in North America by Consortium,
1045 Westgate Drive, St Paul, MN 55114-1065
Telephone: 1 800 283 3572
Distributed in Australia by Bulldog Books,
PO Box 300, Beaconsfield, NSW 2014

Printed and bound in Finland by WS Bookwell

One

THE COCK SHOP

Late on Monday afternoon, with four cold bottles of beer sitting nicely inside him, Dale Summer was feeling pretty good about life. He was not drunk, just relaxed and extremely happy; happier than he had been in a long time.

As he came out of the XL bar and sauntered down the street towards the promenade, he found himself humming a tune – something the DJ had been playing before he stepped out, which had now wedged itself firmly in his head. It was a massively overproduced disco-stomper and he didn't know its name. Maybe Luke would know, if he sang him the chorus. Though it was hardly important, it was the kind of teaser that would bug him for days if he didn't find out.

This early part of the evening was Dale's favourite time of day. It had rained heavily just a few hours earlier. The pavements were still damp but the sky was now clear; a pale window of blue, touched with just the lightest grain of purple. As dusk began to set across the North Sea, the view was incredible.

The rain had caught Dale unprepared and he had been forced to take shelter in the nearest bar. Fortunately, the weather had broken when he was on the right side of town and the bar he ducked into was a gay one. If he ever needed proof that Newbiggin Bay was a world away from his London home ground then he found it in XL. On a Monday afternoon the bars he knew at home could at best boast a cluster of businessmen and a smattering of tourists. In contrast, XL was two-thirds full. The weather might not be the greatest in this area of the country but it didn't seem to deter the tourists. People came to

Newbiggin Bay to have fun, and even on a pissy Monday afternoon, fun was there to be had.

A glorious-looking drag queen, calling herself Kandi Legz, towered over the bar in a DJ booth, blasting out HI-NRG anthems. It was tacky, camp and garish but no one seemed to mind; they gloried in its excess.

The men here were different to the guys he knew in London too. So they should be, he mused; on holiday, free from work, they had every right to relax. Even the local guys were having fun. What was it about northern men that Dale found so sexy? Their accents? Their laid-back attitude? Northern men seemed a lot brawnier than the guys he knew at home. Their muscle and bulk was genuine, not cultivated in a gym with pills and steroids. He knew he was oversimplifying the comparison, but his opinion of the men back home was somewhat jaded. Even the cruising here was laid-back, less persistent.

This was exactly the kind of freedom Dale needed in his life right now. After the unamicable break-up with Kelly, he wasn't looking for a boyfriend. Sex would be nice but he wasn't ready to go chasing it.

Without intending to, he spent a couple of hours in the bar. He sat alone, enjoying his beer, listening to the music and repartee from Kandi Legz. There were plenty of good-looking men around. A few showed interest in him and a couple of warm smiles were directed his way. Dale smiled back but didn't pursue it; there would be other opportunities.

As the earlier storm cleared away, the night turned warm and sticky. Dale took a leisurely walk down the street, his sleeves rolled up, his jacket flung casually over his arm. The top four buttons of his shirt were undone, showing the dark chest hair beneath. His lips relaxed into a broad smile – a pleasant side effect of the beer.

For once he didn't care about anything. He was just happy. He had good reason: he was on holiday, with the freedom to do what the hell he wanted. Like sitting in a bar for two hours, drinking beer on a Monday afternoon.

But you haven't had sex for two months, a little voice needled.

There was nothing wrong with that. And nothing wrong with him. He hadn't been in the mood much, lately. Not since Kelly left. Kelly was the best. He couldn't see the point of jumping into bed with someone new when they could only disappoint him. Still, maybe this holiday was the perfect opportunity to end his self-imposed celibacy.

Maybe I will. When I'm ready. He would know when the time was right.

He crossed the road with a vague sense that he was heading in the right direction. He wanted to get back to Luke's. It was still early. He decided to follow his senses. They would lead him home eventually.

The infectious song continued to float around his head. Up ahead and to the left, a minor side road led off from the main street. Dale stopped to read the sign; he was on The Strand. *The Strand*. That seemed to ring a bell. He remembered reading the *Gay Times* listing for Newbiggin Bay on the train last week. There was definitely mention of something on The Strand; a bar or shop, or something.

The street was lined on either side with bars and shop doorways. It was hard to tell them apart from the end of the road. Dale decided to take a look. It couldn't do any harm. Besides, if his sense of direction was correct then The Strand was on the route back to Luke's. If nothing else, this would be a short cut home.

The first bar he came across was called Allyson's. Loud Euro-dance was blasting through the open doorway. He glanced inside. A man and woman sat over by the window and a lone cashier cleaned glasses behind the counter. Other than those three, the place was deserted, and his first impression was not good. It seemed to be the very worst kind of straight bar, the type that catered for tourists and drunken stag parties. On a Monday night there were very few of either around.

He continued down the street, past a couple of clothes stores that had long since shut for the day. The next three bars didn't show much promise; they either looked very straight, very quiet or very boring. He was beginning to think he had made a mistake about The Strand. Then his eyes were drawn to a doorway on the left and he had to look twice to be sure he wasn't imagining things.

The sign above the solid red door read 'Cock Shop'.

The windows were blackened so there was no way to see inside. Dale stepped nearer, somewhat incredulously. There was a small, neatly printed sign attached to the front door. It read: 'COCK SHOP. GAY ADULTS ONLY. OPEN. PLEASE RING FOR ENTRY.' A small door bell was fitted into the side of the frame.

He laughed out loud. *What a great name!* Whoever thought of that was a genius. He surmised there were no prizes for guessing what they sold inside the Cock Shop.

Once, with Kelly, he had gone to Clone Zone on Old Compton Street, where they specialised in accessories for gay men: swimsuits, rubber, leather, videos, sex toys, books, cock rings, etc. He guessed the Cock Shop offered more of the same.

He hadn't actually bought anything in Clone Zone, though he'd been tempted by a pair of sexy white retro-style swimming shorts. He was too nervous to go to the counter. He didn't have enough cash to cover the purchase and was cautious about a sex shop showing up on his credit-card statement. He knew that was ridiculous, but still, it bugged him.

He didn't even own a dildo. He had never *used* a dildo.

In that moment Dale Summer had an epiphany. He was thirty-three years old. He had been comfortable with his sexuality since the age of twelve. He had his first serious relationship at eighteen. And not once, in the whole of his sexual life, had he ever had a dildo up his arse.

How did that happen?

He was a top by preference, but had never been afraid of a little arse-play. He wasn't one of those butch guys who found his masculinity threatened by just the thought of having something inside him. He used to let Kelly fuck him all the time.

But he had never used a dildo. It was hard to credit.

So what are you gonna do about it?

The sign said ring for entry. His index finger hovered above the doorbell and he felt a delicious thrill shoot up the back of his spine.

He hesitated. Should he really go through with this?

Of course you should. What's the big deal? Millions of guys do it.

He looked up and down the street and found it deserted. There was no one around to see him go in. He pressed the bell and heard the faint ringing inside. He waited, glancing nervously left and right. A small camera was positioned above the door. Whoever was inside must check to see who was there before letting them in. He guessed it was a security measure to keep out rowdy stag parties.

A sharp, electronic buzz sounded within and the lock clicked open. With beer-fuelled bravado, Dale pushed open the door and entered the Cock Shop.

The interior was a decent size; decent for a local sex shop anyway. It was about thirty foot long by fifteen wide. A blond guy, in his late twenties, was standing behind the counter. He glanced up from a magazine as Dale entered, and smiled.

'Hi,' the blond said. He was extremely good looking.

'Hi,' Dale replied, shutting the door behind him.

A dance song was playing loudly. Dale had heard it a few times already over the weekend. The interior of the shop looked pretty much as he expected it. Down the left-hand wall were two displays: one of erotic greetings cards and another of CDs. Camp, HI-NRG stuff sat with some current chart releases, Kylie and the like. There was a book stand in the corner, all gay titles, mostly porn, and next to that, a massive display of porn magazines. Against the wall, directly opposite the door, was a clothing section. On one tiny bit of wall hung full rubber bodysuits, jockstraps, underwear and swimming shorts, as well as whips and harnesses.

Further round from the rubber section was the counter where the blond was reading his magazine. Over the man's shoulder, Dale could see an array of cock rings and leather straps, a variety of masks and the largest assortment of amyl nitrate he had ever seen. To the left of the counter was a video unit. And finally, to the right of the door was a huge cabinet of sex toys.

There were no other customers.

Too nervous to start browsing the various dildos straight away, Dale went across to the magazine rack. There was the usual selection of British skin mags filled with pictures of cute Brit boys, tasteful and inoffensive. The Cock Shop also stocked a huge array of imported skin-mags. These were hard-core titles from central Europe, where the laws were more liberal, as well as US publications like *In Touch*, *Freshmen* and *Playguy*.

Picking up a recent issue of *Freshmen*, Dale skimmed through the photographs, captivated by a set of extremely revealing anal shots. He glanced casually over his shoulder. Behind the counter, the blond was watching him. He smiled. Dale nodded.

He was incredibly handsome. As he smiled, his eyes creased with strong laughter lines. There was something quite rugged and organic about his face. He was five foot eight or so, with a slender, sinewy frame. His hair was dark blond, cut into a short, boyish crop. His skin was tanned and there was at least two days' worth of blond shadow on his square jaw.

He was definitely hot, but not really Dale's type. Dale preferred guys who were a little younger, a little smoother.

'Is there anything I can help you with?' the blond asked. He had a Geordie accent.

Dale shook his head. 'Not just yet. I'm browsing.'

'Okay then. Have a good look round. Let me know if you see something you like.'

'Thanks, I will.'

Dale put the magazine back on the shelf. It was time to get what he really came in for. He turned and strode over to the toy section.

Christ, he didn't know what to look for. He had never seen such a vast selection of rubber cocks. Spread across five shelves, the dildo display seemed to comprise every size, shape and colour of toy imaginable. The collection began on the top shelf with a huge, three-foot-long, double-ended monster, and went all the way to the bottom where there was a selection of small, finger-sized plugs. There was every possible combination in between.

Dale stared in awe. He wasn't sure what it was he wanted. Certainly not one of the top-shelf beasts. He wasn't equipped to lose his dildo-virginity to one of those brutes. But then again, the little finger plugs would be a complete waste of time and money; he could shove his own finger up his arse if that was all he wanted. He needed something from the mid-range; just a nice dick size.

He picked up a vibrator. It was packaged in a black box with a plastic window. The blurb on the side of the pack said it was eight inches long: *A full eight inches of vibrating pleasure to make you squirm and beg for more*. It was moulded in flesh-coloured plastic and designed to look like the real thing, with a big crescent head and a string of veins running all down the shaft.

He wasn't sure. It wasn't the length that put him off, so much as the girth. This thing was huge, like his wrist. He didn't think his arsehole was ready for that kind of duty yet.

He put that vibrator back and selected another. This was more of a classic design, basic white plastic. It was about seven inches long and dramatically slimmer than the previous model. The surface was smooth, and he reasoned it would insert easily into an orifice with enough lubrication. It just wasn't very sexy. The thought of stuffing a hard piece of plastic up his arse didn't excite him. He put it back and gazed along the shelf at the remaining vibrators. None of them was suitable, none of them excited him.

On the next shelf down were the dildos. These were a more reasonable size than the creations above. They came in flesh-toned colours or black. He was drawn to an 'Uncut Gem'; an eight-inch latex cock complete with balls and a foreskin. This was more like it. He could see himself having fun with this piece. It was a little on the large side, but made out of soft, spongy latex. He also found the detailing on the balls and foreskin a big turn-on. He would bear it in mind.

His attention wandered lower, to the range of butt plugs. Some of these were so small that they were barely worth considering. But others were promising. Dale had never before understood the idea behind butt plugs. What were you supposed to do with them anyway? Did you stick it up your arse and jerk off with it inside you? Or were you supposed to leave it up there? Holding it deep while you went about your business?

His cock gave a sudden jerk, seeming to like this idea.

Suddenly, he imagined himself in all kinds of situations with a plug up his arse; doing everyday stuff, like shopping, working out, riding the tube, going on a date. He was excited by the possibilities. What a great secret it would be. He imagined sitting in a meeting with his bosses, or a client, and they wouldn't have the slightest inkling of what he had inside him.

His mind was made up. He was going to buy a butt plug.

The next problem was deciding which one.

Excluding the ones that were obviously too small or too large, he narrowed his choice to three. There was a black five-inch plug that was roughly shaped like a real cock, a flesh-coloured model of similar design and a traditional-shaped plug made from flesh-coloured latex. He picked up each model in turn and inspected it carefully. They were all wrapped in a protective sheath of plastic. After careful analysis, he opted for the traditional plug. It was five inches long, with a narrow tip that widened to a two-inch circumference at the base. If he had been completely sober, he might have thought the toy too wide, but as it was, he felt that his arsehole was more than capable of taking this thick piece.

He took the plug to the counter.

The blond closed his magazine and put it away. He wore a name badge that read Sam. He smiled again as Dale stood the plug, base down, on the counter.

'Nice choice,' Sam said.

Dale was well beyond the point of embarrassment. He returned Sam's smile. 'Yeah. I didn't expect such a huge selection. I had a hard time making up my mind.'

'Like the name says, this is the Cock Shop. I sell the usual sex shop fare but really I'm a specialist in dildos and vibrators. If I don't have what you want in stock, I can get it for you. I even have a catalogue and a website.'

'A specialist! Is there much demand for a service like that?'

'It's a struggle keeping up with the demand. Men are always looking for something new to shove up their arses.' Sam smiled again. He had a very natural, quite dynamic smile. One of his two front teeth was slightly out of line with the other and, rather than marring his features, the minor imperfection bestowed an additional layer of charisma to his friendly face. The effect of his smile was incredibly horny.

'So,' said Sam, leaning on the counter, 'do you want anything else?'

Dale's eyes were drawn to the open V of his shirt, to a nest of natural blond curls that covered his chest and extended to the hollow of his throat. Dale had a preference for smooth men, but like everything else about Sam, his hairy chest was extraordinarily sexy.

'No,' said Dale, meeting the gaze of those cool blue eyes. 'I don't think so.'

'Poppers?' Sam asked, cocking an eyebrow. 'That's a pretty thick plug you've got there.'

Dale regarded the object on the counter. Sam was right. 'All right. Yeah, that's a good idea.'

Sam cast his hand over the choice of amyl nitrate behind him. 'Rock Hard, Liquid Gold, TNT, KIX+, Pure Gold. Take your pick.'

He shrugged. 'Which is the best?'

'It's a matter of taste. TNT has a kick but personally I like Liquid Gold.'

'I'll take Liquid Gold then.'

Sam grabbed one of the small bottles wrapped in gold foil and set it on the counter beside the butt plug. 'Anything else?'

He shook his head. 'I don't think so.' There was lube in his bag back at Luke's.

Sam took Dale's money and rang in his purchase. Dale paid cash. Sam handed him his change and a receipt. He nodded at the object on the counter. 'Do you want me to wrap that for you... or would you like to try it now?'

Dale gazed into his eyes. Sam leaned forward, a crooked smile played on his lips. Dale wasn't sure he had heard correctly.

'What?'

'Why wait until you get home, when you could put it in right here? I'll be happy to assist.'

'You'd do that?'

'I said I was a specialist, didn't I?'

Dale's throat was dry. 'What if someone comes in?'

'They can't. I control the door from here. Besides, it's been a slow night. I was planning to close up.'

Dale looked at him. There was no doubting it, this guy was serious. Dale was about to tell him a bag would do fine, when the more adventurous side of his nature took over. The side that drew him into the Cock Shop in the first place was determined not to back down. Now that he was here, he might as well go all the way.

'All right,' he said, sounding more confident than he felt. 'Where? Just here?'

'Here will be fine,' Sam said. 'Take down your pants.'

Dale put his jacket on the counter. His fingers trembled when he unfastened the buckle of his belt, not through fear but through excitement. He undid his jeans and shoved them down to the knees. His cock was rigid, showing clearly through his white briefs, leaning along the left hip. He hesitated, just a second, before pushing down the briefs. His dick lengthened, jutting at a right angle. He looked at Sam.

Sam's eyes travelled back and forth between Dale's face and his cock. The smile continued to hover on his lips. 'Big fella,' he said, before picking up the plug. He tore off the wrapper and tossed it in the bin and then retrieved a bottle of lubricant from beneath the counter. It was a large bottle with a pump lid.

'Bend over,' he told him.

Dale breathed deeply, the sound loud in his ears. He bent forward, resting his elbows on the glass counter. Sam came around behind him with the butt plug and the lube. He squatted on the floor.

'You have a nice arse,' he said. 'Stick it out a little further.'

Dale's cock throbbed. He pressed his hips back and widened his thighs. This was so out of character for him. He couldn't believe he was baring his anus to a perfect stranger.

'Is that okay? I can't get my legs any wider.'

'It's perfect,' Sam said. 'I'm just gonna lube your hole.'

He put a hand on the cheek of Dale's arse and spread his buttocks. Dale felt the cool conditioned air on his exposed crack and then the warmth of Sam's breath as he moved in closer. He felt a finger, slick with lube, press against his ring. Sam circled the hole slowly, teasing the ring to relax the muscle, then he pressed firmly inside. Dale groaned. Sam pushed in further, shoving the lube into his passage.

'What are you into, then?' Sam asked. 'You like getting fucked?'

Dale steadied himself, dipped his knees a fraction. Sam's finger felt good. 'I prefer to do the fucking.'

'Really?' He sounded surprised. 'So what's this all about?'

'I've never owned a dildo before.' His arsehole was really loosening up. 'I thought it was about time I did.'

'It's as good a reason as any, I suppose.' He withdrew his finger slowly. 'Okay. Are you ready for this, baby?'

'Just a minute.' Dale reached for the poppers and broke the foil seal. He unscrewed the lid and held the bottle beneath his nose.

'Okay,' he said, 'do it.'

As he felt the tip of the plug slip past the lips of his arse, he inhaled the chemical fumes. The effect was instant. There was a sudden rush to his head and his tight arsehole relaxed further. Sam pressed the toy deeper into him. His hole widened around the thick circumference and suddenly he had it all inside him. His sphincter tightened around the squat base and held it firmly.

He had never felt so full. He screwed the top back on the bottle and breathed normally, allowing his body to adjust to the intrusion. He slowly straightened, getting a feel for his new-found attachment. His cock was harder than ever.

Sam's hand still rested on Dale's arse. 'How does that feel?'

He laughed. 'It's awesome. I can't believe how horny this is.'

'Yes,' Sam said, rising to his feet. 'You're horny, all right. Would you like to do something about it?'

'Definitely.' Sam might not be his usual type, but Dale felt freer and more liberal than he could ever remember. Sam was gorgeous. For Dale's first fuck in two months, he could do a lot worse.

'It's not what you think.'

Dale stroked his cock slowly, showing off its ample length. 'What do you mean?'

'I get the impression that you came in here looking for more than just a dildo. You're looking for adventure, aren't you?'

Dale squeezed his butt around the plug. His arse felt like warm liquid. 'I want to shoot my load,' he gasped helplessly.

'I know you do.' Sam slipped his hands around Dale's waist and brushed up against him, trapping Dale's cock between their bodies. 'But I can take you on an adventure that you'll never forget. It will blow your mind. Are you interested?'

Dale was crazed with ecstasy, way beyond the point of reason or choice. He ground his leaking cock against Sam's hips. 'I'm interested,' he said. 'Take me with you.'

Two

THE CHAIN

Dale's rectum began adjusting to the presence of the plug. His orifice had stopped trying to reject the blunt object and the initial discomfort caused by its insertion had evaporated quickly. He couldn't decide whether he enjoyed having the great chunk of rubber inside him or not, but it was definitely doing *something*. He couldn't ever remember being so aware of his hole, perceiving its being with every move he made. It tingled and quivered.

When Sam finished kissing him, Dale pulled up his pants. He had to clench his hole to keep the plug from shooting out. He pocketed the amyl nitrate and waited for Sam to cash up the shop's takings. Sam locked the money in a safe somewhere out the back, returning to the front with a lightweight jacket hanging over his arm. He began switching off the cabinet and counter lights.

Sam smiled. Dale was definitely attracted to him. So what if he wasn't the kind of man he usually went for? He was little older, a bit more rugged; what did that matter? There was no denying a chemistry existed between them. Dale reasoned that a change could do him good after a rush of younger men.

'When are you going to say where you're taking me?' Dale asked.

Sam grinned, heading for the door. 'I thought you wanted an adventure.'

'I do.'

'So don't spoil it for yourself. Come with me.'

Dale followed him slowly, careful of every step. Trying to walk with an arse full of rubber would take some getting used to. Sam waited, holding the door, and he walked outside. It wasn't quite dark yet but the sky was a deeper shade of blue than when he'd entered the Cock Shop and the streets lights had come on.

Sam activated the alarm and locked the door, pulled a set of metal shutters over the front door and windows, and fastened them with sturdy bolts. The street was deserted in both directions.

'It's quiet around here,' Dale remarked.

'It is. Monday is the slackest night of the week. You're lucky to have found me open. I usually close early.'

Sam stuffed the keys into an inner pocket of his jacket and extracted a pack of cigarettes. He offered one to Dale.

'No thanks. I don't smoke.'

Sam stuck a cigarette between his lips and lit it. 'Good for you. As for me, I couldn't get through the day without them. My name is Sam, by the way, if you hadn't already realised that from my badge.'

'Dale Summer.' They shook hands.

'What are you doing in Newbiggin Bay? Holiday?' Sam struck off down the road at a steady pace before realising Dale's awkward gait. He slowed down.

'Yes, on holiday, visiting friends. I live in London, Blackheath. I haven't had a proper break in eight years. I thought it was time.'

'Eight years,' he drawled. 'What do you do?'

'I'm a lawyer.' He laughed. 'You probably don't get many of us in the Cock Shop.'

'I dare say I do. Nothing surprises you when you work in a place like that. I have a broad range of customers, many of them are professionals. But they just don't share it with me. Usually I mind my own business, anyway.'

'I thought you were giving me special treatment,' he teased. 'Don't tell me you do the arse plug thing for all your customers.'

'Ha. No, not all of them, just a special few.'

They reached the end of the narrow alley where it opened out onto the main road. Dale followed Sam down the street and around a corner to an open car park. At that time of evening it was relatively quiet, with just a dozen or so vehicles parked there. Sam led the way towards a silver Nissan Almera.

'She's not the flashiest of cars but she does her job.'

'It's better than mine,' Dale said.

'What do you drive?'

'I don't.'

Sam unlocked the doors and they climbed in.

A spasm of pleasure-pain shot through Dale's body when he sat down. The seat pushed the plug deeper into his anal cavity. He drew a sharp breath. The pain didn't last more than a second and was replaced by a disconcerting, strangely uncomfortable pleasure. He squirmed, getting used to the new sensation.

Sam opened the window and tossed his cigarette butt away. When he put his key in the ignition and turned it, the CD player throbbed to life along with the engine. The frame of the car vibrated with a hard-bass dance track. Sam adjusted the volume, turning it down.

Northern guys really seemed to love dance music, though this was in a different vein to the stuff Dale was used to hearing here. It had a deeper, darker sound with a mad over-the-top rhythm. The singer was female, her voice enigmatic and hard, soaring to a point of dementia above the frantic chords. There was an almost frightening poetry to the lyrics. It didn't sound like a new song but it was quite unlike anything he had heard before.

He fastened his seat belt as Sam put the vehicle in gear and shot across the car park and through the exit. Dale was unfamiliar with the roads, and though he knew they were heading out of town, he had no idea where they were going. There was virtually no other traffic on the road.

Sam shot him a sideways glance.

'Don't look so nervous,' he said.

'Wouldn't you be?' Dale said. 'I don't know anything about you and I'm in your car, driving into the night to God only knows where. This is insane. I would never do anything like this in London.' But there was something genuine about Sam. A gut instinct told Dale he could trust him. He wanted an adventure and this was it.

'Don't worry. I'm not some nutcase. Besides, you're a big enough fella, you could knock me out any time you wanted to. There'd be no contest.' His left hand drifted from the steering wheel into Dale's lap. 'Is your cock hard?'

It was. When Sam's hand moved higher, closing over the bulge in Dale's jeans, it throbbed even harder. Dale raised his hips, working the plug in his arse at the same time as pushing his cock into Sam's hand. Sam squeezed and kneaded the bulge.

Dale groaned. 'Oh God. I wanna come so badly.'

Sam returned his hand to the wheel. 'Just hold onto it. Not far now. You'll soon be shooting gallons. I can promise you that.'

Dale closed his eyes, breathing slowly in and out through his nose. He controlled his breath, calming himself, soothing his hunger. He concentrated on the music. The track seemed to seep through his pores, into his soul. It managed to reach a far deeper level of consciousness than the catchy disco tunes he'd been listening to earlier. This song was filled with sadness, desperation and raw sexuality.

They were driving along a dark coastal road, winding further and further from town. Dale glanced between the black sea on his left and Sam at the wheel.

Sam turned, sensing his apprehension. 'It's okay,' he said softly. 'We're nearly there.'

The plug in Dale's rectum pressed directly against his prostate, causing his cock to leak a heavy flow of precome. His briefs were moist, the crotch area wet with seminal fluid, the rear damp and sticky with lube. He shifted his weight, readjusting himself, giving his cock the room it needed. He repositioned the large shaft along his pelvis, with the damp head resting on the top of his thigh.

Sam turned into a side road which was little more than a dirt track. The headlights picked out a group of low buildings ahead. No lights shone from any of the windows but Dale could see at least a dozen cars parked in front of the nearest structure.

'What is this?' he asked. 'A farm?'

'It used to be,' Sam answered. 'It's not used for that anymore. The buildings are privately owned, currently in a process of conversion. Some of them are already in use, as you're about to find out.'

He pulled over at the side of the road, parking behind a massive red station wagon. As he turned off the engine, killing the music, the silence was uncanny.

Dale eased himself out of the car, still not used to the intrusion in his rectum. It was dark. He discerned little more than a shadow as Sam came towards him.

'Follow me,' he said. 'I'll take you in.'

Dale followed his broad silhouette past the other parked cars and around the side of the nearest building. They stuck to a broken track close to the wall. Dale was nervous and filled with doubt. If anything happened to him out here, he knew he might never be found. None of his friends knew where he was. They would never trace him to the Cock Shop.

Halfway around the building, Sam stopped and Dale collided with his back. It took a moment for his eyes to adjust and see that they were standing in front of a door. His heart seemed to stop as abruptly as his feet.

This was it. Last chance to turn around and get the hell out of whatever situation he was about to get into. But he couldn't do that; despite the fear and trepidation, he could not remember the last time he had been so excited. It had taken courage and trust to bring him this far. He trusted Sam to take him all the way.

The blond man knocked slowly on the door, four times. And then again, twice – fast. Dale held his breath. His arsehole tightened around the plug. His sphincter almost loosened its grip when he heard a bolt draw back on the other side. He held on tight.

The door slowly opened to a gap little more than six inches wide. He could not see the figure behind.

'Yeah?' The voice was deep and mature.

'Edward de Souza,' Sam said clearly.

The door opened wider.

'It's Sam. I brought someone with me.'

The man beyond the door seemed to consider this a moment.

'Has he been before?' he asked eventually.

'No, it's his first time,' Sam said. 'But he'll be okay. I'll vouch for him, let us in.'

Dale waited, expecting the man to slam the door in Sam's face. Another moment and it slowly opened wide. Sam stepped inside. Nervously, Dale followed.

The door closed behind him and the lock was slammed home.

They were standing in a small hallway, in what was obviously a barn conversion. The floor was concrete and uncovered, the red brick walls raw and exposed. A naked bulb hung from a low ceiling beam, casting a stark light.

The doorman reminded him of a Tom of Finland drawing. He was huge, naked from the waist up, with a massive barrel of a chest. A gold sleeper dangled from his left nipple. With broad shoulders and thick arms, he was covered in wide peaks of impossible muscle. His head was almost too small for an enormous neck. He had a steely grey crew cut and neatly clipped tache. His eyes were shadowed by a thick, overhanging brow. The harsh light added some severity to the furrows of a scowl.

It was hard to put an age on him. He could have been anything from thirty-five to sixty. His chest and stomach were covered in a pelt of dark brown hair, peppered with grey. The trail of hair descended over the ridges of his gut and dipped below the belt into his denims. He was wearing black leather chaps over an ancient pair of Levis. His feet were encased in heavy-duty work boots and his hands were covered in black leather gloves.

Dale was tall at six foot one. This guy towered over him by at least another five inches.

Sam introduced him. The doorman was called Big Harry. Dale couldn't conceive of a more appropriate title.

'What are you?' Big Harry growled.

'What am I?'

'A man or a cunt? Top or bottom?'

'Er… top.'

Big Harry's lips curled back in a wicked sneer. 'Of course you are.' He turned to Sam. 'You gonna chaperone him?'

Sam nodded. 'All guests must be chaperoned by a member,' he explained. 'As I'm introducing you to The Chain, then you're my responsibility. If you cause any bother, then my membership will be revoked. So make sure you behave.'

'Strip,' Big Harry barked.

'What?'

'You can't go in dressed like that,' Sam told him. 'You don't have to get naked, not yet. Just down to your jeans or your shorts for now.'

Big Harry indicated a wooden stall behind him. 'Leave your stuff in there. It'll be safe enough.'

Dale followed Sam behind the wooden screen. Sam pulled off his jacket and shirt and hung them on a peg along the far wall. Dale's eyes were drawn to his bare torso. He was lithe and lean. His chest and stomach were covered in a layer of dusty blond hair. The muscle beneath was impressive, firm but not overly developed.

Dale had come too far now to be modest about his body. He hung up his jacket and removed his shirt. He had no reason to be shy of his own physique. He was lean and sinewy. There was a smattering of black hair between his pecs and a little around his navel, but other than that he was smooth.

'Are you gonna go further?' Sam asked, pointing at his jeans.

'Not yet. I don't know what I'm letting myself in for. I'm in the middle of nowhere, with a plug up my arse, taking off my clothes in a barn.'

'You can leave whenever you want. Stay close to me and you'll be fine.'

'What is this place?'

'It's called The Chain,' he said, as though that explained everything.

They went back into the entrance. Big Harry waved them towards another door. Dale followed, close to Sam; he didn't want to lose him. Sam opened the creaky door and they stepped inside.

The old barn was about a hundred feet square. Although there were four strips of fluorescent tubing across the ceiling, the place was relatively gloomy. Bales of hay had been stacked up around three walls and covered in blankets, to form the basis of a makeshift auditorium. In the centre of that auditorium, an orgy was taking place. Dale counted twenty bodies, there could have been more.

Off to the side of the floor stood a small, circular cage. Inside it was a boy. He looked to be around twenty-two. He was dark with a stocky build and completely naked. Four men were gathered around the cage. They were all big and brawny, more Tom of Finland types. Two of them were naked, the others were dressed in leather. They stuck their cocks through the bars of the cage and the puppy boy took them in turn, working his way around the circle to suck each shank of meat.

A handful of guys were sprawled on top of the hay, beating their dicks. A couple waved at Sam as he entered the arena of man-sex.

Dale noticed another boy. His head and his hands were restrained in wooden stocks. He was on his knees, his bare arse raised high in the air. Two older men took it in turn to whip him with their belts. His small buttocks were red and sore but, through gritted teeth, he thanked his abusers for each stroke.

On a bare mattress on the floor, a blond guy, naked, somewhere in his mid-twenties, was on his hands and knees. A well-built man in leather squatted behind him, ramming his dick into the blond's arse. He slammed the boy's buttocks with his hips, burying his cock fast and furiously. While he took one cock in the arse, the blond attempted to deep-throat another man, who knelt in front of him.

A skinhead, covered in tattoos, leaned over the back of a wooden chair, while another tattooed man munched on his arse.

Dale's eyes swept compulsively around the barn, drawn from one scene to the next. He was transfixed. In the whole of his life, he had not seen anything like this. He enjoyed sex and experimentation, but it had always been one on one. He hadn't participated in so much as a threesome, let alone a full-scale orgy.

Sam's hand was on his shoulder.

'What do you think? Is this the kind of thing you were looking for?'

He could not speak. His mouth was bone dry. He coughed and let out a nervous laugh. He suddenly felt foolish, way out his depth with this crowd.

'I think... I think I should go,' he managed to say at last.

Sam came closer, slipping his arm around Dale's waist and leaning against his body. 'Give it ten minutes,' he said. 'You might like it when you relax. Give it a chance.'

Dale ran his tongue over his dry lips and said, 'Okay.'

With his arm around Dale's back, Sam drew him to the circular cage. Dale wanted to pull away but as he got nearer to the cage and saw the boy inside, he was drawn to him.

The boy was older than Dale first imagined, in his mid rather than early twenties. He squatted on his haunches, gripping the bars with both hands, while his face was stuffed with cock. His jaw gaped wide and he swallowed a shaft down to the base, pressing his face into the guy's wiry pubic bush. He pulled back to the round crown and then lunged all the way down again, closing his eyes as he swallowed. The cock was big. When he pressed his face to the root, the shaft must have been lying halfway down his throat.

The boy was stocky. It was difficult to estimate his height from his prone posture but Dale guessed he was around five foot eight. His legs were covered in silky black hair which grew thickly on his calves and the back of his muscular thighs. There was also a fine dusting of hair on the cheeks of his arse. His fat cock jutted between his chunky thighs and the foreskin was retracted to reveal a shiny pink head. The underside of the shaft was sticky with precome.

He had a tattoo on his right arm, some kind of tribal band that twisted all the way around his bulky biceps. On the other shoulder he had a Celtic cross. A huge black panther decorated his back – it looked as though the cat was clawing its way up his spine. His left nipple was pierced with a steel bar that caught the light and glistened amid the dark hair on his chest.

His body was magnificent and, for the second time that night, Dale found himself attracted to the kind of man who would not normally appeal to him. Dale liked chickens: young, slim and smooth. The guy in the cage was anything but a chicken, he was mature and well developed. But he was divine.

There was something extraordinary about his looks; he was perversely handsome and yet strangely angelic. It was his face, distorted and bulging with cock, that captivated Dale the most. Although he worked his head back and forth like some cock-hungry monster, he seemed virginally pure. Dale was spellbound by the boy's innocent beauty.

His hair was as black as coal and cut into a short crop. He had a broad, noble forehead, with thick eyebrows. His eyes were shut as he gagged on more and more cockmeat. His long lashes were as dark as his hair and he had a straight nose and high, chiselled cheekbones. His jaw was stretched to its widest capacity and his lips bulged around the fat dick. There was a dark shadow on his broad chin. He didn't give a damn about anything other than the fat cock between his lips.

All Dale knew at that moment was that he wanted him.

The man spat out the cock he was currently worshipping and moved round to the next. He ran his tongue around the head of this fresh dick and then shoved it deep into his mouth.

'Who is he?' Dale asked Sam, his voice lowered.

'He calls himself Charlie,' Sam said quietly. 'Every man here has had him, and hundreds more besides. Charlie is addicted to cock. I've never met a man who can take it the way he can. He keeps coming back for more and more. You see that fella over there?'

Sam was pointing across the barn. Three guys, butch types, were lying back on a stack of hay, beating off. They were big men with matching dicks. One of them had a close cut of pale blond hair, the other two were dark.

'Which one?' he asked, trying not to stare while taking in the scene.

'The guy with the blond hair. That's Max, Charlie's lover. Or master. I don't understand the dynamic of their relationship.'

Max was too far away for Dale to get a full impression of him. He was naked except for a pair of black boots and a leather harness crossed around his bare chest. He was sprawled across a bale with his legs splayed wide. He held his huge cock in one hand and calmly slipped the foreskin back and forth across the juicy head. His other hand was between his legs, tugging at his balls, stretching the shaven sac.

'Doesn't he mind all these other men fucking his boy?'

'Fuck, no, why should he?' asked Sam quietly, careful not to be overheard. 'Besides, there's more between these two than you would think. Charlie has a wife, for a start.'

Dale glanced back to the man in the cage. He had stopped sucking. He knelt on all fours with his face pressed up close to the bars. His eyes were closed, his mouth open, expectantly. Three of the men on this side of the cage were tossing off over him.

The first shot of spunk hit him full in the face. It spattered across his nose and hung down his cheek in a long white rope. Charlie smiled but kept his eyes shut. The second blast landed across his upturned brow. The third caught him full on the lips. His tongue shot out of his mouth and lapped up the sticky white come.

The expression on his face was total ecstasy. His skin glistened in the dull light with an amalgam of sweat and come.

'You've got to be kidding.' Dale was incredulous. 'This guy has a wife?'

'Uh-huh,' Sam whispered. 'Not just a wife. A kid too. A little boy; he must be over a year old now.'

The guy in the cage, his face dripping with spunk, the spunk of three different men, was a father.

'I don't get it,' Dale whispered.

'None of us do. Charlie isn't the average married man who likes to suck a few cocks on the side. He likes it hard-core. Not S&M. Probably doesn't want the marks to show at home. He's into extreme fucking. I've seen him gangbanged by more than twenty guys for two or three hours at a time. Shit, I'm completely queer, I've never been near a pussy in my life, but even I couldn't take as much dick as this boy does. Not that I would want to,' he added.

'What's the story with Max, then?'

'I don't know the full history but Max has been with Charlie for years, from before Charlie was married. Max brings him here every couple of weeks or so, and this is what happens. Charlie sucks cock like his life depends on it, he gets fucked and then Max takes him home to his family.'

'*Jesus*.'

'I know, but who are we to judge, eh?'

'He's gorgeous,' Dale said, thinking aloud.

'Well, if you want him,' Sam said, 'you don't have long to wait.'

'What do you mean?'

'If you want him, you can have him.'

Charlie had aroused something deep within Dale. The kind of primal, all-consuming passion that had plagued his adolescent years. A sudden and incomprehensible desire for someone he could never have.

He noticed Max standing up and, along with the other two men, climbing down from the bale to approach the cage. Charlie, sensing the presence of his master, opened his eyes. He turned to face Max, giving Dale an unlimited view of his arse.

What an arse it was: smooth, firm and juicy. His pale buttocks were glazed with a layer of fine black hair. His prone position caused his cheeks to open and Dale could just make out the dark jewel in the centre of his cleft. Dale's gaze flickered between Charlie's arse and Max.

Max was handsome in a mean, almost brutal way. His short hair was nearly white. He looked to be around forty, maybe older, with a large, brawny build of well-developed muscle. His face was striking with a broad nose and strong jaw line. His eyes were like steel. There was something cruel-looking in the set of his thin lips.

His cock was a monster. It jutted out straight from his body. It was eight, maybe nine inches long. A Prince Albert piercing dangled from the piss slit. His body was perfectly smooth; chest, belly, armpits, legs – all were shaven. There was a neat thatch of pubic hair above his dick, only a shade darker than the hair on his head.

He was good looking with an incredible body and a big cock but there was something in his aura that Dale found deeply unattractive. He was dangerous, frightening. He put Dale in mind of Robert Shaw, when he played an assassin in the Bond film *From Russia with Love*. Dale avoided any kind of eye contact with the big man.

Max approached the cage and unfastened the bolt that held his young man captive. The door screeched noisily on its hinges. Max took a step back. No one uttered a word.

The silence was palpable as, with his gaze lowered to the floor, Charlie crawled out on hands and knees. He followed his master across the straw-covered concrete like an obedient puppy.

Max stopped beside a leather sling, suspended three feet from the ground. Charlie did not have to be told what to do. He stood up slowly, hitched his white arse into the sling and lay all the way back. He lifted his knees up to his chest, hooking them around the suspension chains, and spread his butt wide. His spectacular body was open and ready. Suspended. Waiting.

Max squatted in front of Charlie's dark hole. He spat a huge gob onto the wrinkled orifice and spread his saliva around the rim. He straightened and pointed at his slave's arsehole.

'There you go, boys,' he said with a sneer. 'He's all ready. You know what to do with him.'

The first guy stepped forward. He was tall and athletic, in his early thirties. He was already wearing a lubed rubber on his cock. He grabbed the back of Charlie's thighs, holding him steady, and shoved straight in.

A line began to form. Four other men were already waiting.

Dale was unable to take his eyes off the boy in the sling.

'If you want to fuck him, this is your chance,' Sam said.

'What? He'll let *anyone* fuck him?'

'I already told you, he'll let *everyone* fuck him, if they want to. This happens every time. His hole is there for whoever wants to use it.'

Sam sensed Dale's trepidation. He took his elbow and led him to the sling.

'Come on,' he said. 'Let's get in line before the queue gets too big.'

There were six other men in front of them.

'You can go before me,' Sam said, pushing him forward.

Dale stood on tiptoe to gaze over the shoulders of the men ahead. He couldn't see anything of Charlie, just the back of the athletic man. His buttocks were moving fast as he delivered short, sharp jabs to Charlie's hole. Charlie moaned loudly. It was clear from the tone that his cries of ecstasy were genuine, not part of a performance.

Max stood away from the sling, stroking his pierced cock, with a look of pride on his darkly handsome face. He glanced slowly down the line of men, all eager for a piece of his lover's rectum. Dale stared straight ahead, avoiding Max's gaze. He felt the heat of the older man's eyes, scrutinising this stranger. After a moment of burning, Max's attention moved down the line.

The athletic guy had finished and the next man took his place inside Charlie.

'Fuck, yeah!' Charlie cried, as the new cock was inserted.

Dale clenched his own sphincter, tightening his grip on the plug and experiencing a fraction of what Charlie was feeling at the front of the line.

As each man emptied his balls into Charlie's arse, he stepped aside, allowing someone else to take his place. Dale and Sam drew closer and closer to the object of everyone's desire.

'Here,' Sam said, passing Dale a condom.

Dale opened his fly, tugging out his cock. The crown was soaked with a slick spread of precome. He wiped his dick, then opened the foil wrapper and stretched the sheath down over it.

The man in front of Dale withdrew his dick slowly. The shaft of his cock had started to soften and the tip of his condom drooped with a heavy load of jism.

Finally, it was Dale's turn. He stepped forward, his heart hammering in his rib cage. Out of the corner of his eye, he saw Max watching him intently. He ignored the older man and concentrated on the beautiful boy in front of him.

Up close, Charlie was indeed beautiful. He raised his head slightly and gazed at Dale through half-lidded eyes. He was dazed with sex. His face was red and dripping wet. His chest rose and fell as he sucked in great lungfuls of air.

Dale's gaze shifted lower, towards Charlie's arse. He saw nirvana – a wet, honey-brown vision of buttery man-flesh. There was a cluster of saturated black curls around the sticky orifice. The hole was loose and wet, the pink inner flesh clearly exposed.

Dale held his cock and inserted the tip slowly into the gooey ring. Charlie's resistance was well worn by the men before him and Dale's cock slipped into the warm passage with no opposition. He leaned forward, pressing all the way into the boy's body, feeling the heat of him all along his sensitive cock shaft.

He planted his hands on the back of Charlie's thighs and started to build an immediate fuck rhythm, jabbing at his sphincter. Charlie grunted with each inward thrust, his cock drooling a steady stream of clear fluid, the dark hair around his navel matted with the strongly scented juice.

'Oh yeah.' His thighs jerked spasmodically as Dale directed a long jab at his prostate.

Their eyes met and they looked deep into one another. As Dale stared into the brown liquid pools, he felt himself losing the battle for control. Charlie was humping against him, gripping the suspension chains and thrusting hard and fast.

'*Come on, fuck me harder, you bastard!*'

With each stroke, Dale felt his orgasm building. Then it began. He felt the first spasm deep inside his arse and it gradually started to spread towards his cock. The sensation, the intensity was building. He could barely breathe. He couldn't see for the sweat in his eyes. This was it. *This was it!*

He screamed, burying himself to the hilt. The pleasure flooded his balls and surged along the narrow tube of his cock. He came in an eruption. His knees trembled as he emptied himself, body and soul, into Charlie's sweet, fuck-worn arse.

Two o'clock in the morning. They did not say much on the journey home. Dale was physically and emotionally exhausted. The rubber plug was still wedged inside him.

His thoughts dwelled on the events of the night. He couldn't think of anything other than Charlie.

When Dale had finished with Charlie, Sam had taken his place. And after Sam, another man. And then another. One by one, they screwed him. Charlie's enthusiasm never faltered. When the tally reached twelve, Dale had stopped counting.

Sam drove with the window down, a cigarette clamped between his lips. The roads were quiet as he steered back towards Newbiggin Bay. Dale gave him vague directions to Luke's house and Sam said he knew where to go.

'So, was this the kind of adventure you were looking for?' Sam asked, glancing across at him.

Dale stared straight ahead at the empty road as he replied, 'I don't know. It was like nothing... Christ, I can't believe what that boy put himself through. Why would he want to do that?'

'Look, Dale, you'll be doing yourself a big favour if you forget all about Charlie. He's gorgeous. It's easy to fall for him, but don't. You can never have him, not in the way that you want. You'll never find out what makes him tick. I've known him for years and he's still a mystery. He'll come back to the lodge in a week or so and he'll do it all again with as many of the men as want him. That's the way he is. It's what he does.'

Dale sighed. He knew Sam was right. He would get over it, but for the moment he couldn't get that face, those eyes, out of his mind.

'How long are you going to be here?' Sam asked.

'I'm not sure. At least until the end of the week. I haven't planned anything definite.'

'Do you want go out with me sometime? I'd like to see you again, show you round.'

Dale searched for something to say. Sam was stunning but he just wasn't Dale's type. 'I... er, I'm not looking for a boyfriend right now. I've just come out of a pretty serious relationship. I don't want to get into another so soon.'

Was it his imagination or did he detect a twinge of disappointment in Sam's features?

'That's all right,' Sam said bravely. 'I just wondered if I could take you out sometime. Just for a laugh, nothing serious. As well as working at the Cock Shop, I DJ one night a week at a local bar. I thought you might like to come along and see me play. I do Wednesday nights at XL. How about coming down to check it out?'

Dale stifled a yawn. He was tired, his pants were soaked with come and his arse was aching to be rid of the rubber plug. He wondered how Charlie's hole was bearing up at that moment.

'So, are you coming, or what?' Sam asked.

'What?' His mind was somewhere else.

'To see me DJ on Wednesday night.'

Dale dragged his tired brain back to reality. He forced a smile for Sam's benefit. 'Sure. I'd love to.'

Three

THINKING IT OVER

The house was quiet when Dale got back. Luke and Paul were in bed. Dale wasn't surprised – it was gone half two. He eased the front door shut behind him and quietly turned the key in the lock. Rather than turn on a light, he waited for his eyes to adjust and went up the stairs in the dark. His anus was loose and he had to concentrate on holding his sphincter tight; the motion of climbing threatened to dislodge the embedded object.

He smiled for getting himself into such a situation. It was ridiculous. The last six or seven hours had been surreal.

At the top of the stairs he turned down the landing and entered the bathroom. He closed and locked the door before turning on the light, wincing at the sudden glare. Before he did anything he had to get this plug out of his hole. Taking off his jeans and soggy underpants, he placed a towel on the floor and squatted over it. He reached for the toy, holding its base, and was about to wrench it out of his hole when a sudden burst of curiosity made him stop. He wanted to see how it looked.

Luke's shaving mirror was propped up against the window. Dale reached for it, clenching his ring. Excitement and an illicit sense of fun sent a surge of blood to his cock. Though it continued to hang low, the aroused flesh lengthened and began to fill.

He held his breath, listening for any sign that Luke and Paul were not asleep. There was nothing to hear but silence. He placed the mirror on the floor, on top of the towel, and squatted over it. To begin, the reflected image was a blur. He had to move his arse, adjusting the position, before its image filled the mirror. He felt silly and excited; he hadn't seen himself from this angle since practising the same manoeuvre as a kid. Back then the view from below was dramatically different to the one he saw now.

His butt was white. A pattern of hair ran up the back of his thighs and over his perineum, growing more thickly in the cleft between his cheeks. The hair was darker in the crack, the colour reminded him of strong black coffee. Wet with sweat and lube, the swirling hair was plastered to his skin in a complex formation. There was a small mole at the top of his left leg, just below the crease of his buttock, that he had forgotten he had.

His view of his hole was obscured by the base of the object jutting out of it, which was oblong with curved edges, roughly three inches long and two inches wide. He gripped the base and eased it to one side, the motion stirring him within. He could see part of his hole now, stretched around the creamy rubber. The puckered lip was dark pink, slightly swollen. He gave the toy a gentle tug and watched the hole bulge outwards, ready to expel the plug. He let it be, enjoying the sensation for a few moments longer. He pushed it up inside himself and released his hold. The pull of gravity weighed heavily against his hole.

He groaned, forgetting for a second that he was not in his own home. It didn't matter, the sound was not loud enough to wake his friends.

He contracted the muscles of his anus, sucking the plug inside, and then allowed his rectum to relax, enjoying the dragging sensation as the toy slipped back down. He repeated this motion. Once. Twice. The feeling was divine.

He was curious to see what had become of his hole. Would it have stretched beyond recognition? Dale planted his feet wide, steadying himself with one hand on the side of the bath. He gripped the squat base and pulled gently, bearing down with his arse. His eyes were fixed on the mirror, watching his anus expel the toy. The rim stretched and widened as it gave birth to the fat, weighty object.

Coming out, it seemed bigger than it had going in. He pushed, feeling himself open wider. With a final effort it burst free. For a brief moment he saw his hole wide open, forming a perfect O shape. Almost immediately it began to contract, just like a mouth, the lips shrinking back to their original size.

He touched himself, exploring his anus and its fresh sensitivity; it was soft and hot and wet. His index finger entered the hole effortlessly, he moved around inside himself, where he was hot and squishy. He withdrew and watched, fascinated, as his arsehole pouted, hungry for more. It seemed to be alive with a separate will and identity to the rest of his body.

With his eyes fixed on the mirror, he grabbed his dick and stroked it – slowly to begin, but building speed rapidly. His come shot high, arching from his dick to splatter the floor tiles in five rapid spurts. The spasms rocked his lower body, from the depths of his arse to the tip of his cock.

Dale slouched back on his haunches and waited for the pleasure to subside.

He wiped himself with the towel and stood up. His thighs ached from sustaining the same position for too long. He ran hot water into the sink and dropped in the butt plug, cleaning it thoroughly with liquid soap. After drying his new toy, he cleaned the floor, then gathered up his clothes, the plug and the dirty towel, and carried them to his room. He returned to the bathroom to finish cleaning himself. It was too late to run a shower, so he washed as thoroughly as possible at the sink and brushed his teeth.

The guest bedroom was a good size with a large double bed and a pine wardrobe, made from reclaimed timber. Dale's suitcase sat on the floor at the bottom of the bed. Although he intended staying with his friends for at least a week, he hadn't bothered to unpack. He bundled the dirty clothes into a separate bag and stashed the sex toy at the bottom of his case, beneath his clean socks and underpants.

It was after three and he was knackered.

Dale whipped back the covers and crawled into bed. After turning out the light, he was asleep within minutes.

The alarm clock said seven. Despite sleeping for less than four hours, Dale was wide awake. His dreams still lingered clearly in his mind. He'd been dreaming about Charlie; swinging round crazily in his sling, legs raised wide, his dark hole exposed and winking. Dale fucked him in the dream. It seemed to last forever, with Charlie refusing to let Dale stop or come. The younger man gritted his teeth and goaded him to fuck faster and harder. He lay in the sling and brutalised his nipples, twisting and squeezing the swollen peaks until they stood erect. He tugged at his piercing, threading the metal back and forth through his flesh.

All through the dream, Dale heard music, the same song Sam had been playing in his car with its rabid, frenetic rhythm.

The imagery and the music lingered in his mind now he was awake. Sunlight peaked through the wooden slats of the bedroom blinds, suggesting a beautiful morning. Shrugging off his tiredness, Dale rolled out of bed and stretched. He drifted to the window and opened the blinds. It was a bright morning with just a scrap of cloud to trouble the azure sky.

Luke and Paul wouldn't be up for another half-hour. He wandered naked to the bathroom and took a difficult piss through his morning erection. He washed his face and couldn't resist the urge to check his arse in the shaving mirror once again. Squatting, he was relieved to see his hole had returned to its normal proportions, a tiny, dusty pink pucker. No permanent harm had been done by the seven-hour plug session. What a relief.

He thought about Charlie and wondered what state his hole was in this morning. Surely he was experiencing some discomfort after such a heavy drilling.

Five minutes later, dressed in a blue T-shirt and grey shorts, Dale jogged to the end of the street and took a route that would lead him to the promenade. The main roads were already filling with traffic and pedestrians; he passed a couple of joggers headed in the opposite direction and a cute young lad taking his Labrador for its morning exercise. The early air invigorated him, increasingly so as he moved nearer to the sea. It dissolved the last dregs of fatigue from his mind.

The tide was out, way down the beach. Dale jogged from the promenade to where the sand was damp and firm, and followed the line of the shore to the north. All along the front were the usual tourist shops and arcades; restaurants, fish and chip shops, theme pubs, discos, ice cream parlours. At this time of day they were closed, nothing would open for another three or four hours. Newbiggin Bay had a reputation for being tacky, which it deserved. But it was also a lot of fun and hugely entertaining; a notion the snobs and purists failed to grasp. Along with its west coast rival Blackpool, the bay was an ideal location for a few days of frivolous fun.

Dale's mind was on fun of a different kind. The kind of fun he'd had last night.

Even now he was finding it difficult to believe. If his memory wasn't so vivid, he could convince himself it had been a dream, and he had imagined it all. That he'd downed one too many beers that afternoon and in a drunken faint had fantasised the whole scenario.

The organisation of it all amazed him – that these men could have the foresight, as well as the desire, to establish such a group. How did they find each other? How did they recruit new members? Was it by invitation only? Sam said they had pretty strict rules. Were there other places like it? Other groups? Other chains?

Dale concluded that, sexually, he led a naive existence. Perhaps this was normal for a lot of people. Maybe there were other groups, links in The Chain all over the place and he was too provincial to notice.

Dale pushed on across the sand.

After the split with Kelly, he realised he was in an emotional rut. He'd been repeating the pattern for years, in all of his relationships. Dale valued romance and the notion of one true love. He just made the mistake of thinking every man he met was his true love. Kelly was his sixth serious relationship in as many years.

It was a predictable pattern. He would meet a man, usually someone several years younger than himself, always pretty, always full of life – lads in their prime. After several intense weeks of sex and courtship, he asked them to move in with him to his small, one-bedroom apartment. The length of these relationships varied; Alex stayed with him for three and a half weeks. At eighteen months, his relationship with Kelly was a record breaker. Dale gave his boyfriends everything: love, attention, compliments, money. He paid for one boy to learn to drive, and subsidised another's addiction to Dolce & Gabbana. Ultimately they always left him, often with apologies and affirmations that it was their fault, not his; he was a great guy, they didn't deserve him, they had to find themselves, needed space to grow up. The excuses varied but they meant the same thing – he was dumped. Again.

Kelly was twenty-three when they met and Dale was thirty-one. It didn't matter. Kelly was mature for his age. He was a waiter in a Covent Garden cafe; five foot seven, slender, blond, tanned. He liked Ronan Keating and watching made-for-tv movies, the kind based on true stories. He was out to his friends but not his family. Dale encouraged him to have faith in himself and supported him through a difficult confession to his old-fashioned parents. Kelly was *the one*, Dale had been sure of it.

But Kelly met a forty-two-year-old restaurateur from Soho, who gave him a trainee manager's position in his restaurant and a more physical position in his bed.

It was now just two months since Kelly had moved out. They hadn't seen each other since. He'd been spotted on the scene by a couple of Dale's friends but, because of the hours Kelly worked at the restaurant, Dale was unlikely to bump into him himself.

Dale was faithful to all of his boyfriends and, without exception, they all cheated on him. He blamed himself. He was too soft, too grateful. He had to stop. He had to break the pattern.

Last night proved there was another life out there; a world entirely different from the one he knew. Dale wanted to be part of it.

Luke and Paul were in the kitchen having breakfast when he returned to the house by the back door. His blue vest was several shades darker from his profuse sweat. 'Morning,' he gasped, putting his hands on his thighs and bending over to catch his breath. He'd overdone it on the final stretch.

Luke and Paul were ready for work, Luke in a well-cut navy suit, Paul more casual in black trousers and checked shirt. They sat at the breakfast table, set for three, eating muesli with skimmed milk. There was a carton of orange juice in the centre of the table and large pot of tea. The BBC breakfast news played on a small television, mounted on the wall.

'Morning,' the two men said concurrently. They exchanged a glance, grinning slyly.

Dale met Luke at law school in Nottingham; as the only openly gay men in their year, they bonded instantly. The friendship they formed had lasted ten years. Despite working in different fields and different parts of the country, they kept in touch, meeting up for weekends and parties two or three times a year.

Paul came on the scene when Luke moved to Newbiggin Bay. He was a probation officer, working in the County Durham area. They had been living together for five years (which restored some of Dale's faith in gay relationships). They were in their early thirties and physically very similar. Both around five foot ten, medium build. They wore their hair almost identically, short with school boy quiffs and neat sideburns. They were good looking, healthy and happy.

Dale sat down at the third place setting and helped himself to juice. His heart rate was returning to normal. He wiped his brow against the back of his arm.

While Paul occupied himself with the newspaper, Luke looked

straight at Dale. 'Well?' he said, raising an eyebrow. 'Are you going to share your joy or do we have to beat it out of you?'

Dale laughed. 'What joy?'

'What joy?' he mimicked. 'If he kept you out until two in the morning, I'm assuming that at least you got his name. Come on, tell everything. Was he a local boy or a tourist?'

Dale poured himself a cup of tea with milk and sweetener. 'You automatically conclude I was shagging around?' he said slyly.

Paul put down his paper. 'Yes.'

He smiled and sipped his tea, maintaining the suspense. 'Well,' he said, at last, 'you have a limited imagination if shagging is the best you could come up with.'

'So what were you doing?'

'Have you ever heard of a place called the Cock Shop?'

'Yes, it's on The Strand,' Luke said. 'I buy our porn there. There's this lovely blond who owns the place.'

Dale told them his story from the point of being caught in the rain through to meeting Sam at the shop and his invitation to The Chain. He took great pleasure in their stunned expressions as they listened, their jaws slackening further as the story unfolded.

'Woah, hold on a minute,' Luke said. 'You let a man you'd only just met drive you out into the middle of nowhere to an abandoned farm. Are you insane? He could have slaughtered you.'

'I realise that. Going with him is the most foolish thing I've ever done. It was madness. But after what happened in the shop, I felt I could trust him.'

''Cause only a normal, totally sane individual would offer to shove a plug up the arse of a customer. It's a wonder you're still here to tell this tale.'

'Ssh,' said Paul. 'He is here, so let him get on with it. What happened at the farm?'

Dale proceeded with the story. 'There was a password to get in. It was a name, I can't remember it now. I didn't know if it was significant or meant anything.' He described the procedure; undressing, going into the main barn, the whole scenario.

Luke nearly choked on his tea. 'You're making this up.'

'I swear I'm not,' he laughed. 'So, this isn't usual, is it?'

'Hardly.'

'I just wondered whether it was a regular thing around here, if everyone knew about this group. To tell the truth, I thought you might have been.'

'No.'

'You would know if we had.'

'There were a lot of men involved. There must be some kind of promotion for these events.'

Paul began clearing the dishes. He couldn't stop smiling. 'You've made my day. Fancy it, Luke, a sex group right here in the bay and we didn't have a clue.'

'I still think you're having us on,' Luke said.

'I swear I'm not. What more do you want me to say?'

'Why are you laughing?'

'I'm laughing at your reaction. I thought *I* was supposed to be the prudish one.'

'Obviously not.'

'I'm not finished.' He told them about Charlie and the brief history that Sam had given about him. 'You should have seen him. He was insatiable. And gorgeous isn't the word, it's not nearly enough to describe him.'

'I've never understood bisexuals,' Paul said, closing the dishwasher.

'Have you logged onto Gaydar recently?' Luke asked. 'Just about every man I've chatted to is married and looking for a bit of dick on the side. They're all at it.'

'This isn't the same. Charlie couldn't get enough of the men last night, it's like he was addicted to cock or something.'

'He wouldn't be the first.'

'I can't get my head around him. According to Sam, Charlie was into some pretty heavy stuff with Max years before he was ever married. If he was just your average gay man in denial, he wouldn't have been doing all that. Most of them start playing around with other men after the wedding, not before.'

'I wonder if he goes on the scene. We could have seen him around. We've probably had him.'

'We would remember,' Paul said. 'He doesn't sound like the usual anonymous trade.'

'I don't think he does go out. I think these gangbangs are the only scene he knows.'

Luke and Paul had to leave for work. 'Are you going out again tonight?' Luke asked.

'I'm not sure. I'll see what the rest of the day brings.'

'Have a good one then. If we don't see you before, Paul and I will be in XL or Bassey's from around eight-thirty.'

'If I'm not here when you get home, I'll meet you there.'

When his two friends left, Dale finished clearing the kitchen. He went upstairs, stripped naked and bundled up his jogging clothes with the dirty towel and clothes he'd been wearing the night before. He took them back to the kitchen and started the washing machine.

What now? he wondered.

In the bedroom, he booted up his laptop and logged onto the internet. There was a backlog of e-mails that he hadn't checked since the weekend. Scrolling through the list, he realised there was nothing there but junk, and deleted the entire contents of his in-box.

Sitting on the bed, naked, cross-legged, he logged into a search engine and typed in 'cock shop'. That there was more than one website using the title did not surprise him. Scanning through the list of options, he eventually found the URL for the site he required and clicked on the link.

Clicking past the adult content and over-18s warning, he accessed the main menu of the Cock Shop website. 'UK specialists in adult toys, leather, rubber and erotica' read the bold header. Dale was impressed.

Whether Sam designed the site on his own or licensed it out, it was a professional-looking website with a clear layout and animated graphics.

He learned that the shop had opened in Newbiggin Bay in 1998. There was a full catalogue of products, probably an even greater selection on-line than was available in the shop itself. The company promised to dispatch any items that were in stock within twenty-four hours of receiving the order. There was an e-mail link for enquires and a gift-wrapping service available.

Skimming through the catalogue was enough to get Dale's cock swelling.

On the side-bar menu, he noticed a link that read 'Customer Galleries'.

'No way,' he said, double clicking the icon and waiting for the page to load.

Just as expected, he found an exhibition of satisfied Cock Shop customers, together with their purchases. Some men had no reservations when it came to putting themselves out there. The pictures in the galleries were as explicit as they could be; arseholes stuffed with every conceivable size of dildo. Some of the guys were more into it than others, sometimes posting as many as a dozen shots of themselves, before, during and after their sessions. Some of the men had obscured their faces, either keeping them out of the frame or blurring the image, others were not so shy. Each of the pictures was about an inch square, though instructions at the top of the page said 'click any image to enlarge it'.

Dale was drawn to a photo showing an enormous black dildo. He double clicked. The image loaded. The man, whose face had been pixelated, looked to be around twenty. His chest and stomach were smooth, natural rather than shaved. The picture wasn't very well lit but he was sitting on a single bed in a nondescript room. On his lap lay the black dildo. It had to be at least sixteen inches long, if not more. It obscured his own cock and balls.

Dale clicked for the next photograph. He was lying on his back, face still pixelated, knees bent, legs open. His cock and balls were tied with a length of cord, the veins bulging. It wasn't a big cock. It didn't matter, not with the black monster he was holding near his hole. His arsehole was smooth, again it looked natural. Even in the poor light of the picture, Dale could see it was wet; lubed and prepped for action.

Next picture. The huge black head of the toy was inside him. His knees were tight in to his chest. The sight was incredible.

Dale began playing with his cock, left-handed, working the laptop with his right.

In the following shot, the man had two-thirds of the toy inside himself. Double click. Even deeper. That had to hurt. Then it was all the way in. He held the base, pressing it into himself. Dale wished he could see the expression on his face right at that moment.

The final shot was too much. It was an extreme close-up of the man's hole, looking much worse for wear; open, tired, sore. Dale could see all the way inside to his mushy interior.

'Jesus,' he grimaced, returning to the main gallery.

He scrolled through the thumbnail menu again, now looking for one in particular. He clicked into the second gallery, studying each tiny image carefully. Into the last gallery. He reached the end and sat back, disappointed. It was too much to expect Charlie to be in there. Why would he? It was too dangerous; even if he obscured his face, there would always be someone likely to recognise him by his physique, the pattern of his chest hair, his tattoos.

Dale looked down at his cock which throbbed persistently. He shut down the laptop and took himself in his right hand. That was better. He lay back, stroking himself, thinking about Charlie, remembering the desperate look in his eyes when Dale fucked him. The way he ground his teeth, hissing and groaning, demanding more; always more. Was he ever satisfied? Was Max enough for him? Was his wife?

Apparently not. None of them was.

He was a mystery. Maybe even to himself. Did Charlie know what it was that made him tick, what drove his hunger?

Dale gasped as the sensation in his dick increased. He rolled onto his stomach and shoved a pillow between his legs, thrusting his hips, burying his cock in its soft pleat. He dug his knees into the bed for leverage, grinding. The pleasure was exquisite. He stretched and twisted, murmuring in ecstasy and thinking about Charlie. He closed his eyes and pictured Charlie beneath him, kissing him, wrapping his strong hairy legs around Dale's waist and levering himself from the bed to take even more of his cock inside. Dale gave him more and more, knowing he would never be satisfied, fucking his greedy, married hole.

Dale shot off into the pillow, long and hard, biting the bedclothes as he came. He panted to the rhythm of his throbbing, squirting cock and then collapsed, the tension draining from his body along with his sperm.

He lay there, not moving, eventually dozing, still dreaming of a man called Charlie.

Four

SAM

It had been a busy afternoon. Sam was grateful for the trade but didn't take any of it for granted. He couldn't afford to. Even in peak season, at the height of the summer madness, there was no guarantee of customers. The back alley location of the Cock Shop left many tourists oblivious to its existence. There was a high number of tourists around today, which was unusual for midweek. Sam was pleased he'd had the foresight to ask Stuart to work overtime, as he could not have coped on his own.

He was tired. Last night's excursion to The Chain had taken its toll. By the time he'd dropped Dale off at his friends' place, Sam didn't get home himself until nearly three-thirty. He was ready to drop. Strange then that, despite his tiredness, he did not sleep well. He tossed restlessly back and forth as his mind refused to shut down. He lay there for ages thinking about Dale. He didn't know why. He liked him all right but it was fairly obvious Dale didn't feel the same. Apart from when Sam inserted the plug, there was no physical contact between them. Even that was something he had done so often for so many customers, it ceased to be important; however much he liked the guy he was plugging, it was just part of his job.

He stifled a yawn as he swiped a credit card through the system and waited for the print-out. He smiled at the customers, a couple of guys in their twenties down from Newcastle. It was a good sale; the latest issues of *Indulge* and *Inches*, a three-pack of stainless-steel cock rings, a HI-NRG CD, *Personal Trainers Part 2* on DVD and a set of Tristan Paris anal eggs. Stuart packed their purchases into plastic bags and shoved in a couple of free safe-sex kits.

While one half of the couple signed the credit-card slip, Sam noticed the other guy checking out Stuart. He was a popular lad, fair haired and slender, with a pierced eyebrow – the chicken hawks went gaga for him.

'Stick the kettle on,' Sam said, when the two men left the shop. 'We might as well take a break now, while there's a lull.'

The young man nodded and stalked through the door behind the counter, into the small warehouse. He was always *on*, strutting his arse and prowling even when there was no one there to watch him. If the performance was for Sam's benefit, then he was wasting his time, as Sam had no interest in chickens. Sam changed the CD that was playing, bored with Stuart's choice, replacing Justin Timberlake with the latest Almighty compilation.

Stuart returned with two coffees, handing Sam the mug with an 'I Take It Doggy-style' motif. They stood at the side of the counter, drinking. Stuart flicked through the latest edition of *Heat* magazine and commented on the fashion sense of a bunch of D-list celebrities. In his skin-tight T-shirt and candy-pink pants, Sam wondered how Stuart had the nerve to criticise the way other people dressed.

'Did you see the way those last two customers were looking at you?' Sam asked, when he couldn't stand any more. He would rather hear Stuart ramble on about himself than listen to another word about a bunch of soap-opera stars he had never heard of.

The younger man looked up from his magazine. 'Mmm,' he said, tight lipped.

'What's that mean? I thought you would approve of their attention.'

'I saw them in the club last night, they were eyeing me up then too.'

'You love all that. What went wrong?'

'Nothing,' he said. 'I can do better than those two, that's all.'

'Oh, right,' he laughed. 'I forgot you were so fussy these days. Where were you? Chaps?'

'Aye. I wasn't going to go clubbing, but everyone in the Feather

Boa said they were going and I was supposed to be sharing a taxi with my friend Mick and he wanted to go clubbing too, so I went with them in the end.'

'Did you have a good night?'

'Aye, it was all right. I met this fella from Exeter. He was staying at Xanadu.'

'Nice?'

Stuart blew on his coffee before sipping. 'He was all right. Shag-worthy. Dick like a family-sized tin of rice pudding.'

'Nicely put. How long is he staying?'

'Oh, I don't know,' he said airily. 'I didn't bother asking. That Xanadu's a right dump, you know. I couldn't believe the state of the rooms. The shower was minging.'

'Did you bother to get his name?'

Stuart shrugged, turning back to his magazine. 'I'm not very good with names. John or Robert, something like that.'

Sam drank his coffee, hoping it would revive him. He promised himself an early night. Tomorrow night would be another late one, when he performed his set in XL.

XL was only a pub. Sam played an early set, finishing at eleven. Most weeks he was so excited after the gig that he went clubbing to work off the energy he had created.

'I didn't see you last night?' Stuart said.

'Since when have I gone clubbing on a Monday night?' he asked.

'I thought you did.'

'No.'

'What did you do then? Stay home and wash your hair?'

'Watch it, slag, you'll find the end of my foot up your arse if you're not careful.'

Stuart wagged his tongue. 'You'd enjoy that more than me.'

'You're not my type.'

'You've been chasing fossils too long, Sam. I'm a peach compared to those old men you go for.'

'Your modesty knows no bounds,' he quipped. 'Get back to work. You can start by tidying the magazine stand – the back issues are all mixed up. And you can dust the dildo cabinet before you go home, you didn't do it right last time. You're supposed to empty it first.'

Stuart closed his magazine and did as he was told. Sam walked behind the counter. It was ten to six, just over an hour left. He yawned, stretching his back.

He was still thinking about Dale, wondering if he would keep his promise and check out his set tomorrow. Sam hoped he would but it was better not to expect it. There was little chance of anything occurring between them anyway. It would have happened last night if it was going to.

The thought that he might not see Dale again before he returned to London caused an unusual sensation in Sam's stomach, like a knot in his guts being slowly pulled tighter.

Dale reminded him of a man he knew years ago; one of his first loves. Martin was his boss when he was training to be a manager on a supermarket development course. Sam was twenty at the time, Martin was thirty-five, a few years old than Dale was now. There were other similarities: height, build; Martin was going thin on top and kept his dark hair cut as short as possible. Despite a high brow, Dale didn't look like he was losing his hair, but he cut it in the same short style that Martin used to. They shared the same features, a strong face full of lines and character. Martin had intense sapphire eyes, the exact same shade as Dale. Their body types were similar too. From what Sam saw last night, Dale was magnificent, with a body of long, sinewy muscle; strong like a panther. There wasn't a scrap of excess on his impressive frame. Martin was the same – or at least, he was when Sam knew him.

He had no idea what Martin would look like now. That was eight years ago. It was a defining moment in Sam's development. He'd been with other lads before but Martin was something else entirely. Martin was his first *man*. When Martin found out Sam was gay, he promised he would fuck him and, true to his word, he did it. Later that very same day. In a locked cash office, Martin bent him over a desk and screwed him hard and fast. Sam couldn't get enough of him. In the seven months they worked together, Sam made his boss come at least once every day. He used his hands, his mouth, his arse, anything to make Martin happy. Sam loved him.

But Martin loved Gary, his boyfriend of twelve years. Sam was just a pleasurable diversion at work, like a cup of coffee or a cigarette. He was convenient. When Martin transferred to another branch, he did not keep his promise to stay in touch, and Sam missed him so much that he dropped off the course – all the fun and motivation had vanished from the job.

He got over Martin eventually, but never forgot him. Sam was still hopeful they would see each other again – that Martin would wander into the shop, in town on holiday perhaps, or appear in XL one night. Sam wanted Martin to see him, just once, and realise what he'd missed. He'd be in his forties now and, if they were still together, Gary would be pushing that age too; while Sam was only twenty-eight, attractive and healthy, a man in his prime. Martin would bend over backwards to have him now.

Sam chided himself for such resentment. That was in the past, he had a present to live for. It was a pity that present didn't look like it was going to include Dale.

Sam logged onto his computer and checked the web pages. There had been three new orders since he last looked at lunch time. All of the items were in stock. He took a print-out and began to process the dispatches.

The door bell sounded.

'Can you get that?' he called to Stuart.

The younger man checked the image on the CCTV screen and released the lock. While less than ideal, the security measure was necessary due to the location of the shop. There was trouble a couple of years back when a rowdy stag party barged their way in and trashed the place. Sam was on his own at the time. He ended up in hospital with concussion and a broken rib. It could have been a lot worse.

The door opened.

Busy with paperwork, Sam didn't take any notice of the new arrival, not until a shadow fell across the counter and a familiar voice said, 'Hello Sam.'

He started, looking up, then attempted to cloak his surprise with a smile. 'Dale. Hi. I didn't think I'd see you until tomorrow.'

Dale shrugged and grinned. 'I was passing this way, back to Luke's. When I saw the shop was still open, it seemed rude not to drop by.'

He looked great, even better than Sam remembered. He was dressed casually in a short-sleeved, pale blue shirt, unbuttoned to the breast bone, with expensive-looking jeans and cream shoes. An affable, sexy smile lifted his face. He looked like he had caught a bit of sun; a faint show of freckles had surfaced on his brow and across the bridge of his nose that hadn't been there yesterday. Sam approved; the freckles added a smoky, smouldering facet to an already handsome face.

'You look great,' he said.

Dale laughed. 'Rested,' he said. 'I got up early to go running on the beach but I was back in bed by nine o'clock. I didn't move again till noon.'

Stuart watched them with brazen interest, one hand on his hip. Sam passed him the print of internet orders. 'Package these up,' he said, knowing the task would keep him occupied in the storeroom for a while. Stuart rolled his eyes, snatched the paper from Sam's hand, and headed through the door behind the counter.

'He doesn't know anything about The Chain,' Sam explained when his assistant was out of sight. 'I want to keep it that way. He'd be an obliging enough addition to the group but his big mouth would also be a disadvantage. He would broadcast its existence the length and breadth of the county.'

'How do other guys get to hear about your meetings?' Dale asked quietly.

'Private invitation.'

'How did you get involved?'

'A couple of guys invited me, not long after I opened the shop. I didn't have a clue what I was getting into. They were my best customers in the early days and I couldn't afford to offend them.' He laughed.

Dale nodded. 'I owe you a huge thanks, then. You'd only just met me and you trusted me enough to share this. Why did you do that?'

He shrugged. 'Just a feeling I had about you. Luckily my instincts were right. How's your butt? Still wearing the plug?'

Dale laughed, reddening beneath his suntan. 'No. I haven't used it at all today.'

'No?' Sam teased. 'I thought you might have come by to pick up a bigger size.'

'It's more than enough for me at the moment.' He nodded towards the cabinet and the collection of monster specimens. 'I can't imagine anyone getting one of those things inside them. The body can only take so much.'

'For you or me maybe, but for some guys it's never enough.'

Dale stared at his feet, shuffling from one to the other. 'What about that guy last night? Charlie? Is anything ever enough for him?'

'Not that I've seen.' So that was it. Dale's visit to the shop had nothing to do with seeing Sam again, it was just a ruse to learn more about Charlie. Sam concealed his disappointment. 'That was an average session for Charlie. I've seen him take much more than that.'

Dale crossed his arms and frowned. 'Why?'

'You'd need a psychologist to answer that one. I have no idea what makes that boy tick.'

'Is it Max? Does he force him into it?'

'Sometimes, but it's part of their game. Charlie does exactly what he wants to. Don't ask me why. I've never understood him.'

It was clear that Dale wanted to know more.

'I'll tell you what I know,' Sam resolved with a sigh. 'For a start, Charlie's not his real name. He's actually called Adrian Foster. I didn't have much to do with him when we were at school, he's a year younger than me so we didn't mix. I knew who he was, though – by the time he was fourteen he really stood out. He was a great-looking lad. He played on the football team and always had loads of girlfriends. There were rumours he got a couple of the girls pregnant; he was a horny bastard even then. I didn't see him again after leaving school, not for about three years. You could have knocked me over with a feather the night he first came out with Max. Adrian was the last lad I'd have expected to be gay.'

'You knew Max then?'

Sam made a face. 'Everyone knew Max. He's always had younger lads hanging round with him. Gullible, disposable totty. He tried to have me when I first came out, but I already knew what he was like and I kept well away. The man's a bastard. He's been locked up a couple of times for assault. There's a rumour that one of his boys left him for another master; neither of them has been seen again.'

'When was this?' Dale gasped.

'It was before my time. I don't know if I believe the story or not, but it seems to have stuck. Max is a violent man, I know that much.'

'What else?'

'Well, Adrian could only have been eighteen when he started hanging round with Max. That's when he began calling himself Charlie.'

'Why?'

'Fuck knows. Maybe Max gave him the name. I was going out a lot at the time but they weren't regulars on the scene. I used to see them about once a month, sometimes not even that. Max used to show up other nights with other lads. But Charlie only ever came with Max, never on his own or with another man. I didn't bother with either of them. I had my own friends and, to be honest, they used to scare me. When Max went to jail, Charlie disappeared from the scene entirely.

'I got to know them better when I opened this place and then later, when I joined The Chain. Charlie was a regular in here, he still is. I wouldn't say we're friends. He keeps himself to himself, emotionally at least. I got the shock of my life when I found out he was married. I don't know his wife but I think her name is Julie. Poor cow. They have a little boy, he must be nearly two now.'

'If Max is really so possessive, how did that happen?'

'I've no idea. They're an anomaly, the pair of them.'

'What do they do?' Dale asked. 'For a living?'

'I don't know about his wife but Charlie's a carpenter. He has his own business. So does Max, he's a roofer. It fits their butch image,' Sam said surreptitiously.

Dale sighed. 'Interesting men.'

'Or scary, depending on your point of view.'

'Max maybe, not Charlie.'

'You're really taken with him, aren't you?'

'I've never met anyone like him. What he did last night... it was incredible.'

'He's enthusiastic, I'll give him that.'

A faraway look had come into Dale's eyes. 'I'd love to see him again, just once before I leave. Do you think there's a chance? Where could I see him this week?'

Sam looked at him directly. 'Do you remember what I said to you last night? Don't fall in love with him. He'll never love you back and you'll only hurt yourself.'

'I'm not in love with him,' he said. 'I just fancy him. Who wouldn't want to see him again?'

Sam knew that Dale was lying but there was no point trying to dissuade him. He was under a spell. Charlie had the ability to affect men like that. Everyone he met went nuts over him. Everyone except for Sam – Charlie didn't appeal to him at all. 'All right,' he sighed, 'but I think you're making a mistake. The best thing you could do is forget all about him, but I can see you won't do that.'

'You'll help me then?' Dale said hopefully.

'Stick around,' he said, looking at his watch. 'He doesn't come by every week but Tuesday is his most regular night. Usually after six-thirty.'

Dale's face lit up. 'Really? You're expecting him tonight?'

'No, I'm not expecting him. But this is your best chance of seeing him before the end of the week. He doesn't go to the bars and there isn't another Chain meeting. He didn't come by last week so he may come in tonight.'

Dale took a deep breath and exhaled slowly. Suddenly he seemed nervous. He looked at his watch. It was six-fifteen. He glanced expectantly towards the door.

'Don't get your hopes up,' Sam warned.

'No, of course not.' He chewed his bottom lip. 'But all the same – thanks.'

Sam sighed. What a waste. He had hoped Dale would turn out better than most of the men he met. It didn't look likely. 'Are you still coming tomorrow night?' he asked cheerfully.

Dale was distracted. 'Tomorrow?'

'My set at XL,' he explained. 'You said you might check it out.'

'Oh, right. Of course. What time do you start?'

'I set up at seven but it doesn't get going until nearer eight. Any time after then will be great. It's a good night, I think you'll enjoy it.'

'I'll be there. I'm looking forward to it.'

'I usually go clubbing afterwards. You could come with me, if you feel like it.'

He nodded, not really paying attention, and wandered over to the magazine rack where he browsed absently through a couple of issues. Sam gave up and busied himself tidying the counter, secretly hoping Charlie wouldn't show. He'd decided he would give Dale another chance and ask him to come for a drink when the shop closed. Maybe over a few beers he could persuade him of his own virtues, rather than those of an amoral carpenter.

Charlie arrived at twenty-five minutes to seven. Sam's heart sank when he saw movement on the CCTV screen. Charlie stood in the doorway for a moment before pressing the buzzer. Dale started at the sound.

'Is that him?' he asked.

Sam nodded, releasing the lock.

'Hi,' he said, smiling at the competition as he entered.

'All right?' Charlie nodded, not smiling. He looked like he had come straight from work; wearing a black vest and baggy cargo pants. He closed the door and turned to look at the sex toys. If he noticed Dale, who was feigning interest in the magazines, he didn't acknowledge him. 'Anything new?'

Sam came out from behind the counter and crossed to the cabinet. He pointed out the latest arrivals: a nine-inch, multi-speed vibrator, a small flesh-coloured dildo and a selection of butt plugs in various sizes. 'Got anything in mind?' he asked.

Charlie looked over the contents of the cabinet, giving each item serious consideration. He seemed taken with a substantial butt plug, moulded from black rubber and one size up from the version Dale had bought yesterday. He picked it up and turned it over in his work-worn hands. 'How much is this one?'

'Twenty-eight,' said Sam.

Charlie gave a slight nod. 'I'll have it. Got any new films?'

'Not since you were last in,' Sam said, taking the toy to the counter. Charlie was fond of the more explicit tapes produced by American studios like Falcon International; the kind of movie that showed big men having extreme sex. He was especially keen on films that included heavy arse work, dildo and fisting action. 'There are a bunch of new titles due at the end of the month. I'll let you know when they arrive.'

He nodded again, reached into the pocket of his pants, pulled out a roll of notes and peeled off three tens. He glanced towards Dale, lowered his voice and said to Sam, 'Are you going to give me the usual service?'

'I can, if you like,' he answered. 'Or maybe you'd like a fresh approach.'

A thick black eyebrow lifted. 'What did you have in mind?'

He hailed Dale over. Dale put down the magazine he was looking at and approached the counter. 'Dale was at The Chain last night as my guest.' He formally introduced them.

Charlie studied Dale as they shook hands, deliberating. 'I remember now,' he said indifferently. 'Fifth or sixth in the line, weren't you?'

'Something like that,' Dale said, remaining cool. Sam was impressed. With an ego like Charlie's, seeming too interested wouldn't do. Dale was playing it just right.

Sam opened a drawer beneath the counter and produced a small Yale key which he handed to Charlie. 'You know the way,' he said. 'You've got half an hour before I go home. Make the most of it.'

Charlie nodded but didn't manage a smile. He picked up his plug and motioned Dale to follow him. Sam watched them disappear through the door into the back of the shop and experienced a sudden pang of jealousy. He hoped Charlie appreciated what he was about to receive.

Dale followed Charlie through a small warehouse. Cardboard boxes were stacked high on either side and they had to walk sideways as the route narrowed in several places. Sam's young assistant was sealing up a small parcel as they squeezed by. If he was surprised to see two men wandering through this private area, he didn't show it. Charlie led Dale to a tight stairway. The steps were rickety and narrow. The old boards juddered beneath Charlie's work boots as he went up to the first floor.

Dale followed, admiring the hard contour of Charlie's buttocks through his baggy pants. He couldn't believe his luck. It seemed like he had thought of nothing else all day. After his wank that morning, he fell asleep and dreamed about Charlie again. Incited by a fear that he might never see this magnificent man again, Dale had returned to the shop. He'd hoped Sam might be able to direct him to finding Charlie, but had not expected it to be this easy.

At the top of the stairs, Charlie paused to switch on a light. The naked bulb illuminated a tiny landing with three doors leading off from it. The plaster walls were bare and the wooden doors were scarred and cracked. The place smelled of dust and damp.

'What is this?' Dale asked.

'Just storage. Sam lets us use it as a fitting room if he has enough space.'

Inside, another naked bulb illuminated a sparse room. There was no furniture, just a dozen assorted crates and a seedy mattress on the floor. The boards were bare and there was no plaster on the walls, just red brick. The window was shuttered so the only light came from the single low-watt bulb.

Dale waited by the door; his big cock was hard and pressing in his briefs. Charlie opened one of the smaller crates and pulled out a frayed bundle. He unrolled a scruffy towel, revealing a large bottle of liquid lube with a pump-action lid.

Is this it? Dale wondered. No small talk or chat, just straight down to action without nicety or finesse.

Charlie turned to look at him, leaning against one of the larger crates. Dale took a deep breath, returning the look, taking in the beauty of his face and body. There was serious intent in Charlie's expression. He brushed his fingers across his stomach, slowly circling lower, moving towards his groin.

Dale caught the butt plug as Charlie threw it to him.

'Have you ever used one of these before?' Charlie asked.

'Not before last night.'

'Doesn't matter,' he shrugged. 'You'll learn. Take off the wrapper.'

Dale tore the clear plastic seal and ripped open the wrapper. It was huge, three or four inches wide at its thickest point. 'Can you take all of this?'

Unbuckling his belt, Charlie said, 'We're about to find out.'

He shoved his trousers down and pulled them off over the top of his work boots. He was wearing a white jockstrap. Turning to give Dale an unrestricted view of his meaty buttocks, he lifted a leg and climbed up on to the top of the crate. Squatting, he looked back over his shoulder and beckoned Dale towards him.

The posture gave a Dale a nice view of his rear, the shape of his arse and a brief hint of anus, framed within the white straps. He ran his hand under Charlie's thigh, following the curve to his arse. He moved into the crack and gently massaged the hole with two fingers, feeling its heat. Charlie made a noise deep in his throat.

'Is it sore?' Dale asked, fondling the hot orifice. 'After last night? You took some serious abuse.'

'God, no.' Charlie moaned. 'Last night was nothing.' He rolled down onto knees and elbows, sticking up his arse, exposing his hole. 'See any damage?'

He didn't. Charlie's arsehole was a beautifully puckered jewel, the colour of dark honey. Dale put his hands on those buttocks and lowered his head into the crack. His nuzzled the crevice with his nose and mouth, inhaling its savoury aroma. He flicked his tongue across his lips, tasting hot, puckered flesh. Charlie groaned. Dale's initial hesitance vanished and he glutted himself on Charlie's hole.

Charlie thrust back, grinding his arse into Dale's face. 'Oh God,' he growled when Dale forced his tongue into the tight hole. Charlie lowered his head onto his forearms and wriggled his body backwards, giving himself entirely. 'That feels incredible.'

'You taste incredible,' Dale told him.

When Charlie's hole was dripping, Dale forced a finger into the opening. Charlie went nuts, arching his back, squirming his butt. Dale worked another finger into his sphincter and fucked him with a slow twisting action. His hole clenched, sucking Dale's fingers like a mouth.

'The plug,' Charlie grunted. 'Grease me up and stick that fucker in there.'

Dale removed his fingers from Charlie's tense hole and picked up the black toy and the bottle of lubricant. While he pumped a good squirt of lube into his palm, Charlie changed position, rolling over onto his back and pulling his knees into his chest. His arsehole pouted and opened slightly. He watched Dale expectantly.

Dale coated the entire surface of the plug in lube and then worked another squirt of juice around Charlie's hole. He shoved his fingers back inside, greasing his passage. The hole grasped his fingers.

Charlie pulled his knees up tight when Dale placed the plug into his crack and pressed the tip to his sphincter. Dale pushed gently, watching the conical tip sink into a delectable ring of flesh; half an inch, an inch.

Charlie's brow furrowed. 'Give it to me. Give me all of it. *Push!*'

He shoved further, watching the hole unfold to accommodate the object. Charlie tugged the pouch of his jock aside and started pumping his cock. He was panting. His arsehole resisted. Dale applied more pressure. He looked at Charlie's face, afraid of hurting him. His eyes were shut, his face set in concentration. Dale pushed the plug the final distance, sinking it deep into Charlie's arse.

As his hole embraced the weighty toy, Charlie's brow knitted, his abdominal muscles contracted and he splattered his black vest with a brilliant white jet of sperm.

Five

THE COCK ADDICT

With the release of orgasm came a release of tension: Charlie's face relaxed and the strain ebbed from his body. With the plug still in his rectum, Charlie's head dropped back and he lowered his legs over the side of the crate. He still held his dick in a tight grip. The organ was dark red, thronged with protuberant veins. His semen began to cool and lose its brilliant white colour, becoming translucent. Its impressive range extended from his navel all the way to his left shoulder. His chest expanded as he filled his lungs to capacity.

Dale leaned against the edge of the crate and stroked Charlie's inner thigh. Charlie twitched as Dale's fingers brushed across the sensitive flesh high on his leg.

'It tickles,' he gasped, pushing up onto his elbows. His face was red, a deep blush that also covered his neck and shoulders. 'Thanks, man. What's your name again? Dale, was it?'

'Dale Summer,' he said.

'Charlie,' he replied. Their eyes met and held. Charlie's lips parted, it seemed that he was about to speak, and then, as though thinking better of it, he closed his mouth and shuffled forward to the edge of the crate. He reached for the frayed, washed-out towel and began to wipe himself down. Dale watched quietly as he towelled his cock, meticulously cleaning the underside and around the head. He wiped spunk out of his pubes and turned the towel over to wipe down his vest. Although dry, the stains were still discernible afterwards.

'This stuff gets everywhere,' he said. As he smiled, his mouth was bracketed with dimples, giving his face a look of innocence.

Charlie turned and kissed Dale full on the mouth, catching him off guard. The kiss was brief and Charlie pulled away before Dale could return it.

'Want me to do you?' he asked softly. 'We've got another ten minutes before Sam wants us out. I can blow you if you like.' He came forward, his cock still erect, poking sideways from his jockstrap. He reached for Dale's fly.

Dale caught his wrists, keeping him from going further. 'You don't have to do that.'

Charlie looked at his face. He was confused. 'But you didn't come.'

'It doesn't matter,' he said. Before Charlie could answer, he pulled him closer and kissed him again. Charlie responded, opening his mouth, tilting his head to the right until they fitted perfectly. When they broke apart, they both smiled.

Charlie retrieved his cargo pants from the dusty floor and stepped into them. His buttocks splayed when he bent to pull up his pants and the base of the plug could be seen clearly.

'How long will you keep it in for?' Dale asked.

'Just until I get home.' He returned the bottle of lube to its home inside a packing crate and dumped the dirty towel on the floor. 'Shall we go then? Sam will want to lock up soon.'

They headed for the door. All Dale had wanted before this encounter was the chance to see Charlie again. He'd convinced himself that once would be enough, bringing closure to unfinished business. He was wrong. Incredibly naive. How could an expeditious tryst in a damp storeroom be enough? It couldn't end like this.

'Do you want to grab a beer?' he asked. They were on the landing, about to go downstairs.

'Now?'

'I'm in town until Friday, then I'm going away for the weekend with some friends. I may be back for a few days next week, but then I have to go home. Whenever you are free.' He was slightly short of breath and the blood was coming to his face. He hoped he didn't sound desperate.

Charlie seemed surprised by the offer. He paused halfway down the stairs, giving it some thought. 'Why do you want to have a drink with me?'

'Why not? Does it always have to be so anonymous? I'll be gone in a few days, I'm not trying to intrude on your life. I'd just like to spend some social time.'

'You've been inside me. How much more sociable could we get?'

'One drink. Half an hour.'

He waited for the reply, certain of rejection.

'All right,' Charlie said. 'I'll have a beer with you. But I'm not going to any of those scene bars, I can't be bothered with those bitches. I don't know what would please them more, seeing me dressed like this or seeing me with you.'

'That's okay,' he said with relief. 'You choose where we go.'

Sam was counting the day's takings when they returned to the shop. His assistant had gone. Most of the lights were out. Charlie handed him the key.

'Thanks,' he said.

'Everything all right up there?'

'Yes,' he answered. 'I left the dirty towel out.'

'I'll get it tomorrow.' He looked at Dale. 'Okay?'

He nodded. 'Thanks Sam. I'll see you tomorrow night. I owe you a drink.'

'Actually, I'm pretty thirsty now. Feel like joining me in XL for an hour?'

'Oh,' he said, feeling awkward. 'I'd like to but I've agreed to have a drink with Charlie. We were going to avoid the scene.'

Sam looked from one to the other. Dale felt himself shrink under the withering stare. 'Oh well,' Sam said acridly, 'I'll see you tomorrow then.'

'Definitely,' Dale said, overly cheerful. 'Eight o'clock. I'll be there.'

They left the shop and turned left. A warm, sun-filled afternoon had given way to a pleasant evening, more akin to the coast of the

Mediterranean than the North Sea. In short-sleeved shirt and vest respectively, Dale and Charlie were ideally dressed for the uncharacteristic heat.

'Sam didn't look too happy,' Charlie remarked.

'He'll be okay. We didn't have anything planned for tonight.'

'He's soft on you, can't you tell?'

'I don't want to encourage him.'

Charlie looked at him. 'I think you'd be good together. You're exactly the type Sam goes for, and he's not exactly ugly, is he?'

'No, he's extremely attractive, but I'm single for the first time in ages and I'm not looking for a boyfriend.'

'Is that what you think Sam is after?'

'I don't know. It's just a feeling.'

'You're probably right,' Charlie said. 'You're single again? Were you married?'

'No,' he said quickly. 'I'm not bisexual. I'm gay.'

They went to a pub called The Castle with a large beer garden overlooking the promenade. Charlie managed to find a table outside while Dale went to the bar. He bought a bottle of beer for himself and a pint of ale for Charlie. Charlie was sitting facing the sea, arms folded on the table, when Dale returned with the drinks. Music was pumping out onto the terrace through the wide open windows.

'Cheers,' they both said.

Condensation dribbled down the side of Charlie's pint glass. He drank with his left hand, showing a plain gold wedding band on the fourth finger. He took a long draught, clearing the rim of foam, and his tongue flicked across his lips afterwards.

'I see you have a wedding ring,' Dale said, deciding he would play dumb. 'Do you have a wife or boyfriend?'

Charlie looked down at the ring and turned it slowly around his finger. 'Didn't Sam tell you?'

'He didn't say anything.'

His brow lifted. 'Really?'

'Nothing,' he lied, wishing he had chosen a different tactic.

Charlie looked into his glass and spoke quietly. 'Yes, I'm married. I have a son who is nineteen months old. The reason I don't like all those scene bitches is because they just don't get me. I don't fit their bill. I don't go cottaging like the other married men. I don't cruise for sex on the net. I didn't get married until years after they all knew me.'

'Does your wife know you go for other men?'

'I'm not going to tell you about my wife,' he said firmly. 'You don't need to know. The only reason I tell guys up front is so they don't get the wrong idea. You said you were enjoying being single and didn't want to get involved with anyone right now. Well, I enjoy being married. It's part of my life. The sex part is something else. Do you understand?'

'Not entirely.'

Charlie smiled. 'Don't worry. You're not alone. Just don't try to make me see the error of my ways. You wouldn't believe some of the crap I've heard these last few years. Every little queen to climb out of the closet seems to view themselves as a graduate of psychology and human behaviour.'

He took another drink and swallowed; a look of bitterness had crept across his face. Dale didn't respond immediately. He waited, digesting Charlie's story.

'I don't judge people on what I don't know. I make my own decisions about what men and women do,' he said at last. Then he added, 'I'm a lawyer,' hoping to lighten the mood.

Charlie looked at him and then smiled. 'So what was a lawyer doing at a gangbang?'

Dale swigged beer from the bottle and said, 'The same as a married man, I suspect – having fun.'

'Ha. And did you?'

'How could I not? I was dubious to begin with.' He related his story – meeting Sam, the drive to The Chain. 'Part of me thought I was about to be murdered.'

'Sam must really like you. It sounds like love at first sight to me.'

'You're reading too much into it.'

He leaned over the table. 'I don't think so. He just meets you and an hour later he takes you to a highly secret group. Do you know how hard it is to get an invitation to that place? I was with Max for months before he took me along.'

'What about Max?'

'Do you know him?'

'I saw him. The huge blond guy, right?'

'Yes, that was Max. You know I don't talk about other people, though. If you want to know anything about Max, you'll have to ask him yourself. If you go to XL tomorrow, you'll get your chance. He goes there most weeks.'

'Tell me about you, then. How did you meet Max and get involved with The Chain? I'm not looking for gossip. I seriously want to know. The things I've seen in the last twenty-four hours are like nothing I've ever known. This is a new world for me. I'm fascinated.'

Charlie looked him squarely in the eyes. 'It's a long story,' he said thoughtfully, 'and not one I really want to tell, not now. Max is my lover. That's right, *is*. I've been with him for years. I'm not going to tell you how we met, it's private, but I do love him. He's another part of my life; equally as important as my family. I suppose he is family. Max was already a Chain member when we met. The Newbiggin link has been active for years.'

'Link?'

'Link in the chain. You didn't think this was a one-off, did you?'

'I hadn't really considered.'

'I don't know the full history. The original Chain started in Amsterdam, in the mid-1980s. A bunch of guys got together and set up a party palace in a garage or warehouse, I can't remember which. They started assembling all the usual stuff: swings, mattresses, harnesses. They'd get together ever week or so to fuck, suck, lick, rim, whatever. Then sub-groups began to form across Europe. There are five links in the UK. They link up now and then for bigger parties. Actually, there's a big meeting coming up. It's a well-organised machine.'

'Apparently so. How is it all financed?'

'From within: donations, investment, fundraising. It's no different to any other social group.'

Charlie's glass was empty. Dale reached for his wallet. 'I'll get another round in.'

'No,' said Charlie, looking at his watch.

'Do you have to go?' The earlier feeling swept back over him. He didn't want it to end, not just yet and not like this.

Charlie put his elbows on the table and leaned closer. 'Not yet. But if we only have a limited amount of time together, it seems like a waste to spend it in a pub.'

Dale's pulse quickened.

Charlie continued, 'I've still got the plug in my arse, remember. It's about time I exchanged it for a real cock, don't you think? Where are you staying?'

'With friends.'

He screwed up his face. 'We can't got to my place either.'

'No,' said Dale. 'It's okay. My friends are going out. The house will be empty until eleven.'

They rode in Charlie's van the short distance to Luke and Paul's. Both cars were parked on the drive when they arrived but the house was empty, the town centre being an easy distance on foot. Dale unlocked the front door and led Charlie into the house.

'Can I get you anything?' he asked, hovering nervously in the hall. 'A beer? Wine? Vodka?'

Charlie slipped an arm around Dale's waist and kissed him. 'We don't have long. I didn't come here to drink.'

They continued kissing. Dale's hands slid under Charlie's vest, feeling the hardness of his body, fingers raking through his hairy chest. Charlie flung an arm around Dale's neck, pulling his head down, to devour his mouth. Their tongues united. Dale could feel the hardness of Charlie's cock through his cargo pants, and wondered whether the erection was fresh or whether he had been hard all this time – the plug in his arse stimulating his arousal.

'Where's your room?' he asked.

'This way.'

They separated and bounded up the stairs. Dale closed the curtains and turned on a bedside lamp. Charlie waited by the open door, standing soldier-straight, chest out, his hands behind his back, waiting. He looked magnificent in the half-light of the room.

Dale kissed him again, exchanging saliva, breathing into him. He'd heard of married men who refused to trade mouth action with other guys, but thankfully Charlie was not that type. The kisses intensified. Dale dragged the younger man's vest up to his shoulder and caressed his chest with wild, exploitative sweeps. His palms brushed through soft hair and felt the hardness of Charlie's swollen nipples, while their mouths continued to yield.

Dale wanted to be inside him. Last night he'd had to share this beautiful man with a room full of others. Tonight, he would have him to himself. Charlie belonged to him; not to Max or his wife or anyone else. He was Dale's.

Dale broke the kiss. Charlie's head moved back, mouth open, eyes wide. His breath came in short bursts.

'Take your clothes off, carpenter! I can't fuck you as you are.' Dale's commanding voice cracked through the bedroom. He didn't know where this assertive impulse came from, but his instincts told him Charlie would get off on being told what to do.

He was right. Charlie's dark brown eyes sparkled as he tore the vest over his head and tossed it aside. Dale stood back, watching while Charlie unfastened his trousers.

'Do you want me to take off all of my clothes?'

'The whole lot. Strip!' Dale was used to standing up in court and asserting his presence; dominating Charlie wasn't so different. 'I want to see you naked as the day you were born.'

Charlie removed his boots and socks and stripped off his trousers. Dale admired his hard body, the fluid motion of strong muscle. It was the body of a man used to robust, manual work, thick set and hardy. His hard cock tented the front of his jock.

'Get it off,' he ordered.

Charlie skinned the jockstrap down his thighs and kicked it aside. There was an upwards curve to his cock, which also listed to the left at a slight angle. It was a stocky tool, suiting his build perfectly. He assumed the military stance again, his face impassive. His cock jerked under Dale's intense gaze. The dark pink head poked through his foreskin.

Dale ordered him onto the bed. Having overcome an initial stab of shyness and embarrassment, he was starting to enjoy this game. 'On your hands and knees,' he commanded

Charlie obeyed in an instant, climbing onto the mattress and shoving his arse in the air. It was probably the most natural position in the world for him to adopt. Dale stared at his arse, at the full, round swell of his buttocks, at the wide open cleft. It was the most perfect butt he could ever recall, outclassing every other man he'd had, even Kelly.

With his forehead resting on his arms and his big, beautiful arse splayed out, Charlie's balls hung low between his thighs. The only obstacle to a near-perfect sight was the object that plugged his anal cavity. The broad base of the toy covered his anus entirely.

'I want you to unplug your hole,' he said.

Charlie's right hand moved back towards his arse.

'No,' Dale snapped. 'No hands. Make your arse do the work. Shove that thing out of you.' He sat on the edge of the bed, his face level with Charlie's butt. He stroked his big arse. 'Come on, spit it out.'

'Yes, sir!'

The plug gave a little, bulging outwards as he pushed from within. Dale's cock was painfully hard. Charlie relaxed his anus and the plug settled back inside him.

'That's no good,' Dale barked. 'You need to work your hole. Push that fucker out of there.'

Charlie inhaled and shoved his arse back further. He concentrated, bearing down.

'Push, carpenter, push!'

Charlie screwed up his face, straining. With a loud groan, he expelled the fat black toy from his anus with such force it shot clear off the edge of the bed. His anal ring remained open for a brief second before folding shut; liquid lube dribbled from the opening. That sight alone was nearly enough to make Dale shoot his load.

He slipped a finger into the wet hole, feeling the muscle quiver. Entry was effortless. Charlie groaned and arched his back. The greed he had exhibited the night before was evident again, his hole ready to take everything it could get. 'Squeeze my fingers,' Dale told him, sinking a second digit to the knuckle.

His fuckhole obeyed, chewing the intrusive digits. Dale manipulated the ring of muscle and felt it give.

'Want me to fuck you?'

'Oh, yes,' Charlie groaned, wriggling his toes and grinding his hips uncontrollably.

'Tell me.'

'I want you to fuck me.' It was like he could talk with his arse as well as his mouth. The orifice chomped at Dale's fingers, communicating its own desire. 'I want you to put your cock in my hole and fuck me. Fuck hard and fast. Fuck this worthless piece of shit, sir! Fuck me. *Fuck me*!'

'I'll fuck you all right, carpenter, but first you're going to get my cock nice and juicy.' The force of his own conviction surprised him. This kind of talk was new to Dale and yet the words poured effortlessly from his mouth. He was like an actor, finally getting the chance to shine as a character he was born to play. 'Don't just lie there, get your fucking lips around my cock, now!'

Charlie turned around, eager to please. He reached for Dale's fly. Dale stood up and unbuttoned his shirt, making Charlie's task easier. Charlie pulled Dale's jeans open and dragged them halfway down his thighs. Dale was wearing his uniform briefs, black. The designer-branded waist stretched a good inch from his pelvis, tented by the intensity of his erection. Charlie rubbed the side of his face against the bulge, feeling its length. He opened his mouth and followed the line from the base to the leaking head. Dale groaned, feeling the warmth of Charlie's breath through the soft cotton.

Charlie tucked his fingers into the waistband and pulled the briefs down. Dale's cock extended up and then forwards, guided by Charlie's hand to his warm and open mouth. He gripped Dale's thighs and leaned forward, stuffing his face, taking it all the way into his throat. His skill was unparalleled – none of Dale's previous lovers could deep-throat with such agility. There was no gagging from Charlie as he swallowed Dale's meat.

When Dale's dick was good and wet, Charlie pulled back and began nursing the head and shaft. He kissed the juicy end, flicking his tongue around the tiny opening to devour its sticky fluid. He traced the thick vein along its underside, following it down to the ball sac. Slobbering over the hairy nuts, he sucked each ball into his mouth, one at a time, tugging gently, stopping just before the pleasing discomfort could turn to pain.

Back to the top, he took the cock all the way inside him again. Dale put his hands on Charlie's shoulders and began riding his face, pulling back, shoving deep. Charlie's forehead glowed red with a translucent sheen of sweat. He slurped noisily.

'Time for your arse,' Dale said.

Charlie nodded, wide eyed, open mouthed. While Dale discarded the rest of his clothes, wiped his cock and then sheathed it in rubber, Charlie assumed the position on his hands and knees, his buttocks poised and open at the edge of the bed. The height was perfect. Dale fisted lube over his swollen cock and dribbled even more of the clear juice over Charlie's bull's-eye. He grabbed a hip with one hand and guided his cock to the best angle with the other, bumping up against the hole. Charlie stared back over his shoulder, waiting breathlessly.

Dale lunged forward, skewering his helpless arse.

Charlie growled, his ring unfurling around the head of Dale's dick.

'Come on, carpenter, push back. Fuck yourself on me.'

Charlie lifted his arse, shoving upwards and back. Dale's cock vanished inside a hot, spongy tunnel of flesh. Charlie drove backwards, spearing himself, taking it all until his hard butt rested against Dale's pubic bone. Once in position, he paused, squeezing his hole.

'Come on, carpenter, fuck yourself.'

'Yes, sir!' he barked.

Charlie dragged his arse forward, until just the head remained inside, and then shoved all the way back. He repeated the motion, once, twice, moving at a deliberately lazy pace. 'Like this, sir?' he asked, without breaking his rhythm.

'A bit faster now.'

'Yes, sir!'

Dale looked down, spreading Charlie's buttocks. The arse lips were swollen, bulging around Dale's shaft, as Charlie worked his hips up and down, back and forth. He grunted and groaned, increasing the speed.

Dale pulled out, leaving Charlie's hole empty and gaping. He grabbed Charlie's ankles and flipped him onto his back. Then he lifted the young man's legs high and wide, giving himself a clear shot at that hole – and shoved back in there.

'Oh,' Charlie drawled, looking straight into his eyes. Dale got one foot on the bed for leverage and fucked him long and deep. Charlie's own cock was straight as a girder, spattering his furry belly with clear juice.

The sound of sex intensified; a rhythmic slap-slap of skin on skin, laboured breathing, grunting, moaning, the squelch of Dale's cock impaling Charlie's squishy hole.

He pounded, ready to let himself go. 'I'm gonna come, carpenter,' he gasped.

'Yes, sir! Shoot your load in my worthless hole, sir!'

Charlie writhed and bucked as Dale's cock began to spurt. He shot again and again, filling the condom inside Charlie. He gripped Charlie's legs to his chest, unable to speak, giving in to the feeling in his dick, allowing the throbbing, spurting sensations to fill his entire body.

He felt Charlie's arsehole tighten and through blurred vision he saw the eruption that shot high and splattered the younger man's chest with a succession of white waves.

The only sound was the gentle undertone of their breath as they lay together on the bed, side by side, staring at the ceiling. Dale's heart was still beating fast but, as the moments washed by, he felt a gradual deceleration in his pulse. The come-filled condom, tied off and swaddled in tissues, lay on the floor beside the bed.

'Mmm,' Dale sighed contentedly. 'That was good.'

'Absolutely,' Charlie drawled. 'Full points, man.'

Dale wanted to ask if this kind of intimacy was common for him. Did he share these quiet post-coital moments with his wife? With Max? There was no intimacy evident with the men at The Chain last night; that was just detached, mechanical sex. Anonymous and empty. What they were sharing now was something entirely different. Dale kept his query to himself. He didn't want his uninformed curiosity to spoil what had just occurred between them. He stretched luxuriously, savouring the squishy afterglow.

The melody of the song he had heard in Sam's car last night returned to haunt him. Instead of associating the unusual tune with Sam, his mind seemed intent on connecting it with Charlie. He found himself humming softly.

Charlie reached over to the bedside cabinet and grabbed a handful of tissues. He raised his hips from the mattress and began to mop up the lube from his crack. He balled the tissues and grabbed another.

'Do you want to take a shower before you go?' Dale offered.

'No thanks. I'll have a bath when I get home. It always relaxes me after a day at work.' He glanced at his watch. 'I should make a move. I didn't intend staying this late tonight. I'll have missed the bairn's bedtime.' He swung his legs over the end of the bed and stood up.

Dale rolled over, rising onto one elbow, watching Charlie retrieve his clothes from the floor. His broad cock swayed between his thighs as he moved. Was his appetite satiated now? Would this be enough for today? Or would his hunger for sex return?

Maybe later, after his bath, his cock would harden and the hunger would return. Would Charlie go out again or would he fuck his wife?

Dale chided himself for such pointless speculation; that way lay madness.

'What kind of lawyer are you?' Charlie asked, pulling up his jockstrap, tucking his cock inside, bending to retrieve his socks.

'I do mainly criminal work,' he explained. 'A little bit of conveyancing, a bit of family law.'

'Divorces?'

'Sometimes.' *Interesting he should ask that.*

Dale lay naked on the bed while Charlie finished dressing.

When he was ready, he leaned over and kissed Dale softly on the lips. 'Thanks for a lovely time. It was fun.'

Dale kissed him back. 'Could we do it again? Maybe before I go home?'

Charlie pulled away. 'One on one, like today?'

'Yes.'

He shook his head. 'No. Once is fun. Twice is serious. You're nice, really nice, but my life is complicated enough.'

Dale nodded. 'I understand.'

Charlie moved to the door. His butt plug was stuffed in the pocket of his cargo pants. 'I'm going to The Chain next week. There's going to be a big meeting, the Blackpool and Glasgow groups are joining us. It should be a lot of fun.' He smiled. 'I'll see you there if you're around.'

Dale did not move. He heard the front door open and close, and a few minutes later the sound of Charlie's van starting up and pulling away. He raised his fingers to his face and inhaled the scent of the other man. The smell of him was all that remained.

It was finally over. Dale had got what he wanted – another chance with Charlie. He should be content, he told himself.

But he wasn't.

Six

THREESOME

While Dale fulfilled his desires with Charlie, Luke and Paul met for a dinner at Ricardo's, an Italian restaurant on a road parallel to the Cock Shop. Tuesday night and the place was two-thirds full. The atmosphere at Ricardo's was always friendly, the food was excellent and reasonably priced. It was a traditionally decorated eatery. One wall was exposed brick, decorated with prints of Italian landscapes, while the other walls were burnt orange. The delicious aroma of good food permeated the room, adding to the warm atmosphere.

The head waiter had seated them at a table by the window. They had a superb view of the crowd standing in line across the road, waiting for the opening of Luscious Lipstick, a revue bar that staged an extravagant drag show seven nights a week. Though the residents tended to avoid it, Luscious Lipstick was a major tourist attraction for Newbiggin Bay. Luke and Paul usually went twice a year, whenever the content of the show was changed, usually around April and October. This season the troupe were staging a potted version of *Cabaret*.

Luke had called Dale before leaving the office at six-thirty, to invite him to join them for dinner. The mobile switched straight to the answer service. Luke left a message saying where to find them if he decided to come along. Dale still wasn't home when Luke and Paul met at the house to shower and change out of their work clothes into something less formal, so Luke scribbled another message telling him where they were and stuck it to the fridge.

'I feel guilty,' Luke said, tasting the strong Merlot they had ordered to accompany their food. It was delicious. 'Leaving Dale to fend for himself. Some friends we are.'

'He's coping all right,' Paul said.

'He shouldn't have to cope. He came up here for a break. I wish I'd been able to take some time off to be with him.'

'How could you, at such short notice? Besides, there's the weekend to come. We'll have plenty of time to spend with him then.'

Luke and Paul had arranged the hire of a cottage in County Durham with two of their friends, William and Colin, for the coming weekend. They'd made the plans months ago. When Dale announced his intention to visit, Luke thought they may have to cancel, but a phone call to the letting agency clarified that there were three bedrooms in the cottage. William and Colin were happy for Dale to join their party, though they took the liberty of inviting one of their own friends, Eddie, an out-of-work actor, in the hope of fixing them up. Luke deliberately kept this information from Dale so he wouldn't have a reason to back out. Once they were there, out in the remote country, he'd have no choice but to bunk up with Eddie.

'Anyway,' said Paul, 'what are you so concerned about? Do you think Dale would have swung an invite to an orgy if he was hanging around with us? He's having a great time on his own.'

Luke was about to swallow and almost choked when he started to laugh. 'Christ, I know.' He coughed into a napkin. 'I thought I was still dreaming at breakfast. Dale Summer at an orgy. He's the last person I'd have expected to join in.'

'You underestimated him.'

'I don't think so. When we were at college, I had a threesome with a couple of guys from the gaysoc. Dale was horrified; he called me the biggest slag on campus for months after. No, he's definitely changed since Kelly. Maybe it's for the better.'

Their food arrived. They had both ordered pasta. The waiter, an authentic Italian with a pert butt and impossibly tight trousers, refilled their wine glasses, hoping they would order a second bottle.

'Enjoy your meal,' he grinned, flirting as he walked away.

They skipped dessert but, as they weren't driving, ordered coffee with dark rum afterwards. Paul, feeling totally relaxed, leaned back in his chair and said, 'I'm kind of jealous.'

'Of what?'

'Of Dale,' he said. 'He's been here three days and he discovers a side to the scene we knew nothing about; orgies and gangbangs. We've been here years and what adventures have we had? A handful of drunken shags after Chaps on a Saturday night.'

Luke laughed. 'It's not the same, we live here. Remember the fun we had in London last summer with those Australian guys? Everyone behaves differently when they're away from home. Dale's been in London eight years and what's he ever done until now? He's had an unsatisfying sex life with half a dozen chickens. Now he's had his heart broken by another one. He deserves all the fun he's having now.'

'That's not what I was saying.'

'What are you saying?' Luke asked. 'Do you want to go to an orgy?'

'I might,' he said wistfully. 'At least I'd like the opportunity.'

'We've played around before, had threesomes and foursomes. How many cocks do you want at one time?'

Paul laughed and sipped his coffee. He put the cup down. 'I used to have this fantasy. I suppose I still do. I'm on a bus and I'm naked on the back seat. All of the other passengers are men. No particular type of man, they're all ages and sizes, some are gorgeous, some are repulsive, but I have the lot of them. They line up down the aisle, taking turns to fuck me. When they're finished, the driver stops the bus and these men grab me by the arms and legs and throw me out into the road.'

Luke leaned in, excited. 'Why didn't you tell me this before?'

He shrugged. 'It's just a fantasy.'

'It sounds like the scene Dale talked about. What did he call that boy? Charlie? Hanging in a sling while everyone fucks him.'

Paul nodded, licking his lips. 'That what got me thinking again.'

Luke's eyebrows arched. 'So what are you saying? That you want to be fucked by a room full of strangers?'

Paul leaned back and shook his head. 'I'm not sure. I don't know if I would go that far, not with so many men. The fantasy is still a turn-on.'

Luke was fascinated. Paul had always been the more passive partner in their relationship. He was a great bottom and he liked to get fucked. Sometimes they would change and Paul would fuck Luke from time to time, but it didn't happen often. Luke was versatile but he liked it on top. They were perfectly matched.

Paul's confession opened up possibilities. They had an active sex life. They didn't screw around behind each other's backs but they enjoyed other men. They had fun together. The sight of Paul riding another man's cock took Luke's breath away. It had been a while since their last adventure, three months or more.

'Let's go to XL,' he said, draining his coffee cup, 'and see if there's any talent in tonight.'

Every night of the week was busy in XL. Competition between the local bars was fierce, although not unpleasant. XL contended with its rivals by offering a popular mix of music, cabaret, karaoke, strippers and games. Every night was a lavish party, conducted by Kandi Legz, a stunning drag queen and local celebrity. Just last month Kandi had been in the newspapers when she presented a £5000 cheque to the baby care unit at the local hospital – money raised from charity collections in XL. Decked in *Carry on Nurse* drag, Kandi was pictured on the front page of the evening papers cradling a baby under each arm.

Tonight she was dressed as Velma Kelly in a black bobbed wig, sequinned dress and sheer stockings. She sipped lime-flavoured Bacardi Breezers through a penis-shaped straw while blasting an old Kylie tune from her DJ pulpit.

'We've got cabaret for you later this evening,' she announced over the outro of Kylie in a heavy Geordie accent. 'All the way from Soho, it's the Bananarama Experience. They'll be on stage a bit later on.

You'd better clap tonight, you miserable bastards! Not like last fucking week, I could hear a bloody pin drop.' The audience laughed. 'And after the girls we've got a male stripper for you; Tornado or Turbo... something or other. I can't think what the fuck he's called. But I'm assured he has a big cock and that's all we care about in this place. Anyway, he won't be on until later on so here's another record for you. I'm ready for another Breezer if anyone's buying.'

A HI-NRG reworking of 'Dance Yourself Dizzy' started playing.

Luke and Paul pushed through the crowd to the narrow bar. The barman, a pretty young thing called Ben, saw them waiting. 'The usual?' he mouthed over the deafening music. Luke smiled and nodded.

The customers that night were a typically mixed bunch of regulars and new faces. Unlike Luscious Lipstick, XL was as popular with local lads as it was with the tourists. The layout of the bar was fairly traditional, with a DJ booth and dance floor that doubled as a stage during cabaret, a raised seating area adjacent to the bar and a pool room to the rear. Although it was busy tonight, there was comfortable standing room. On Friday and Saturday it was virtually impossible to move.

Luke and Paul carried their drinks from the bar and found a place to stand against the wall, opposite the stage. There was a shelf there at shoulder height for glasses.

Tuesday, Saturday and Sunday were their regular nights for coming here. Occasionally they ventured out on a Friday too, if they could be bothered after a heavy week at work.

Luke cast his eyes about. 'I can't see Dale,' he said.

'Stop going on about him,' Paul admonished. 'You're not his mother. He knows where we are; he'll join us if he wants to.'

The place was buzzing and, by the time they bought another round of drinks, so were Luke and Paul. They shuffled closer as the space around them began to fill. A massive Muscle Mary in his late forties elbowed Luke on his way to the toilets, spilling his drink over his shoes.

'Bastard!' Luke hissed, shaking his leg.

'He's just done the same to me,' said a guy behind them, brushing off a damp stain on his jeans. He spoke with an American accent. 'What an asshole.'

'Yeah,' said Luke, sympathetically. 'Total wanker.'

'Do you know him?'

'Not really. He comes in about once a month. I don't think he's from round here. I can't say I care to find out.'

The American held out his hand. 'Hi. I'm Matt.'

Luke and Paul shook hands and introduced themselves.

Matt was around five foot ten and porn-star beautiful. His short black hair was parted loosely on the left and a tousled lock fell over his forehead. His face was strong and even, with a clean jaw line and huge hazel eyes. He had a wide mouth with even teeth, very white. There was a natural cast to his skin, suggesting, along with the darkness of his hair, Latin blood.

His body was perfectly pumped – broad shoulders, flat gut, massive arms. His soft cotton T-shirt stretched tight across an impressive chest. His nipples were large and prominent. Luke guessed him to be somewhere in his late twenties. He was the model all-American boy.

Matt was originally from Connecticut and now worked in the Manchester office of an international bank. With a couple of days' leave due, he'd decided to explore some of the country.

'Why Newbiggin Bay?' Paul asked. 'Wouldn't you have rather seen somewhere with more culture and history? Like York or Edinburgh?'

Matt laughed. 'No. I wanted a laugh and I was told this was the place to come.'

He enquired about the local scene. The guys explained the venues to him in detail, illustrating their merits and failings. Matt listened with interest and asked questions. They checked him out as he spoke; his crotch, his abs, his thighs. He had a quirky habit of tilting his head when he spoke.

'Are you here on your own?' Paul asked when they had been chatting for half an hour.

'Yeah. I'm staying at a hotel on the promenade. It's pretty nice.'

'Do you have a boyfriend?'

'No, I'm single. I haven't had much experience with guys,' he said shyly.

Luke found that hard to believe, looking the way that he did. 'What do you call not much experience? No serious relationships?'

'Just that,' he said. 'Not much experience. This time last year I was engaged to be married.'

'You've got to be kidding!'

'If only I was. But I'm being completely straight with you.'

'There's a lot of it about,' Paul deadpanned. Luke elbowed him.

'Excuse me?' said Matt.

'Ignore him,' Luke said. 'A friend of ours met a man last night – let's just say, under unusual circumstances – but the man turned out to be married.'

'What's your story?' Paul asked. 'Gay? Bi? Greedy?'

'I was always expected to marry and I never questioned it. I met this really nice girl, my family adored her, and that was it – we were engaged.'

'So then what? You woke up one morning and decided you'd rather take a dick up your arse instead?'

'Paul!' Luke snapped.

'I'm just saying.' Paul raised his hands. 'It's not the way most guys go about it.'

'No,' Matt said, good-naturedly. 'I know it's weird. I didn't just wake up one morning and decide anything. I always knew. I was in denial. That's why I took the job in England, to get away from home and accept this for myself, without any pressure from anyone else.' He folded his arms across his huge chest and shrugged.

'What happened to your fiancée?'

Matt laughed. 'She's engaged to someone else now. I think she just wants to get married, it doesn't really matter if it's to me or somebody else.'

'Can we change the subject now?' Paul asked. 'This talk of marriage freaks me out.'

'Sure, let me buy you guys another drink.'

Kandi Legz continued to play her music, while Luke, Paul and Matt got to know each other better. It became evident pretty quickly that Matt found the couple just as attractive as they found him. There was a definite frisson between the three of them. They chatted and laughed; they teased, the mood becoming increasingly flirtatious.

'I've been wanting to do something all night,' Paul giggled, after another drink.

'Oh, yeah,' said Matt, his hazel eyes sparkling. 'What's that?'

Paul reached over and tweaked Matt's left nipple.

Luke's heart collided with his chest, astonished by his lover's audacity, yet grateful he could be so bold. Matt grinned, leaning closer, and Paul gave his nipple a firm twist. The American moaned, the sound lost below a blaring Madonna tune.

Matt put down his drink and slipped a hand around each of their waists, pulling them close to him. He kissed them on the lips, Luke first, then Paul. His hands slipped lower, cupping their buttocks.

'Would you like to come back to my hotel?' he asked, having to shout. 'I've got vodka and something to smoke, if you're into that.'

Luke slid a hand under Matt's T-shirt, tracing a six-pack. 'You don't need to lure us with booze,' he said, nuzzling the side of his neck.

Matt was staying at one of the better hotels in the bay. The four-star Sulik was five storeys high, with plush bedrooms and impressive leisure facilities. Used to their guests bringing home visitors, the doorman and receptionist smiled as Matt led the boys towards the elevator. They kissed again on the ride up to his fourth-floor room.

The room was decorated in a modern but classic style – various shades of red and gold merged on the walls and carpets. Instead of the usual landscapes found in hotels, the walls were adorned with solidly framed Rankin portraits of Debbie Harry and Björk. In another photograph, the face of Robbie Williams had been grafted onto the crotch of a pair of ladies' pants.

'I'll get those drinks,' Matt smiled.

Luke sensed a sudden nervousness now that they were alone in his room. They'd been in this situation before, but the thrill and apprehension was something that never went away, however experienced they became. They sat on the edge of the bed, while Matt poured three hefty slugs of vodka into plastic tooth mugs and a coffee cup and added a dash of Diet Coke from the minibar. He tuned the television to a music channel.

'Mind if we take off our shoes?' Luke asked.

'Go ahead.'

Luke and Paul removed their footwear and made themselves comfortable on the double bed. The vodka tasted strong but it was smooth, good quality. Luke felt its effect on his uneasiness immediately. Someone had to make the first move, otherwise they would sit around all night. He edged across to Paul and patted the space he had created on the bed.

Matt took off his socks and shoes and lay down beside them.

Luke and Paul pounced, like lions in an orchestrated attack. They climbed on top of Matt. Luke went for his face, thrusting a tongue into his willing, open mouth. Paul headed lower, peeling back Matt's T-shirt from a magnificently honed and hairless stomach. Matt responded: one hand flew behind Luke's head, pulling him deeper into the kiss, the other went to his jeans, ripping the fly open. He hitched his arse from the bed, allowing Paul to pull down his jeans and underwear, releasing a nice, hard dick. He was circumcised with a thick, rounded head topping off a fat shaft.

His black pubes were trimmed. As Paul undressed him, revealing his balls, then his thighs, he realised those pubes were the only hair on Matt's body. Everywhere else was shaved and smooth – his balls, his thighs, his calves. On other men the effect could be disconcerting, possibly unattractive, but with Matt's well-developed muscles and creamy brown skin, it was stunning.

Paul threw Matt's jeans and boxers into the corner and crawled between his thighs. Matt opened them wider. Paul realised he'd been mistaken. Although Matt's balls were utterly smooth, he had allowed the hair to grown underneath them. The result was a trail of silky black curls that ran along the ridge beneath his scrotum and into the tight crack of his arse.

He started midway up the left thigh, grazing his tongue slowly along the sensitive flesh. He could feel Matt's muscles quiver as he ran higher. The American's cock gave a sudden twitch. Paul flicked his tongue over the smooth balls; they tightened and rolled over in their silky sac. He nipped the skin softly between covered teeth. Matt's moans were smothered by Luke's mouth.

Luke rolled on top, straddling Matt's chest. He tugged Matt's tight T-shirt above his nipples and their size amazed him. He circled their outer edges with his fingertips and spread his hands across Matt's chest. His pecs were huge and could only be the result of spending hours each week in a gym. He tweaked the hard brown stubs.

'Oh,' Matt exhaled a long breath. He lifted his shoulders from the bed and Luke tore off his T-shirt. He was completely naked while Luke and Paul remained fully dressed.

Luke leaned down to kiss him again, still working his tits. He tugged Matt's juicy lower lip with his teeth before breaking away, nibbling his way along the jaw line to the tender flesh of his neck. He gnawed, very gently, careful not to leave a mark.

'You guys are fantastic,' Matt exclaimed. *'Oh yes!'*

Paul had Matt's cock clamped in a firm fist, working the swollen head with his lips and tongue. The sensation was exhilarating. Paul opened his mouth wider, swallowing the head. His lips tightened, forming a seal just behind the ridge, and he focused his entire attention on the mushroom head. The organ throbbed against his teeth, a living, pulsating thing. He sucked, tasting man juice. He flicked his tongue across the ultra-sensitive area below the slit and Matt's cock continued oozing.

With Luke sitting on his chest, Matt could not see what Paul was doing. Paul reached across the bed for his drink and poured a measured splash of vodka over the head of Matt's cock.

'*Holy shit!*' Matt groaned, curling his toes.

Paul moved quickly, chasing the cold alcohol as it dribbled down the shaft. He sucked and slurped the liquid from Matt's balls and out of his pubes, where it formed a froth among the hair. He returned to sucking cock, moving up and down, working it all: the head, the shaft, using his hands on Matt's balls.

Matt's lips were red and swollen. 'Take off your clothes,' he said to Luke.

Luke raised his arms and pulled his shirt over his head, not bothering to undo any of the buttons. His torso was not in the same league as Matt's gym-perfect physique, but he was in decent shape. He had a firm, shapely chest, coated in hair. His stomach was not defined like Matt's but it was flat and compact. Neither Luke nor Paul went to the gym much, but they were keen joggers and went swimming when they had the time. Their bodies were lean and athletic without being overly muscular.

Matt clearly approved. He reached for Luke's belt, unbuckled it and opened his jeans. He reached inside and pulled out Luke's impressive, uncut dick. He caressed the foreskin, tugging gently, and precome oozed across his fingertips. He put his fingers in his mouth and licked them clean.

'What do you guys like to do?' he asked, palming Luke's dick.

'We're easy,' he replied. 'Both versatile guys.'

'I haven't taken it up the ass yet,' Matt said. 'I'm not sure I want to.'

'That's okay,' Luke assured him. 'You don't have to do anything you don't want to.'

Paul released Matt's dick from his mouth and said, 'You can fuck me.'

Matt looked at Luke, seeking approval.

'Go ahead. You can fuck us both if you like.'

Luke and Paul climbed off the bed and hurriedly undressed. Matt padded into the bathroom, his hard cock sticking out in front of him, and returned with a couple of safer-sex kits. Luke gave Paul's arse a playful slap and he jumped onto the bed, wriggling round into a position on his back. He shoved a pillow beneath his hips and opened his legs.

Luke and Matt ducked down and pressed their faces close to Paul's arse. They kissed the back of his thighs, both working their way to his butt. He rolled his hips higher, exposing his hole. Matt moved closer and kissed the inviting orifice. Paul groaned as Matt's tongue tickled his hot sphincter. He worked his tongue all the way around the rim for a couple of minutes before pressing into the tight muscle. Paul bucked and writhed as the American slipped his tongue in and out, pushing deeper each time.

Luke opened one of the safer-sex kits and handed Matt a condom. 'Why don't you fuck him now? You can see how much he wants it.'

While Matt put on the rubber, Luke tore open a sachet of lube, emptied the contents into his hand and began shoving it up his lover's arse. Paul's hole grasped at his fingers. 'He's ready,' he told Matt, wiping the rest of the lube over the American's rubbered cock.

Matt knelt in front of Paul, leaned forward, hooking the prone man's legs around his elbows, and allowed his dick to find its way to the opening. Hot and throbbing, he pressed against Paul's hole. With a forward roll of his hips, Matt slid his cock into Paul's warm, velvety gut.

From the edge of the bed, Luke had a magnificent view of the two men: of Matt's hard buttocks, his densely hairy crack, his smooth balls, and his cock – buried inside Paul's upturned arse. He could just about see Matt's pinky butthole through the forest of black hair. As Matt started to move his hips, pumping in and out, it became more visible.

Paul wrapped his legs around Matt's waist, pulling his body down so they could kiss as they fucked. They humped and twisted. Paul's arse swathed itself around Matt's hard, thick pole, pulling it inside. Soon Matt was pumping wildly, driving it deep, sweat dripping from his brow and down his face to his chin, where Paul licked it off.

With Matt's cock still inside, they changed position. Matt moved back into a kneeling position with Paul sitting on his cock, facing him. Now Paul was in charge of the action. He moved his arse up and down, supporting himself on Matt's shoulders and grinding his dick against Matt's hard belly. They were both hot and dripping with sweat. Luke moved closer, kissing them as they fucked, stroking Matt's strong back.

Paul's head suddenly flew back and he tensed his entire body. Through gritted teeth he cried out and shot after shot of white come burst from his dick, splattering Matt's chest. Matt held on tight to his trembling body.

When Paul was done, he climbed aside. Matt ripped off the condom and reached for another.

'It's your turn,' he said to Luke.

Paul lay flat on his back. Luke climbed on top to kiss him and shoved his own lubed arse towards Matt. Matt entered from behind, holding Luke's hips and feeding his meat into the hole.

'Fuck him hard,' Paul urged.

Matt fucked with long, slow strokes to begin. Luke held onto his lover as the American quickly found his rhythm again. He was soon pumping wildly, groaning each time he slammed his cock in to the root. Paul slid a hand between their bodies and gripped Luke's dick. With each rapid jerk it spat precome onto his belly.

When Matt's cock grew unbelievably harder, Luke knew he was about to shoot a massive load. 'Make me come,' he pleaded to Paul. His lover obliged, tugging his dick even faster. Matt kept his cock inside Luke as he came. He groaned helplessly and buried a wild load deep inside Luke's rectum. Luke roared and fired his own load in every direction, soaking Paul's chest, his face and the pillows beyond.

'You guys are fantastic,' Matt gasped, carefully pulling his cock out of Luke's rectum.

As was typical in these situations, not one of the three men knew what to say after the sex. What is there to say? Luke wondered. See you around. That would be an outright lie when they would never see each other again.

They settled on a string of complimentary remarks and humble thanks.

The kiss Matt gave each of them as they were leaving his room said enough for everyone.

Seven

INTIMATE AND LIVE

Sam loved music. His weekly spot at XL was a dream vocation for him. He got to play the kind of records he loved, quality dance and pop, for an appreciative audience. The gig had begun as a favour a couple of years ago with Sam covering two nights a week when Kandi Legz took a holiday to Ibiza. Of all the guest DJs to play during her break, Sam was the most popular, so he was offered a regular slot by the manager, Roy, to cover Kandi's night off. His reputation soon grew and, as well as the casual tourists, a faithful crowd of locals came every Wednesday to hear him play.

It led to bookings in other bars; he was the preferred holiday cover for most of the DJs in the bay. Sam hoped that a residency would one day be available to him. If the opportunity ever arose, he planned to hire a manager for the Cock Shop, and DJ full-time. He could think of nothing more satisfying for the future than turning his cherished hobby into a career.

The Cock Shop was too much of a success to give up, but the exertion of running the business on a daily basis was wearing him down. Working in a sex shop, day in, day out, was a grind. Selling dildos, porn and poppers had ceased to be fun. It was work – bloody hard work – and Sam found it a bind. Even if his gigs didn't provide a full-time alternative, he was starting to think it was time to appoint a manager and get out of the business, for a while at least. He could afford it, if he was careful.

Every Wednesday afternoon, he finished work at five, leaving Stuart in charge of the shop for the last two hours. He followed the same routine each week, driving straight home to his modern, two-bedroom apartment on the quayside. He had been there less than a year, having previously shared a house on the other side of the bay. The apartment was part of a new luxury development, intended to attract professionals to the town and dispel its reputation as a tacky seaside resort. His apartment was large and distinctive with huge, floor-to-ceiling windows and a sea-view balcony. He paid cash for the premises and took care that none of his yuppie neighbours found out about his business.

Sam undressed, performed fifty slow push-ups on the bedroom floor, and jumped in the shower. He decided to shave as he'd skipped the task that morning in favour of an extra ten minutes in bed. A day's worth of stubble wouldn't usually bother him or the crowd he played to, but tonight it was important to look good. He doubted that Dale would turn up, but if he did, Sam wanted to look and feel his best.

He put on snug cotton boxers and rummaged through his wardrobe. After rejecting three possible outfits, he opted for dark blue jeans and a tight red sleeveless T-shirt. He checked himself in the full-length mirror, mussed up his hair, and was finally happy with the way he looked.

'If you can't compete with that short-arsed carpenter,' he told his reflection, 'then no one can.'

He was waiting in the foyer, carrying a case full of CDs, when his taxi arrived. Most weeks he drove himself but tonight he wanted the freedom to drink. He'd asked Stuart to cover the shop tomorrow so there was no reason to get up early. He could get as drunk as he liked.

There were half a dozen customers in the bar when he arrived, who had likely been there all afternoon. The evening crowd wouldn't filter in until nearer eight. Sam went straight to the DJ booth, turned on the equipment and began arranging his CDs. He had a loose idea of the set he would play and would slot in requests when they arose.

It was a grey, drizzly night, but annoyingly warm. The front doors of the bar were propped open as the windows began to steam up. Sam looked up whenever someone walked in, hoping to see Dale. He was nervous. He was also annoyed at himself. This was typical behaviour – fixating on a man who was so obviously not interested in him. He took little solace from the fact that Dale was exactly the same in *his* obsession with Charlie – he would never get close to him, no one could. Charlie was soulless.

Sam had been surprised by Charlie's decision to join Dale for a drink but he knew it wouldn't lead to anything. Charlie would dump him when the newness wore off. He was a user. Christ, he was stringing along a wife and kid while he got his brains fucked out by every man who came near him. He had the most worked over arsehole in the history of Newbiggin Bay. What a bastard! What did they all see in him? Sam must be the only gay man in England not to fancy the fucker.

He put on his first record, 'In the Name of Love', and went to the bar.

Ben and Nathan were gossiping about the previous night's episode of *EastEnders*. They broke it up when Sam approached. 'Just the two of you tonight?' he asked.

'Roy and Adam have gone for a shag,' Ben said cheekily.

'How do you know that?' he asked.

The barmen rolled their eyes. 'They said they were going upstairs to watch *Corrie* and have a bite to eat.'

'A bite of cock, more like,' Nathan guffawed.

'They don't even like *Corrie*,' Ben added.

'Not like us. We'd love half an hour off to watch a bit of telly.'

Sam ordered a pint.

'Will you play Dolly Parton for us?' Ben asked, filling his drink.

'Oh, God,' he groaned. 'Do I have to?'

'Kandi always plays it for us. She plays anything we ask her to.'

'Which one?' he sighed, knowing they would pester him until they got what they wanted.

'"Nine to Five". The remix.'

He supped his pint. 'Bring me over another one of these in half an hour, and I'll think about playing your record.'

He headed back to the booth, wondering whether his own head

had been so vacuous at the age of twenty. Highly likely.

Despite the dismal weather, the place started to fill up nicely. Sam scanned the crowd from his vantage point, but there was still no sign of Dale. He turned on the microphone and introduced himself. He engaged in light-hearted banter with a drag queen called Millie before inviting requests. 'This one is for the slappers behind the bar,' he said, playing the Dolly Parton song.

Soon the bar was buzzing with a cheery atmosphere, full of people who had come out to enjoy themselves. Sam was taking a request from a party from Sunderland when he saw a familiar figure walk through the doors. Absorbed by the sight he'd waited all day to see, he almost forgot that the song he was playing was coming to a close. A volley of jocular heckling greeted the sudden silence at the end of the track.

'Bastards!' he retorted facetiously, hiding his blushes as he played the next song.

Dale waved from the doorway, wiping drizzle from his face. He pointed to the bar, miming a drinking action, and mouthed, 'Do you want one?'

Grinning, Sam shook his head. So he wasn't full of bullshit after all. Sam was glad to be proven wrong. He felt his spirit coming back to life. He was not surprised by how pleased he felt at the sight of Dale. Despite the dampness on his hair and jacket, Dale looked immaculate in casual trousers and a white D&G T-shirt. The sight of him filled Sam's head with wondrous visions.

With a bottle of beer in his hand, Dale had an effort forcing his way through the busy bar towards the DJ booth. Sam busied himself changing CDs, pretending not to notice his slow progress.

'Hi,' Dale said at last, gazing up from the floor below.

'Hey, you made it.'

'I told you I would.' His short black hair was plastered to his brow in wet strands. In the colourful light of the bar Sam could easily imagine that the drizzle was sweat; the sweat of sex on his skin after a hard bedroom session.

When the time came to play the next song, Sam deliberately chose a lengthy remix, which gave him a good seven minutes with nothing to do but chat to Dale. He climbed down from the booth.

'How've you been?' They had to lean in very close to hear each other above the music.

'Pretty good,' Dale answered merrily. 'Another lazy day. I had a lie-in, went for a run, did a bit of shopping; bliss.'

'Isn't that what holidays are all about?'

'I'm only just beginning to learn that.'

There was a long beat in which they looked at each other. Sam wracked his brain for something to say. 'So, what are your plans for tonight?'

Dale smiled easily. 'Nothing yet.'

'I thought you might be meeting Charlie.' The words slipped out before he had time to check them. He hadn't meant to say the C-word tonight.

'No,' Dale said cautiously. 'I doubt I'll see him again.'

Sam wanted to ask why but kept his mouth shut. If Dale said he was finished with Charlie, that was good enough. Dale had probably caught a glimpse of the darker side to Boy Wonder's personality and didn't like what he saw – not that there was much to see in the first place. Charlie was worth a fuck or two, nothing else.

'I end my set at eleven-thirty,' Sam said. 'I'm planning to go clubbing after. Do you want to come with me?'

'Where?'

'Chaps,' he said breezily. 'It's not G.A.Y. but it gets pretty busy most nights. It's definitely worth checking if you haven't been before.'

'Great. I'll join you then, if that's okay.'

'Fantastic.'

For the rest of the evening, Sam spent as much time chatting to Dale as he could. While he was busy in the booth, a couple of guys tried to pick Dale up. It was hardly surprising – a good-looking guy on his own was bound to attract attention in this place. Luckily, Dale wasn't interested.

Towards the end of the night, he asked Sam to play him a record.

'I heard it in your car the other night,' Dale explained. 'I can't get the tune out of my head.'

'What was it?'

'I haven't a clue. I thought you would know. It had a really hard sound and this insane beat. It was very distinctive. It had a woman's voice on it.'

Sam bit his lip and tried to remember what he had been listening to on the way to work this week. 'I'm not sure. If I was playing it in the car, it will still be there, I haven't changed the CDs all week. I'll check it out for you tomorrow.'

'Thanks. Let me know what it is. I'll drop by the shop in the afternoon 'cause I'm going away at the weekend.'

Sam's face fell. 'Back to London?'

'Not yet. I'm spending the weekend with friends. They've got a cottage, somewhere in Durham, I'm not sure where. Sounds nice.'

'When do you go?'

'Friday.'

Sam gulped his drink, his third pint. 'No. I mean when are you going back to London? Straight from Durham?'

'Oh, right. I see what you mean. I don't know. I think I'll come back to Luke and Paul's on Sunday and go home sometime next week.'

He took another drink, feeling relieved. 'So you'll be around a few days yet?'

Dale nodded. 'A little while. I haven't decided what I'm doing yet. I have another full week off work after this. I'll see how I feel next week; I may hang round the bay a little longer or spend a few days somewhere else.'

Sam nodded, wondering if it was too early to make a move. A few words to show Dale he was interested might be all that was needed to give him a reason to stay.

No, Sam was getting light years ahead of himself. He would approach the matter later, in the club. It was better to be careful. He didn't want Dale making unfavourable comparisons with Charlie. Charlie was a cheap piece of meat, and Sam's best play was to show Dale how different they were. Subtlety would win over brazen availability. He knew what he would do, he would ask Dale to join him for dinner one night next week.

The night was a success for Sam, with a boisterous crowd appreciating the music he played. He was on form, chatting on the mike between songs, telling jokes. He couldn't remember the last time it seemed so effortless.

'Those guys love you,' Dale remarked as they walked the short distance from XL to Chaps.

'Thanks,' he said, smoking a cigarette. 'I give them what they want. Too many DJs play nothing but their own preferences these days. They get overly precious about taking requests, like it's beneath them. If someone asks me for a song and I have it with me, I've got no problem playing it.'

'What if they ask you for something really crap?'

'Oh, they do,' he laughed. 'As long as it's not too hideous, I don't mind.'

It had stopped raining an hour ago. The pavements were still wet and heavy clouds blocked out the stars, threatening more rain at any time. There was a queue of around fifty waiting to get into the club when they arrived. They huddled around the block in their flimsy outfits, smoking and rubbing their arms to keep warm.

'Don't any of these people work?' Dale asked incredulously. 'I would never have the energy to go clubbing on a normal week night.'

'Is that what happens when you hit the wrong side of thirty?' Sam teased.

'Ha, thirty! How about the wrong side of twenty-five? I think my party days are well over.'

Dale headed towards the back of the queue but Sam grabbed his arm and guided him to the double-doored entrance. A rumble of disapproval went down the line.

'The guy behind XL also owns this place,' Sam explained. 'My name is on the guest list.'

The club was swarming. Glad-to-be-alive pop music blasted over a packed dance floor. Chaps had that particular aroma found in almost any gay club: a blend of sweat, damp, dry ice and amyl nitrate. Like everything else in Newbiggin Bay, Chaps was ultra-tacky, gaudy and fun.

'Let's get a drink first,' Sam shouted, indicating the bar. He was pleasantly drunk already and being out with Dale seemed to heighten his euphoria. They decided to switch to spirits – vodka for Dale, tequila for Sam – and took their drinks to the VIP area on the first floor.

'They have a VIP room?' Dale gasped.

'But not a lot of VIPs. Claire Sweeney did a gig here last summer. That's as big a name as you're ever going to see in this place.'

A glass-fronted balcony looked out over an active dance floor. Below, a gyrating mass of flesh moved in rhythm with the music. The club was thronged with bodies, most of them half naked: dancing, writhing, cruising. Disco bunnies, middle-aged clones, daddies and Muscle Marys put aside their differences and came together in the name of disco and sex.

Sam nudged Dale's arm. 'Do you see who's down there?'

'Where?' he asked, pressing closer to the window and scanning the floor below.

'Far right of the dance floor.'

He stood motionless at the side of the floor. Even in a crowded club, surrounded by a dozen sets of immaculate disco-pecs, Max stood out as something exceptional. He was naked from the waist up. His pale blond hair absorbed colour from the flashy disco lights, appearing blue one moment and red the next, then yellow, then green. He wore an emotionless expression. If he was enjoying himself, it didn't show.

A younger man clung to him, also shirtless, with a small, lithe body. He was twenty, twenty-two tops.

'Who's the bunny?' Dale asked.

'I don't know his name. One of Max's boys. Charlie isn't alone. This one has been hanging round for a few months now.'

They watched as the boy removed something from his hip pocket – a bottle. He unscrewed the cap, holding his thumb over the rim, and offered it to Max. The older man leaned in and inhaled slowly through each nostril. The boy took a dual hit himself before returning the bottle to his pocket. As the amyl nitrate took effect, he wrapped both arms around Max's waist and pressed against his body, rubbing his crotch against Max's thigh. Max grabbed the boy's arse and they started kissing, open mouthed, uninhibited.

'Another dumb fuck,' Sam said dryly.

'Has he ever taken this boy to The Chain?' Dale asked, seemingly transfixed by the men below.

'No. Only Charlie has that privilege.' He put his hand on Dale's elbow, breaking the spell he was under, and led him away from the balcony.

They sat at opposite ends of a brown leather sofa, facing the window. The sofa was small but there was more space between them than Sam would have liked.

'Do you ever dance?' he asked, changing the subject, surreptitiously hoping they could get closer on the dance floor.

'Not at all,' Dale said, shaking his head. 'I like the music but I can't move. I've got no rhythm at all.'

'It didn't look that way on Monday.'

He laughed. 'I thought we were talking about dancing.'

'We can talk about whatever you like.'

To the left of them a young couple were locked at the mouth, oblivious to their surroundings.

'Tell me more about The Chain,' Dale said.

Sam grimaced. 'Do I have to?'

'Come on. I daresay it's something you take for granted, but this is *major* for me. I hadn't had a threesome before now, let alone an orgy. Charlie said there's another meeting next week – something about a merger with two other links.'

Sam's spirits fell. 'I thought you were over him,' he said with more bitterness than he intended.

'I didn't say –'

'You know what?' he spurted. 'I'm sick to death of Charlie. Even just hearing his name. He's all anyone wants to talk about. God knows why! It's as if the whole world revolves around the little fucker. He's not *that* attractive, you know.'

Dale stiffened. For a moment neither of them spoke.

'Sorry,' said Sam calmly. 'I shouldn't have snapped. God, I sound like a right bastard, don't I? Because I was at school with him, it's like everyone thinks I'm an expert. Ever since he came out, people have been asking me about him. I don't know what you see in him. What's so attractive about a selfish, deceitful bastard? There's not much to admire in the man.' He downed his tequila.

Dale remained silent.

Sam brooded, sensing he'd blown it. Shit! How could he have exploded like that? It had been going so well too – he'd been planning to offer the dinner date after the next round of drinks.

'I'm sorry,' Dale said. 'I didn't realise he was a sore subject. It must really piss you off – me asking about him all the time.'

'It's my fault,' he mumbled. 'I shouldn't have overreacted. It could have happened with anyone, I'm just sorry you're the poor bastard who had to bear the brunt of it.'

Dale slid across the sofa, closing the gap between them, and put his hand midway up Sam's thigh. 'Forget I mentioned him.'

'I was going to ask you to have dinner with me next week,' Sam admitted.

'Oh, really? When?'

'Never mind.'

'No, really.' He squeezed his thigh. 'I'd love to go with you if I'm still around.'

'It was a stupid idea,' he said. 'Forget I asked. I think I've misjudged you. You don't want to go to fancy restaurants – you've had a lifetime of that already.'

He looked bemused. 'Have I? Says who? I like fancy restaurants, especially when the company is fancy too.'

Sam moved closer, delighted that Dale did not pull away from the intimacy. He stroked the side of his face, inched closer again and kissed him on the mouth. Dale responded, moving his hand further up Sam's thigh.

After several moments they broke away, flushed and exhilarated. 'I was beginning to think you didn't like me,' Sam murmured.

'What's not to like?' Dale leaned in, kissing him again.

'I have an idea,' Sam said, when they next broke for air. His whole body was tingling with the effect of the kiss. 'I think you might appreciate it.'

Dale moved even closer. 'What is it?' he asked, moving his lips over Sam's.

Sam pulled away slightly so he could lift his butt from the sofa and remove something from his back pocket. They were tickets. 'I wasn't going to go,' he said. 'But if you're still searching for adventure this could be right up your street.'

He turned the tickets face up and handed them to Dale. On high-quality, gilt-edged black card, three words were printed in bold silver lettering: THE SEX CABARET.

'There's no point getting there early,' Sam had explained, delaying their exit from Chaps until after three o'clock. By then they were intoxicated with alcohol and anticipation. They stayed in the VIP section for most of the night, huddled close on the sofa, talking, kissing, groping. Several times, Sam came close to exploding, and only the force of his will kept him from spilling spunk in his pants.

He bought them each a leather cockstrap from the bar, which they applied in the toilets. Sam fastened his own strap as tight as he could stand, preventing any further risk of ejaculation. His tied cock, hard and swollen, showed prominently in his jeans.

It was raining again. They shivered as they walked the short distance from the nightclub to a former warehouse in the arches of a railway bridge. Outside the town centre, the streets became deserted. There were no lights as they walked along the cobbled path towards the arches. They slid their arms around each other to keep warm. Sam shivered.

'You're freezing,' Dale whispered.

'It'll be warm inside,' he assured him. 'And the sun will be up before we leave.'

Sam led Dale to a small doorway, almost invisible in the darkness. He knocked. A narrow slot opened at eye level, blue light shone from within. Sam handed over the tickets to an unseen figure inside. A moment later a bolt was drawn and the door swung inwards. They had to duck their heads to step inside.

There were two doormen, dressed identically in black leather: loose trousers, boots, hoods. Their chests were bare, hairless, tanned and oiled.

The room was tiny, an antechamber. One of the doormen handed back the tickets and opened another lock. The room must have been soundproofed because as soon as the second door was drawn open they heard music and chatter.

A club had been constructed in the high arch of the railway bridge, retaining much of the original brickwork and concrete floor. Tables and chairs had been assembled in a large central area facing a low stage and dance floor. Well populated alcoves were spaced all the way along either wall, with a bar off to the left. The dance floor was full, with an overspill onto the stage. The music had a harder edge than anything played in Chaps or XL.

The club was crowded with a mixed clientele: pretty young things in tight tops fraternised with beary dads. There were older men, average men, attractive men, ugly, fat, thin and fit – a fusion of gay life. The dress ranged from elegant suits, to trendy clubwear, formal, casual, fetish gear and bare skin.

Waiters moved back and forth between the tables and the bar, distinguished from the customers by their uniform of black leather chaps. They were naked beneath, their cocks tied in a state of hardness by tight leather straps. Their anatomy was as uniform as their wardrobe – they were all young, smooth and muscular.

The host, a tanned muscle god, noticed Sam and Dale waiting by the entrance and approached them. He was older than the rest of the staff, nearer forty. His senior position was determined by a leather harness and wrist cuffs.

'Good evening, gentlemen.' He greeted them and led them to a small table, halfway to the stage. 'The show will begin in twenty minutes.' He called over a waiter. 'Taylor, see to these gentlemen.'

They asked for a bottle of oak-aged Rioja, and Sam, realising he hadn't eaten since lunch, ordered a selection of tapas.

The round table was covered in a plain black cloth. In the centre three candles burned in a wrought iron candelabra. There was an ashtray and a dark glass bowl, filled with small metal orbs, slightly smaller than a golf ball.

Dale looked around. There were about fifty tables in the centre of the room, nearly all of them occupied. He looked into the dark alcoves. The dim light made it impossible to distinguish individual features but he could discern the unmistakable spectacle of sex. In the small archways, men were wanking, sucking and fucking. The club was hot and it reeked of sweat and semen. 'How many other secret sex groups are you a part of?' he asked.

Sam laughed. 'Have dinner with me next week and I might tell you.' He lit a cigarette and blew the smoke to the ceiling. 'It's only my second time here. They sent an invitation via the shop. This place has nothing to do with The Chain.'

'What does it take to become a member?'

'I haven't asked.'

Dale's eyes sparkled with excitement. It was the same look Sam had seen two nights earlier when he introduced him to The Chain. He was envious of Dale. This kind of environment – The Chain and The Sex Cabaret – had lost their novel appeal for Sam and no longer provoked the audacious thrill that had enticed him to them in the first place. For Dale this was new and provocative, for Sam it was just another night. Only Dale's presence made it special.

Dale sat up straight, listening to the music.

'Hey,' he said, 'this is it. This the song I was asking about. The one you had in the car.'

'It's Kylie,' Sam said, recognising the track instantly.

Dale looked confused. 'Kylie Minogue? It can't be.'

'It can be. It is. It's called "Too Far", it comes from her experimental indie phase in the mid-1990s. Pretty surprising, eh? It's not her usual pop sound.'

'No. Is it still available?'

'On the album, yes. This track was never released as a single, though there are a few remixes doing the rounds.'

The waiter returned. He was a pretty blond boy in his early twenties. He put down two glasses and set about opening the wine bottle at the table. His hard penis throbbed inches away from Sam's face as he struggled with the corkscrew. It was a beautiful cock, well proportioned, with a juicy foreskin that covered the head entirely, even while erect. Sam tasted the wine, which was excellent, and the waiter filled their glasses.

'Your food won't be long,' he smiled, presenting them with a bill.

Sam checked the amount and opened his wallet, peeling out notes. He took one of the silver balls from the bowl in the middle of the table. Dale watched him curiously. Sam smiled and ran his thumb around the orb, eventually finding a minute clasp. He pressed and the ball opened on a hinge. Sam put the rolled up notes inside and sealed it back up. He handed the metal ball to Dale.

'Here, you can pay.'

His brow creased. 'What?'

'Why don't you show him?' Sam said to the waiter.

The boy nodded and walked around the table. He put his tray on the floor and bent over. Putting his hands on his thighs, he shoved his pretty blond arse to Dale. In the flickering light of the candles, his anus was a small, glistening knot.

Dale glanced between the waiter's exposed rear and Sam. 'What...?'

Sam indicated the metal orb. 'Pay the boy.'

Dale's Adam's apple lifted and fell as he swallowed. The boy widened his stance expectantly. Dale put one hand on his smooth buttock and pressed the orb against his arsehole. He pushed the ball through the ring of muscle and shoved in his finger to push it deeper.

'Thank you, sir,' said the waiter, straightening up and collecting his tray. 'I'll bring your food shortly.'

Dale shifted in his chair, a hand beneath the table to rearrange his cock.

The music on the dance floor came to an end. There was a burst of applause as the dancers cleared the floor, returning to the tables. Sam shifted his chair to sit close to Dale. The lights around the club darkened and men who were gathered in the shady alcoves came out to where they could view the stage.

A single spotlight focused on the stage and a master of ceremonies materialised in its intense glare. He was dressed bizarrely in a white yeti-hair coat that covered him from neck to floor. His short hair was as white as the coat and plastered flat to his head in the style of a 1960s waif. His age could have been twenty or forty, it was impossible to tell. His skin was alabaster white while there were dark shadows beneath his eyes. He wore the dirtiest of smiles on his face.

A smattering of applause greeted his entrance and Sam and Dale sat motionless, holding their breath for what would happen next.

'Gentlemen,' announced the MC in a strong European accent. 'This is it!'

Music began. Hard-edged dance beats were pumped across the club as the MC shrugged his white coat from his shoulders, revealing nakedness beneath. His skin was flawlessly white. He had the hard, lithe body of a dancer or acrobat. His agility was made immediately apparent at he began to move around the sparse stage. It was a flowing routine, intensely choreographed and yet natural seeming. He stood on one leg and raised the other foot high above his head, he walked on his hands, executed audacious back-flips and performed splits and cartwheels. The spotlight pursued him around the stage, illuminating every inch of his body, each intimate crook and crevice, his feet, his navel, his cock, the seam beneath his balls running all the way to his arsehole. The hole itself was frequently seen and more than once, as he performed some acrobatic manoeuvre, the audience was treated to a glimpse of his delicate inner flesh. His body was slightly oiled and it glistened in the brilliant white light.

His naked stomach gyrated in time with the tribal beats. His shoulders bunched, revealing their incredible strength as he lifted himself onto his hands again and performed the splits with his legs in the air. The music thudded faster, a series of complex, orgasmic beats. He flipped back over onto his feet, his hard cock smacking against his knife-flat belly and then he fell forward, face down on the stage. He was shining with a layer of sweat as he began to grind his hips, humping the stage floor. He opened his mouth, leering at the audience, licking his lips as he ground harder and faster. He gasped, pushing back onto his knees, grabbed his cock in both hands and started jerking off, moving them all the way up and down the shaft. His stomach tightened. Sam edged forward in his chair. The MC's hands were moving faster and faster. He rolled his head backwards, exposing his throat, his chest expanding with erratic gasps.

'Come on,' came a shout from the audience.

'Do it,' came further encouragement.

Sam moved his hand below the table, sliding it across into Dale's crotch, feeling the hot, hard length of his cock through his clothes.

The MC leapt to his feet, still jerking off two-handed. His thighs began to tremble, his scrotum tightened. He growled, his stomach tensing. His meat stiffened and a cheer swept over the club as he began pumping his load. Long white lengths of ropy semen shot across the crowd, his impressive trajectory spreading his sperm into glasses, faces and plates.

'Gentlemen,' the MC said breathlessly, 'the show begins.'

The music changed as applause rang out. Strobe lights began to flash across the stage. The MC was gone. Dry ice blasted from the wings as the audience waited to see what would happen next.

Sam squeezed Dale's dick through his clothes. Dale responded, throwing a hand around his neck and pulling him into a kiss.

'Sam, can I come home with you after this?'

'Yes,' he gasped. He shuffled over, sitting on Dale's lap for the next act, feeling the hardness of his cock sticking in his butt. He writhed on the stiffness.

Their eyes were drawn to the rafters above the stage. Four naked men were suspended in slings, legs raised and open, anuses exposed. Slowly they were lowered. On the stage below, waiting as they descended, were another four men. They were dressed in the same leather chaps that the waiters wore, their chests and torsos set off with studded harnesses. Their erect cocks were held stiffly forward by stainless steel rings fitted around the base. The position of the rings, fastening behind their balls, also caused their scrotal sacs to jut forward. The men in the slings were lowered into position, at waist height. For the next half hour they were exhibited. The four masters took each boy out of his sling in turn and with great deliberation showed him to the audience. The exhibition was extreme.

The first boy was forced to stand, bent over, with his back to the audience. One of the masters half-inserted an apple into his anus. The boy had to stand motionless, holding the apple in place while audience members were invited at random to come onto the stage and take a bite.

The second boy was left hanging in his sling. One of the masters retrieved an object from the back of the stage. Sam stretched on Dale's lap, trying to get a peek at what he held in his hand. The master, a chunky man in his mid-thirties, came to the front of the stage and held aloft a dildo, unlike any Sam had seen before. It was massive, at least fourteen inches long, and constructed from clear plastic. The man demonstrated its translucent quality by wriggling his fingers about behind it. He then inserted his cock into the base of the toy, revealing it to be a hollow sheath.

'It's huge,' Dale whispered. 'He'll never be able to take it.'

Sam bit his lip tensely.

While the man with the toy covered its entire shaft in lube, the other three masters worked on the boy's arsehole, taking it in turn to finger lube into the hole until they could fit nearly a whole gloved hand inside him. Sam couldn't see much of the boy other than his willing arse. His skin was creamy brown, several shades darker on his balls and in the arse crack. His body, as much as could be seen, was solid and manly.

When the master with the toy started inserting its huge, blunt head into the boy's hole, Sam could just about feel the pain himself. He reached for his glass and swallowed, unable to take his eyes off the spectacle on stage. Incredibly, the boy was taking it all and in no time the solid piece of plastic was buried all the way inside him.

The audience was so concerned with watching the toy going in, they had not noticed what the other three masters were doing, not until two large screens lit up at either side of the stage and one of the men stepped forward with a narrow, hand-held camera. There was a collective intake of breath as the man moved the camera nearer to the boy's arse. An extremely close-up shot of his stuffed hole filled the twin screens. Though blurred, the image was explicitly vivid. The screens were filled with various shades of pink and red as the camera was inserted into the hollow interior of the dildo, revealing the inside of the boy's rectum.

Sam thought his mind was about to explode. It had gone too far; he was shocked and repulsed. But he could not look away and his cock did not stop throbbing.

There was a smatter of nervous chatter and laughter around the audience.

When the masters directed their attention to the third boy, there was a feeling of anticlimax. They hoisted him down from his sling and forced him to lie on his back. They rolled him onto his shoulders and put his feet above his head. The position brought his arse to a perfect angle for them to empty a bottle of champagne into his rectum. When at last told to do so, the boy squirted the booze back out of him – like a human garden sprinkler, he showered the stage with champagne.

The final boy was fucked by all four masters. It was no light scene after what had gone before. They fucked him at the front of the stage with total abandonment, slamming, slapping, spitting. The boy screamed at his masters, begging for more, groaning and thrusting his arse. The sound of their dicks, squishing out his little hole, was amplified through the sound system.

The audience found it difficult to concentrate on the stage as they began to give in to their own sexual urges. Cocks were freed from pants and slid inside willing mouths and arseholes. Naked men were bent over tables, straddled across chairs, spit-roasted from either end. The cabaret was no longer restricted to the stage.

Eight

RHYTHM OF LOVE

As Sam had predicted, morning had broken by the time they left the club at six-thirty. The sun was beginning to dry the sodden pavements. They eschewed a taxi in favour of walking back to Sam's apartment via the promenade. The heat and dry ice of the cabaret, together with the early onset of a hangover, left Dale with a furious thirst. He stopped at the first newsagent's they past and bought two bottles of fresh orange juice. He downed the contents of the first bottle before leaving the shop. Sam bought a large bottle of water which he drank slowly as they walked along the sea front.

'I love this time of day,' he commented.

'It's lovely here,' said Dale, 'but back home, six-thirty is just as hectic as any another time.'

For a man who'd been up all night, Dale felt surprisingly alert. The lethargy that had crept over him around five o'clock had passed. The energy exhibited on stage and two cups of strong coffee kept him going until he gained his second wind. Now he was wide awake.

The promenade was quiet. They took off their shoes and socks and walked along the deserted beach, holding hands. The sand was cold beneath Dale's weary feet but strangely refreshing. He glanced at Sam and smiled. Sam looked remarkably well, considering he had worked two jobs and spent the night in a sex club since he last slept. The only flaw to his otherwise immaculate appearance was the growth of dirty blond stubble on his chin.

'What are smiling at?' he asked.

'You,' Dale said. 'You're incredible. I've only been out with you twice and look at everything that's happened both times. You set a cruel pace.'

'Are you complaining?'

'Not at all, but I think I'm going to need this weekend just to recover. I'm too old for all this debauchery.'

Sam laughed quietly, kicking sand with his bare feet. 'I don't live like this all the time, you know. I couldn't keep up with it myself. I'm just trying to impress you.'

'It's working.' Dale wished he hadn't said that. It wasn't quite a lie but he wasn't being honest either. He was impressed by the lifestyle Sam had opened up to him, but it was unfair to let Sam believe he was interested in anything more. Dale liked him a lot but, he suspected, not as much as Sam liked him. He tried to make sense of his feelings. Sam was attractive, charismatic, sexy and funny; if Dale was looking for a short-term holiday romance, he couldn't have made a better choice. There'd been times during the night when he felt like throwing caution to the wind and embarking on a full-scale affair. There was no reason he shouldn't; Sam wanted the same thing and they could have a great time together.

But there was Charlie.

Dale couldn't stop thinking about him. The possibility that he might never see the young carpenter again caused an inexplicable pain his chest, like his heart was made of heavy matter, and the weight was too much to carry.

He'd realised while watching The Sex Cabaret that the reason he continued to cultivate this friendship with Sam was all because of Charlie. Sam was the key to seeing Charlie again and Dale was using him. Only Sam could gain him access to the next Chain meeting, and other than ringing every carpenter listed in the local directory, that was his only prospect of seeing Charlie again. He didn't know what he was going to do when he got there, what he would say or how he was going to play it, but he had to get through those doors. Wooing Sam was the only way forward.

In a recess of his mind, not far from the surface, Dale knew that using Sam as a device to get to Charlie was wrong. Exploiting the shopkeeper's desire for him was pretty low, but he was prepared to do whatever was needed to keep Sam onside until the next meeting.

Even now, after another exhilarating night, when he should have been thinking about fucking Sam, it was Charlie he wanted; he'd been on his mind all night. He's probably on his way to work now, Dale thought – early morning starts would be routine for a carpenter.

He wondered whether Charlie knew about The Sex Cabaret? There was no use asking Sam, not after touching a raw nerve with him last night.

When Sam was sitting on his knee during the show, Dale had pretended it was Charlie perching there instead., grinding his hips in excitement. He would love the show, Dale was certain. Christ, it would be impossible to stop him from getting up on the stage. Charlie was born to take part in that show. He would be a natural, hanging in a sling, taking just about anything up his hole. He would be a star, daring to go further than any of the other boys.

At the end of the beach they climbed over the rocks and back onto the promenade, brushing the sand from their feet.

'It's not far now,' Sam said cheerfully, as they continued walking, still carrying their shoes.

Dale was only half listening as he chattered away about local history.

They entered the ornately paved entrance to an apartment complex, passing a well-suited business man on his way out.

'There's something quite satisfying about crawling home to bed while everyone else leaves for work,' Sam said with a chuckle.

They rode in the lift to his apartment, still holding hands. Dale was impressed by the building and its urbane style. It had clearly been designed with fashionable young things in mind. The hall carpet was luxuriously plush beneath his bare feet. His own apartment seemed meagre in comparison; a poky flat that cost him a fortune each month in rent.

Sam opened the front door. The first thing Dale saw as he stepped inside was the incredible North Sea view; long windows extended the entire length of one wall. The decor was plain and tasteful: cornflower-blue walls, cream carpets, a red-wine leather sofa. An impressive stereo system was set up in the living room. Closing the front door, Sam picked up a remote control and activated the sound. A mellow, ambient track started to play, a faultless accompaniment to the marine view.

'Is all this yours?'

Sam nodded, wandering through to the open-plan kitchen. He pulled two cold bottles of water from the refrigerator and came back into the living room, handing one to Dale. 'All mine. If I sell up in a couple of years' time, I'll have made a tidy packet on the place.'

'Is that what you plan to do?' Dale asked, sitting down. The sofa was angled to look across to the horizon. He sank into its comfortable surround, marvelling once again at the lifestyle Sam led.

Sam took the seat beside him, his leg resting against Dale's. 'No plans, just a vague idea. I didn't buy the apartment thinking it was the place I wanted to spend the rest of my life. It's for five years maximum.'

'Why? How could you not be content here? It's perfect.'

'It's a bachelor pad, isn't it? Great for now but I can't see myself growing old here. God forbid!'

'You should see my flat, this place will seem like paradise.'

Sam lifted his feet onto the coffee table; it was massive, wider than Dale's dining table. He picked absently at the label on his bottle and said, 'When I was eighteen I had a one-night stand with this guy I met in Newcastle. He was in his forties; a serial chicken hawk. Ordinarily I wouldn't have given him the time of day, but I couldn't afford the taxi fare home. The first buses didn't start running until six-thirty and I needed a bed for the night. This guy, Vince, was every cliché you can imagine rolled into one. He had a leathery suntan, dyed his hair, bombed round town in a BMW shaggin' wagon with tiger-print seat covers. He used to have a tache but he'd shaved it off by the time I had him. I remember he was wearing this powder-pink vest with a fake rose tattoo on his right arm.'

'Shit, how desperate were you?'

'Very. I had enough change for my bus in the morning and nothing else, not even for a cup of coffee, otherwise I would have stuck it out in an all-night cafe.' He laughed. 'I figured Vince wouldn't be up to much in bed and I could get it over with pretty quickly. Which was right – after a five-minute hand job, he shot his load and I got a decent night's sleep. That's beside the point. What didn't really strike me until years later was his flat; it was a real big boy's pad, flashy, with every modern appliance going. He was in his forties, late forties most likely, and making no attempt at growing up. He had the tan, the flat, the car, he only slept with boys; he did anything and everything to avoid growing up.'

Dale didn't really get it. 'What's wrong with that? If he can afford to live lavishly and can still pull younger men when he's nearly fifty, I think he deserves a pat on the back.'

'If that's the way he wants to live, fair enough, but I don't. I promised myself, years ago, I would never turn out like Vince. That's the reason I don't want to grow old in an apartment like this. I don't even want to be living here by the time I'm thirty-five.'

'I'm thirty-three,' Dale mumbled. 'I wouldn't like to think my time was going to be up in two years. I've barely started.'

'You've got me all wrong,' Sam said. 'I not saying thirty-five is old... or forty or fifty or sixty. Everyone has their own life to live. But I'm tired with this lifestyle already. I can't be bothered with the maintenance on something so unreal. I hate to think of myself living here when I'm older, slapping on fake tan and dyeing my hair to pull a chicken who only wants a bed for the night.' He shuddered. 'It's my idea of hell. Can we talk about something else? This is depressing.'

He wasn't wrong. Listening to Sam made Dale feel ancient. Is that what he'd been doing all these years? Going out with younger men in an attempt to stay young himself? Was Dale just like Vince? Sad and pathetic? You're definitely sad, he told himself, for taking this seriously.

He could only think of one thing that would cheer him up right now. Sam might be a cynical little shit, with the most excruciating outlook on age Dale had ever heard, but he was also very hot. Dale hadn't come home with him to talk about the future, he'd come to fuck him. It was about time he got on with it.

He slithered an arm along the back of the sofa, wrapped it around Sam's shoulder and gathered him close. Sam didn't need any further enticement, suddenly he was straddling Dale's lap. Backlit from the open window, he looked extraordinarily handsome.

'You've got years ahead you,' Dale said, stroking the side of his face. 'Don't throw what you have away too soon.'

Before Sam could answer, Dale pulled his head down to kiss him. Sam's hands were all over him, roaming inside his shirt, kneading his muscular shoulders. As Dale's cock began to harden, he remembered he was still wearing the leather strap Sam had bought earlier. He could feel it squeezing the base of his dick as it hardened.

'Are you still wearing your cockstrap?' he gasped in a moment between kisses.

Sam nodded, fastening his mouth over Dale's again. He ground his groin against Dale's stomach to demonstrate. Its heat and rigidity caused his passion to intensify. He pulled Sam's T-shirt over his chest. Sam raised his arms above his head, shedding the garment completely. Dale pressed his face into Sam's chest, brushing his cheek against golden brown hair. Sam's nipples were small and wide apart. Dale flicked his tongue across the right bud, feeling it swell and harden, then nipping the point between his front teeth.

Sam hissed. He palmed the back of Dale's head, pressing his face to his chest, mothering him.

'Take off the rest,' Dale said.

They separated and stood, peeling off layers. As his jeans came down, Sam's cock poked above the waist of his underpants. Dale dropped to his knees, only half undressed himself, and tugged down the damp pants, unveiling Sam's hard rod. The leather strap was fastened tight around the base of his cock and balls, a network of veins coursed below the delicate surface skin. Dale pushed his face against the shaft, mouth open, and trailed his tongue along the underside, licking a dribble of precome from below the opening. When he mouthed the dewy head, Sam moaned encouragement.

Dale's hands roamed across Sam's body, thighs, stomach, balls, while swallowing his meat. Sam gave a helpless groan as he sank the shaft deeper into his mouth. Dale gripped him at the root, curled his hand around the leather strap, and worked him over. Tightening his lips, he slipped up and down, giving plenty of attention to the juicy knob. Sam leaked precome a mile a minute, strong-tasting juice that was saltier than many of the full loads he'd swallowed.

Dale looked up from what he was doing, lifting his eyes across Sam's flat, hairy belly, over his chest, towards his face. The other man returned the gaze, mouth slightly open, a powerless look in his eyes. He managed a lopsided grin before putting his hand on the back of Dale's head and easing him back into position. Dale sucked and slurped, alternating between deep-throated lunges and gentle tongue work around the rosy head. After further deep activity he let Sam's cock pop free of his mouth, a stream of saliva and precome bridging the space between Dale's lips and the throbbing knob end.

'Turn around,' he said.

Sam did as he was told, lifting one leg onto the sofa and leaning forward, giving Dale unrestricted access to his arse. The view from below was grand, it was a perfect little butt; boyish and peachy. His buttocks were pale and blemish free, apart from a tiny birthmark situated low on the left cheek, no larger than a thumbnail and exactly the same colour as Sam's nipples. Dale gripped his arse with both hands, opening him. A modest track of golden brown hair surrounded the beautiful dusky rose pucker. Sam spread his thighs wider, arching his arse. Dale leaned forward, inhaling the rich, savoury scent of his hole. He blew softly, watching it twitch and tighten. Dale parted the white globes further and kissed deep into the crack. Sam shuddered.

'Feel good?' he asked.

Sam moaned.

Dale ran his tongue across the ultra-sensitive skin that surrounded the hot orifice, avoiding the bull's-eye. Sam went nuts, arching his back, chasing Dale's tongue with his hips. Dale teased, keeping just out of reach. Sam trembled with frustration. When it seemed like he'd had enough, Dale poked his tongue right to the heart, burying into his sphincter.

He tongued him long and slow, pampering his anal ring with extensive care, feeling it ease and give a little more with every stroke. The taste was lush and lightly spiced.

'Dale,' Sam whispered. 'Oh God!'

Everything about Sam was different to Charlie, but Dale couldn't stop himself comparing this arse to the last man he'd devoured. Charlie had a broad beefy rump, Sam was small and boyish. Charlie was dark and dense, Sam was peachy. Charlie's anus was bold and greedy where Sam's hole was sweet and tender, melting like snow beneath the heat of his tongue. If they were wine, Charlie was strong, spicy Shiraz, Sam was buttery, oak-aged Chardonnay. Both different and delicious, there was no way to choose between them except personal taste.

'Where's your rubbers?' Dale asked, tearing off the rest of his clothes.

'Everywhere,' said Sam. He reached behind the sofa, opened a drawer and pulled out a strip of condoms and a pump-action bottle of lube. 'Where do you want me?' he asked.

'Stay exactly as you are,' Dale directed, rolling down a rubber and slathering his pole with lube. He pumped another squirt of lube into his palm and fingered Sam's hole, which was already free and ready for him. One hand on Sam's hip, the other on his own dick, Dale pointed his hard shaft down to an angle, until it was aiming directly at the target. 'Ready for it?'

'Yes. I want to feel you in there.'

Dale pushed his cock forward, feeling the tight anal knot slowly open around the head. A warm ring of muscle gripped him tight, forbidding further access. He pushed harder. Sam grunted as his sphincter surrendered. Dale moved both hands to his hips, locking him in position, and slipped his cock all the way home. Sam's core wrapped around him, sharing its intense heat. They stood motionless, allowing Sam's body to adjust.

'Ready for more?' Dale asked.

Unable to speak, Sam twisted his head and nodded.

Dale edged back a stretch, no more than an inch, and slipped back to the hilt. He repeated the manoeuvre, once, and twice. Sam's anus adjusted and was ready for him to work up a rhythm. He fucked his arse with long, controlled strokes, grazing his cock slowly along every inch of his canal. Sam gripped the leather back rest and ground his hips in a rhythm of his own, pushing back through his entire body to meet Dale's dick full on.

Dale pulled out to change position. Sam got down on the sofa, lying on his back. Dale climbed on top of him, lifting Sam's ankles onto his shoulders, and re-entered his hot, juicy interior. Sam took deep breaths through his mouth, looking into Dale's eyes as he fucked him. His brow was damp with perspiration, which increased as the sensations intensified. Soon there were large beads of sweat rolling down his face.

Dale released Sam's ankles, widened his legs and lowered his own full weight on top of him. Their hearts thudded a rapid tattoo as they shoved against each other. Dale pumped faster. The leather sofa squeaked and groaned as they wrestled on top of it. Sam's limbs were wrapped around him, his hands raking his back, ankles tucked against his buttocks, spurring him on.

Dale's cock tingled, close to coming. 'Sshh,' he hissed, freezing, waiting for the sensation to pass. He covered Sam's mouth with his own. He started again when it was safe, grinding his meat, falling into rhythm. Sam's cock was squashed between their bodies, oozing a sticky juice. Once again, Dale fucked him to the knife-edge of orgasm before waiting, breathing deeply, and holding back until the feeling subsided. He rode him further. His heart felt like it could detonate at any time.

'Oh, God,' he finally cried, 'I... can't... ooooohhhhhh!' It surged from Dale's cock like a river in the rainy season, a furious gush that left him physically and mentally drained. His hips continued jerking in spasmodic, erratic strokes long after the sensations had ebbed.

He eased back a little when his strength returned. Sam's cock was a hard, sticky mess. Dale wrapped it in his fist and finished him off.

When it was over, neither of them could speak

Sam made the first move, ages later, easing out from underneath and cleaning himself with a wad of tissues. He stretched an open hand. Dale took it, stood up and followed him to the bedroom.

They were asleep within minutes.

It was after three p.m. when Dale opened his eyes again. The late afternoon sun came hazily through the drawn curtains. The modern decor of Sam's living room continued in the bedroom. It was large and airy, with tropically shaded walls and furnishings in a pot-pourri of colours – yellow, orange, green and red.

Sam's eyes were closed. Dale yawned and stretched slowly, careful not to wake him. He rolled onto his side, watching Sam sleep.

There must be a million men who would trade places with me now, he thought, and they would be the happiest men in the world. If he had only met Sam a week ago, he would not be so hasty to unseat what was happening between them. He would most likely think he had died in the night and the bed in which he lay was heaven.

Until this week, Kelly had been the best lover he'd ever known. He thought he would never find anyone comparable. But next to Sam, Kelly was an insipid, immature runt. Sam was handsome, worldly, incredible in bed; perfect boyfriend material. A prize catch.

And until Monday that was everything Dale wanted: a good man who would appreciate him and want to settle down.

How could it have happened like this? He found what he had been searching for and, on the exact same day, he met and fell in love Charlie; married, immoral, untouchable Charlie.

Above all the other men he had known, Sam was superlative. But now that there was Charlie, Sam would always be second best.

'You're an idiot, Dale Summer,' he murmured.

Sam stirred and opened his eyes. 'Hmm? Did you say something?'

'Just talking to myself,' he said. 'Take no notice.'

Sam pushed himself up on his elbows. His hair was unruly, flat against the right side of his head, where he'd most recently been lying. Coupled with his sleepy expression and bleary eyes, this made him seem years younger than he really was. 'What time is it?'

'After three,' Dale said.

'You're kidding. Good job I arranged cover for the shop. I haven't slept as late as this since I was sixteen years old.' He shuffled across the space between them and threw his arm across Dale's stomach, settling his head on his chest. Dale felt the warm pressure of Sam's dick press against his thigh. 'I'm glad you're still here.'

He rested his hand in the curve of Sam's naked spine. 'What are the chances of a cup of coffee before you kick me out?'

'I can stretch to scrambled eggs if you're hungry,' he said.

'Coffee will be enough.' He stroked Sam's fine blond hair, smoothing down its sleepy disarray. It was the first he'd noticed that Sam's hair had been cut into a short style to cloak a slightly receding hairline. It was hardly noticeable yet Dale found it secretly appealing.

Just not enough, whispered the voice of conscience.

'I need the bathroom,' he said truthfully. Sam told him where to find it. Afterwards Dale strode naked into the living room to pick up his clothes. Sam was in the kitchen, dressed in navy shorts and pale T-shirt. 'You don't mind instant coffee, do you? I can't be bothered messing with filters.'

'It's all I ever drink,' he said, pulling up his briefs. He sat on the sofa to put on his socks. Sam came round to sit beside him as the kettle boiled.

'So,' he said, exhaling slowly. 'Is this it, then?'

Dale tried to keep his tone breezy. 'I'll be back next week. For a couple of days, at least.'

'How many nights are you spending at the cottage?'

'Two. Luke and Paul are coming back on Sunday evening. If I decide to go home it won't be until Monday.'

'Do you think you will?'

'No, I told you, I'll stick around a few more days. Until midweek at least, maybe right through to the weekend.'

Dale recognised the hope in Sam's eyes and felt like a complete bastard. How many times had he been in Sam's position? Shouldn't he know better than to fuck him around?

But he's your best chance of seeing Charlie, the inner voice contended. *How far are you prepared to go, Dale? How badly do you want him?*

He reached for his shirt. 'Why don't you give me your number? I'll call you when we get back.'

Sam broke into a wide smile and reached for the pen and paper he kept beside the phone. 'How about we go for that dinner?' he asked optimistically. 'Shall I reserve a table? What night is best for you?'

Dale folded and pocketed the number.

'I'll call you on Sunday,' he said. 'I'll let you know then.'

He finished dressing, focusing on his clothes. He couldn't raise his head for fear of the complete trust he would see in Sam's eyes.

Nine

BREATHING SPACE

The cottage exceeded Dale's expectations. The best he had hoped for was a modest bungalow with basic facilities. He was dubious that there would even be an indoor toilet. He toyed with the notion of buying a sleeping bag prior to the trip, in case the beds proved unusable.

He was ecstatic to discover his doubts were unfounded.

Raby Cottage was built in the 1830s and had recently been refurbished to high standards. Situated two miles from the small village of Moordale, with the nearest building being a farmhouse half a mile away, the two-storey cottage faced south, with a picturesque view of the open moors. There was a large living room with a log fire, low-beamed ceiling, twin sofas, television and video. The kitchen was equipped with oven, kettle, microwave, toaster and washing machine. Two bathrooms, one upstairs, one down. The first-floor bathroom contained a huge, old-fashioned bath on cast iron legs, as well as an electric shower. There were three bedrooms, each with double beds, the master room contained a four-poster, and there was central heating throughout. Despite the modernisation, the cottage had been decorated in a rustic style throughout to preserve its traditional form.

As they had left Newbiggin Bay before the Friday afternoon rush hour began, the drive to Raby Cottage took less than an hour. The caretaker was waiting to greet them when they arrived at four o'clock. He'd already lit the fire in the living room and turned on the heating. He provided them with spare keys and a guidebook to the Durham area before leaving.

They were the first to arrive, so Luke and Paul established themselves in the master bedroom. Dale said he didn't mind taking the smallest room at the rear of the house, leaving the middle bedroom for William and Colin. He hadn't met either man before, but Luke assured him they were great guys, and they were all bound to get along.

Dale caught the look that passed between his friends at the mention of the small room. 'What's going on?' he asked suspiciously.

'Well,' Luke said innocently, 'you might not be entirely on your own in there. William and Colin said they might bring a mate with them.'

'We thought there would be two double and two single beds here,' Paul added. 'We didn't think it would be a problem.'

'We had no idea there was only three doubles,' Luke said. 'You don't mind sharing, do you?'

He could tell by the collusive glance that passed between them that this was a setup.

'Who is this mate?' he asked warily.

'I've never met him,' Luke said, 'but William and Colin say he's lovely. He's an actor. He's done a few things for tv and he was a villain in the last Bond movie.'

'What's his name?'

'Eddie Marrs.' Luke said the name like it had great significance.

Dale was a massive fan of James Bond and knew the key cast members of every film. 'I've never heard of Eddie Marrs,' he said.

'Neither have we,' Paul admitted, 'but he's supposed to be very good.'

'And very good looking,' Luke added.

Dale groaned, heading for the bedroom to unpack his bag. The guys obviously meant well – fixing up a couple of their single friends – but this wasn't what he wanted. His objective for this weekend was to sort out his priorities. He'd hoped that time on his own and the fresh country air would clear his head and help him focus on what was important. He felt like a major shit over his behaviour with Sam – using him to get to Charlie. Sam was a remarkable man, sexy, modest, caring, and Dale was pissing him around to get close to a man he didn't have a snowball in hell's chance of winning. The question bugging him was, what was he going to do about it?

He'd hoped this uncomplicated, back-to-basics weekend would help him see clearly. But now, because of well-intentioned meddling from his friends, it was not going to be so clear cut.

After unpacking his toiletries, Dale went down to the kitchen and unloaded the groceries he'd bought that morning: milk, bread, butter, wine, cheese, bacon, eggs, pizza.

While Dale was preparing his shopping list over breakfast that morning, Luke had told him that Colin was a health freak. 'He eats fish but no meat, and I'm not sure if he touches dairy these days. There was a time, when he was on some bloody awful macrobiotic diet, that he hardly ate anything. Thankfully he stopped that one – I think William got sick of it and put his foot down. But don't worry about that, he'll bring his own health food. And William will eat anything, given the chance.'

There was no mention of a sixth guest then.

Dale had also brought a portable CD player. While he was shopping that morning, he went to a record store and found the Kylie Minogue record Sam had told him about. It had been released in 1998, during an experimental but commercially unsuccessful phase in her career. The song Dale had been hearing all week was 'Too Far', the opening track, a noirish, lyrically bleak dance tune. Unlike anything he'd heard from Minogue before, it was a world away from her usual pop style.

As he listened to the chaotic beats and rhythms, Dale thought about Charlie. The song was like a cinematic theme, a soundtrack for Charlie and his hard-core appearances at The Chain. It perfectly captured the essence of his contradictory nature: beautiful, confusing, complicated, compounded by a raw sexuality.

Dale was listening to the CD and chopping ingredients for a salad. As he gazed out of the kitchen window, he saw a silver car pull off the main road and turn down the dirt track, towards the cottage.

'They're here!' he shouted, loud enough for Luke and Paul to hear him upstairs. Their bedroom door was closed and he suspected they were taking full advantage of the four-poster bed.

William was the eldest of the three new arrivals, a great big bear of a man, who smothered Luke and Paul in his enthusiastic embrace, before solidly pumping Dale's hand in a welcoming shake. It was hard to put an exact age on him, but he was somewhere around forty. He was tall and broad, with a ruggedly handsome face and large grey eyes. He had hair everywhere; on his head it was short, a dark brown fuzz, peppered with grey. His upper lip was concealed behind a wide moustache and there were tufts of hair showing above the neck of his white T-shirt. Dale noticed his forearms, which were incredibly thick and also covered in thick brown hair. His body was huge, not fat, but massive, with a broad chest and thickset waist. Despite the rough exterior there was a definite charm about his eyes, and a warm, lived-in quality to his features.

'Pleased to meet you,' he said, still pumping Dale's arm.

Colin, although of similar height and build to Dale, seemed slight in comparison to his partner. His was younger, in his early thirties, with spiky brown hair and smoky good looks. His square jaw bristled with day-old stubble. He studied Dale with intelligent eyes as they shook hands. He wore dark jeans and trainers, with a blue ribbed sports vest and zippered tracksuit top. He exuded an athletic grace.

'It's good to finally meet you,' he said. 'Luke is always going on about the fun you guys had at college.' He had the same northern accent as Luke. Dale didn't know their full history but had always assumed Luke and Colin's friendship dated back to childhood.

The third man stepped forward to shake his hand. 'Hi,' he said. 'I'm Eddie.'

Eddie also spoke with a Geordie accent, though it was more moderate than the other men's – perhaps he'd deliberately dropped it. He looked a few years short of thirty. He was classically good looking with even features and chocolate brown eyes that dazzled when he smiled. He was shorter than the others, but still around five eleven. He wore an open-necked polo shirt and faded jeans, and the body beneath the clothes looked impressive, with strong shoulders and a well-defined chest tapering to a flat abdomen and narrow waist. With his friendly smile and warm manner, he didn't look anything like a James Bond thug.

Dale led him up to the back bedroom. 'We have to bunk up,' he said, indicating the lone bed. 'Did they tell you about that?'

Eddie dumped his bag at the foot of the bed and straightened up. 'The first I heard was in the car, five minutes ago.'

Dale smiled. 'We've been totally stitched up.'

Eddie brushed his fingers absently across his stomach. 'I don't think I snore, if that's any consolation.'

He laughed. 'I haven't had any complaints either.' He sat on the bed while Eddie unpacked. If he had to spend two nights with this guy, he might as well get to know him. 'You're not vegetarian, are you?'

'Absolutely not. I eat anything and everything.'

'Good,' he traced a pattern on the counterpane with his fingers. 'Is it true you were in the last Bond movie?'

Eddie's cheeks coloured as he took toothpaste and towels out of his bag. 'You won't recognise me. I didn't have any lines. I'm just a henchman at the edge of a couple of scenes. You'd only know I was there if you were looking for me.'

'I will,' he said. 'I'm a big fan, I have the series on DVD.'

Eddie's blush increased to a deep shade of red that coloured his face and neck. 'I'm hardly in it. I was only on the set a couple of days.'

'Did you meet any of the leads?'

'Yeah, Pierce is as gorgeous in the flesh as he is on screen.'

'Wow.'

'Yeah. That's why no one knows I'm there. How can I compete when sharing a screen with Pierce?'

Dale found Eddie's humility deeply attractive. He wasn't used to actors and the few he had met had left a negative impression. While at college he'd spent a night with a minor soap-opera star who was appearing in a local pantomime. He thought he was God's gift and the sex was abysmal. One of Kelly's old friends had danced in the chorus of *Chicago* for six months – and what a pain in the arse he was, full of his own importance. The last Dale heard, he was hoofing his way round the provinces in a tour of *Cats*.

On first impressions, Eddie didn't seem anything like those old drama queens, which was a relief.

'What other work have you done? Anything I might have seen?'

Eddie gave up unpacking and dropped, belly down, onto the bed. 'The usual stuff: an episode of *Casualty*, a victim in *The Bill*. I was a photographer in an episode of *Footballers' Wives*. I haven't had the most illustrious career.'

'Where are you based? London?'

He shook his head. 'I share a flat in Manchester but I'm hardly ever home. I have to go where the work is. I'm about to start on a six-month tour of *My Night With Reg*, so I won't see much of Manchester this year.'

'You must love it, though.'

'Well, yes,' he said, 'but I worry about the future. I don't want to be scraping by for the rest of my life. There isn't enough work. I made myself a promise when I started out. If I hadn't cracked a decent-sized part by the time I was thirty, then I would retrain for a proper career before I got too old.'

'You must have a few years to go until then.'

Eddie chuckled. 'Fourteen months. Unless there's a miracle between now and then, I'll be going back to school for my thirtieth.'

Dale thought for a moment. '*My Night With Reg*, I'll look out for that one coming my way.'

'Yeah, come along. Moral support in the audience is always good. I'll get you free tickets.'

'I'll make sure you get a standing ovation.'

Dale was relieved. Sharing his room with the actor would not be so bad. Eddie seemed a friendly sort. The company might do him good. Maybe he would open up to Eddie about his Charlie/Sam dilemma later. Despite years of friendship, Dale hadn't felt able to unburden himself on Luke with this. He knew what Luke would advise – do the right thing – and he wasn't ready to be told that just yet.

He needed an impartial ear.

It was a cold, damp evening. While Dale cooked the pizzas in the kitchen, the other guys laid the table in the dining room, where William lit a fire. A huge leaded window gave the most spectacular view of the surrounding country. The cottage was situated on the bank of a valley. Way below, a flock of sheep grazed on the side of the hill, and further down, a narrow river cut its way through the county.

The others had brought a roast chicken, rice salad, lentils and bread. Colin helped Dale with the final preparations and carried the food to the long table in the dining room. William and Colin sat on one side with Luke. Paul sat opposite Luke, with Dale sitting next to Eddie. They opened three bottles of wine to begin, two red and one white, which everyone drank except William, who wanted beer.

The company was good, with plenty of laughter. William and Colin had just returned from a holiday in Sitges.

'Have you ever been?' Colin asked Dale.

'No. I haven't even heard of it. Where is it?'

There were gasps of astonishment around the table. 'Call yourself a gay man,' Luke quipped.

'Oh, I see,' said Dale, tearing a piece of wholemeal bread, 'it's a gay place. Don't you get enough of the scene at home without going on holiday for it too?'

'No,' the other five chorused.

'It's a small Spanish resort, south of Barcelona,' William explained. 'Really quite quaint. It comes to life at night with around thirty gay bars and a couple of clubs. You should definitely check it out, at least once in your life.'

'This is my first holiday in years,' Dale explained. 'I was planning to go abroad later in the year, but when I do, I want to escape the gay ghetto, not find a hotter version of Newbiggin Bay.'

They laughed.

'Don't knock it,' William said. 'You'll love it. We went for the first time six years ago and we've been back at least once a year ever since.'

'How long have you guys been together?'

'Tenth anniversary in October,' Colin answered.

'Wow!' Dale gasped.

'I know,' grumbled Eddie. 'These guys have been together forever and the longest relationship I ever managed was fifteen months.'

'That's because you're never around to have a relationship,' Colin said. 'Most of your boyfriends finish with you because they never get to see you.'

'So what's my excuse?' Dale asked. 'I've been living in the same place for eight years and I haven't fared any better than Eddie.'

Luke heaved a sigh. 'I can answer that but you never listen to me.'

'Go on,' he said. 'I'm listening now.'

'You go for pretty boys, too young and too dumb for you.'

'Well observed.'

'That can't be all there is to it,' Eddie added. 'Age isn't that important. There's ten years between William and Colin. They've done all right.'

'They've always been equal,' Luke said. 'Dale doesn't go for men who are his equal, he goes for immature chickens. Invariably it fails when they start to grow up.'

Dale frowned. 'I always treat my boyfriends as equals.'

'No, you don't. You treat them like kids, little boys in need of protection. As soon as they realise they don't need a daddy, they piss off.'

'Bummer,' said Colin.

Dale considered Luke's exhortation as the conversation drifted. He remembered Sam's story about the sad old queen sleeping with younger boys to maintain his own facade of youth. Why couldn't he be attracted to men younger than himself without everyone assuming there was something wrong with him or the men he went out with?

He was hardly old at thirty-three, and it wasn't like he had a thing for obscenely young lads. In fact, the youngest lover he'd ever had was twenty, and Dale was only twenty-seven himself at the time.

He didn't understand why none of his relationships had lasted but Luke was wrong, it had nothing to do with age.

They drew out the meal until nine o'clock, at which point William suggested they walk to the nearest pub.

'How far is *near*?' Luke asked suspiciously.

'In the village,' he said, 'shouldn't take us more than forty minutes or so. It'll help walk off some of this food.'

They cleared the dishes and collected jackets from upstairs before setting off. The sky was dark and the temperature was dropping rapidly. They followed the narrow lane, walking in pairs, sticking to the verge. There were no lights on the road and soon the way ahead was pitch black.

William and Paul were in the lead, having set a brisk pace, followed by Luke and Colin. Dale walked with Eddie, trailing along behind. Unused to the country, his eyes flickered warily into the darkness on either side of them whenever he heard movement.

'Creepy, isn't it?'

'Not really,' Eddie said softly. 'I rather like the peace out here. It beats city life.'

Dale could just about discern the features of his face as the darkness deepened. The lights of the village were still a good way off.

'Luke seemed to think he knows you pretty well,' Eddie commented.

'Better than I know myself, it seems.'

The sound of Eddie's laugh was soft. 'So you're single at the minute?'

'Yes,' he said, not quite ready to reveal his hand.

'Me too,' Eddie said. 'Though William and Colin make a bigger deal of it than I do. I can't say I'm bothered. They're lucky, having lasted so long, but I don't believe it happens for everybody.'

'Don't you?'

'One true love? No. Those guys ahead are the exception, not the rule.'

'So what do you think?'

'I think that we meet people at different times in our lives, our paths converge for a while before heading off in separate directions.'

'Isn't that depressing?'

'Is it? I'd be more depressed waiting around for the love of my life, clinging desperately to every bad relationship, trying to make it last, in case he might be the one.'

'I believe in *the one*,' Dale mumbled.

'Hope that works out for you.'

The pub was a traditional country concern, serving an impressive selection of food and beers. The six men found themselves a long table by the window. The jukebox was surprisingly up to date, and Dale and Luke fed it a constant stream of coins to keep the music playing. The out-of-the-way location gave the landlord a certain freedom over his licensing hours – he closed the doors at eleven but was still serving drinks when they left at quarter past midnight.

On the walk back to the cottage, Dale and Eddie strode ahead of the others, followed by William and Colin, with Luke and Paul trailing well behind. Although they had each drunk a fair amount, the nippy country air had a sobering effect.

Out of the village and back on the deserted road, Luke and Paul held hands as they walked, huddling close for warmth.

'What do you think?' Luke asked his lover in a conspiratorial tone. 'Will they get it on?'

'You mean Dale and Eddie?'

'Who else?'

'They seem to be getting on all right,' Paul remarked.

'I hope they do. It's about time Dale had some luck.'

'Ha. I think he's been lucky enough this week. Has he let on to you where he was all Wednesday night?'

'No,' said Luke. 'He reckons I wouldn't believe him. I'm gonna try to get it out of him when he's drunk this weekend.'

'You don't think he was seeing that married bloke again, do you? It could explain why he's been so cagey.'

'I don't think that's it. He wouldn't have been able to stay out all night if he was with him, would he?'

'True,' observed Paul. 'But he's definitely up to something.'

'We'll see.' In the pitch darkness, Luke slithered his hand around Paul's groin. 'How about we get up to something ourselves?'

Paul's groin pulsed. 'There's a four-poster waiting for us.'

Luke squeezed the bulge. 'That's not what I had in mind.' He stopped walking, pulling Paul close against him and kissing him in the dark.

'Here?' '

'Here and now?'

'What about the others?'

Luke marched Paul over the verge until they backed up against the low stone wall. Paul ceased protesting. His hands were all over Luke and it didn't take him long to tear open the front of Luke's jeans and release his dick. Paul stroked it out, getting it harder, milking precome. Luke leaned up against the wall and widened his stance.

Paul felt his way down Luke's body until he was at eye level with his cock, gripped the shaft at its thick mid-section and rubbed the sensitive head across his lips, smearing precome across his mouth.

Luke moaned. The darkness was so complete that he could not see anything of his lover, only feel him, feel his warm breath on his tender organ. Moist lips caressed his head before the warm void of Paul's mouth fully encompassed him.

'Ah, Paul,' he sighed, taking his lover's head in both hands and pulling it down over his pole. Paul was a grand cocksucker, effortlessly deep-throating. Luke guided him for a moment, drawing his mouth right back to the tip before pulling him back down. Luke released his hold and Paul found a rhythm of his own. Luke began to feel the cold seeping through his clothes, but Paul's mouth kept him warm, relaying heat through the delicate skin of his shaft.

'Hey guys!' William's voice cut through the darkness from somewhere up ahead. 'Did you get lost back there?'

'Just... go on,' Luke gasped. 'We'll catch you up.'

Paul paused, listening for an approach. When he was certain they were alone again, he resumed his delightful task, sucking, slurping. He worked Luke with his mouth and hands, rolling his head around the shaft, pulling back the skin.

Luke was close to coming. His breathing became shorter, his thighs trembled. He gripped Paul's hair and started making guttural noises. His hips jerked, face-fucking his way to a climax. A magnificent sensation started in his groin, travelling through his pelvis, his belly, all over his body. He hovered on the edge of orgasm for what seemed like minutes before it finally came, spurting down Paul's throat in long, juddering waves. His hips began to slow.

'Don't swallow,' he gasped, hauling Paul to his feet. They kissed in the dark, open mouthed, swapping semen and saliva. Paul's tongue thrust Luke's load deep into his mouth and Luke swallowed, licking his lips afterwards.

'That was some good blow job,' he gasped, tucking his cock inside his jeans. 'Thanks.'

'You can return the honour when we get back.'

The others were waiting in the living room, a bottle of red open on the coffee table. Luke and Paul headed straight for the fireplace, warming themselves on the log fire that roared in the hearth.

'What took you so long?' Dale asked, cheekily. He was sitting in the middle of the sofa between William and Eddie. Colin was cross-legged on the floor.

'We wanted to take our time,' Luke said, 'to admire our surroundings.'

The others laughed.

Paul poured two glasses of wine, passing one to Luke. 'I've been dying to ask you a similar question,' he said to Dale. 'Where were you from seven p.m. on Wednesday until five p.m. Thursday?'

Dale laughed and rolled his eyes. 'That's for me to know.'

'C'mon, you can't do that. You've learned more about the bay in a week than we have in five years. We're dying to know what we've been missing. What's the latest?'

'Go on, Dale,' Colin urged. 'We're all intrigued now.'

'Okay,' he said, raising his hands. He told them of his experience with Sam, of XL, Chaps and The Sex Cabaret.

'Sex Cabaret!' Luke gasped. 'You're making this up.'

'I'm not.'

'He's not,' Eddie broke in.

They all looked at him.

'It's been going for years. The original cabaret started in Germany in the 1970s. It has quite a cult following. There's more than one production now. I saw a performance in Ibiza two years ago. It's a pretty wild show. I'm amazed they're performing in the UK – our obscenity laws are so arcane.'

'It may only be a trial run,' Dale mused. 'They don't advertise and entrance was by invitation only. Sam only had tickets because of his shop. I think it was quite secretive.'

'It always is,' Eddie said. 'Even in Europe they don't play the same venue for more than a month or so. It's always moving around.'

'Fuck me!' Luke gawked. 'Dale, you are not going out without us ever again. I can't believe the stuff you've got yourself involved in. In fact, I'm going to the Cock Shop straight after work on Monday. All this sex stuff is happening on our doorstep and we're missing out.'

Ten

FREE

Dale's alarm sounded at eight-thirty, rousing him from a dream that was vivid in erotic imagery. The details were hazy and the pictures faded from his mind as soon as he tried to bring them to the surface. His head was muggy with booze. He kept his eyes closed as he reached over and knocked off the alarm. His body registered he was not in his own bed, nor at Luke's, but it took his brain a moment longer to remember where he was. The mattress and pillows were more flaccid than any he would have chosen for himself. But there was nothing soft about the cock poking in his back.

The yield of the bed had caused their bodies to sink, rolling towards each other in the night. Though they slept in their underwear for modesty's sake, there was no mistaking Eddie's morning erection, which rested in the cleft of Dale's butt. As their bodies had gravitated towards each other in a drunken slumber, Eddie's arm had found its way around Dale's chest. He lay against Dale's back in a spoon position, the heat of his body shimmering down Dale's spine. Soft, even breath caressed his neck.

Dale's own cock was rigid and he had a desperate urge to piss. He tried to move without waking Eddie, easing himself out of the dip in the bed. It didn't work. The incline was steeper than he thought and they ended up rolling back together. The giggle from the pillow behind told him Eddie was awake.

'A few nights of this won't do my back much good,' Dale said lightly.

Eddie pulled back to his own side of the bed. 'Hope you didn't mind me cuddling into you,' he said. 'It was so fucking cold in the night. I had two options: get up and find something to put on or share

137

your body heat. There was really no choice.'

He stretched, arching his spine from the mattress.

Dale got up and hurried down the hall to the bathroom, grateful to find it empty. When he returned to the bedroom, his cock had softened. Eddie's hadn't. He was standing at the foot of the bed in his underpants, rummaging through his bag. His briefs were filled with a swollen rod that sloped naturally to the left, leaning along his hip. Dale had been too drunk and tired to take much notice of Eddie's body last night, but he gave it his full attention now: the light triangle of brown hair in the centre of his chest, his stomach with its lean cut of muscle, more hair, a thick path from navel to groin, his strong arms and legs. In build he was closer to Sam than to Charlie.

Dale swatted the idea away before it had formed fully. He couldn't start comparing everyone he met to Charlie.

He stepped into yesterday's jeans and put on an old FCUK T-shirt, before going down for breakfast. Luke, Paul and William were already at the table, the kitchen was filled with the delicious smell of grilled bacon, scrambled eggs and toast. 'It's Raining Men' played on the radio. Colin was on the patio, practising a yoga routine in the hazy morning damp. As Dale watched through the open door, he balanced on his shoulders with his legs straight in the air, slowly spreading them into a wide scissors motion. He then brought his ankles together and lowered his feet over his head into a plough position.

Dale poured orange juice, dropped two slices of brown bread into the toaster and sat down. None of the other men was dressed. They sat round the table in shorts and T-shirts; Paul was bare chested.

'Hangover?' Luke asked, looking rough himself.

'A little muggy,' Dale admitted.

William tossed a strip of painkillers across the table. 'Take two,' he said. 'We're waiting for them to take effect before we even think about getting ready.'

'What about Colin?' Dale asked, indicating the yoga enthusiast. 'How can he do that with a hangover?'

'He doesn't have one,' William grumbled. 'He drank three pints of water before going to bed. He was up pissing four times through the night, but he's brighter than any of us this morning.'

'Clever boy.'

Eddie entered the kitchen in grey sweatpants and a baggy T-shirt, his hair sticking up at crazy angles. He spotted the painkillers and popped two out of the foil wrapper. He glanced at Colin's exertions while pouring a mug of tea and groaned. 'I should be out there with him,' he said, 'but I can't be arsed. You have to relax sometime, don't you?'

'Colin doesn't,' said William. 'He works out every single day. Even on Christmas morning.'

'That's insane,' Luke said, stuffing a forkful of bacon into his mouth. 'We all want to look good but there are limits.'

'I keep telling him that but he won't have it.'

Dale got up to butter his toast. As he caught sight of Colin's perfectly toned physique, his tight waist and flat abs, he decided to omit the marmalade. Maybe he should take up yoga too – that effortless flexibility would come in handy. He made a mental note to check out some classes when he got home. It had to be better than the grind of a gym.

'What are we all doing today?' he asked, sitting back down next to Eddie.

'Paul?'

Paul was studying the local guide that the caretaker had provided. 'It depends what you want. Ramble in the countryside or go into town?'

'Town,' they answered as one.

'All right,' he laughed, backtracking through the flimsy guidebook. 'How about Durham? It'll take about half an hour in the car.'

'I haven't been to Durham since I was a kid,' Luke said. 'My nana used to take us in the summer holidays.'

None of the others had been.

'Well, there should be enough to keep us all occupied,' Paul said, 'especially if the weather breaks. There's a castle, a cathedral, a market, cinema, theatre, restaurants, bars. We should be able to fill a day easily.'

Dale and Eddie cleared the kitchen while the earlier risers took the first turn at the bathrooms. Dale filled the sink and started washing the dishes while Eddie packed away the food. On the patio, Colin had arranged himself in a lotus position and looked like he was in a trance.

'Did you sleep all right?' Eddie asked Dale.

'Like a log. What about you?'

'On and off. I'm not a very deep sleeper. I was worried my tossing and turning might have kept you awake.'

'Didn't feel a thing.'

'Apart from morning wood.'

Dale laughed. 'Yes, that was hard to miss. It's been a while since I last woke up with an erection in my back.'

Eddie found a towel and started drying. 'They're all going to wonder whether we did anything.'

'Let them wonder. They shouldn't be so nosy.'

'They'll just assume that we fucked anyway.'

'Probably. Luke has an active imagination.'

'So do I,' said Eddie baitingly. 'That's partly why I found it difficult to sleep. I lied about the cold. I put my arm around you because I couldn't stand lying there any longer without touching you. It's the first time I've ever been to bed with a gorgeous guy and not had sex with him. Cuddling you was the least I could do.'

'If you feel that way tonight, you have my permission to wake me.'

Dale wondered what was so different about himself this week – everyone wanted a piece. His own out-look had changed too. Until now, casual sex held little appeal, but here he was, gearing up to fuck his third man in a week.

Now that sex was a definite possibility, Eddie and Dale found themselves moving closer to each other. Instead of riding with their respective friends into Durham, they sat together in the back of Luke's

Range Rover and flirted openly. Though their seat belts kept them a decent distance apart, their hands moved freely across the back seats, chasing each other's fingers, goading, tickling. They'd both showered and changed into clean clothes and Eddie looked remarkable in black jeans, a blue striped shirt and dark jacket.

They had no expectations for the day, other than to enjoy themselves.

In the centre of the market square, on a towering pillar, stood a bare-bottomed statue of King Neptune. At three o'clock, Dale and Eddie were sitting at the base of the statue eating hot dogs. They'd had a busy few hours. On arrival in Durham, their party had split up: Luke wanted to shop and took Colin with him, William and Paul went to look at the castle and then take a boat trip along the River Wear. Dale and Eddie had also visited the castle but they then spent an hour in the cathedral, before finding a cafe for lunch.

Eddie's company was a pleasure. They were relaxed and chatty together. Dale felt as though he had known him for much longer than a day. Now Eddie was telling him about his last boyfriend. 'It was more of an affair, I suppose,' he said, mulling over his hot dog. 'He's an actor, fairly well known.' When he mentioned his name, Dale knew exactly who he meant. 'Yes,' said Eddie, 'you're quite right, he is married. We were touring in a play together, a six-month job. He started fucking me in Southampton, the second stop on the tour, and went all the way up to Glasgow. The affair ended along with the play. Handy, eh? Last I heard he was bumming some boy out of *Hollyoaks*.'

From the marketplace, they walked along Saddler Street. Although it was a grey afternoon, the town centre was busy. They moved with the crowd at a leisurely pace. There was no hurry. They weren't due to meet the others until five.

Dale realised that he hadn't thought about Charlie since that morning, then immediately reproached himself for allowing the cause of so much confusion to resurface in his mind at all. He pushed his thoughts of the carpenter away and concentrated on the man he was with now.

'How long have you known William and Colin?' he asked.

Eddie reckoned it up. 'Four years.'

'How did you meet?'

'I met William in Gran Canaria. They take a holiday every year, one week apart from each other. William was staying in the same hotel, on the floor below mine. We got talking over breakfast one morning and, as we were both on our own, made plans for dinner that night. I have no problem travelling on my own but I hate eating by myself.'

'I know what you mean. People always stare at the sad guy on his own.'

'That's exactly what William said when we struck up our first conversation. We were both alone in the hotel cafe and we got talking. It started as a bit of a holiday fling, nothing special, just fun. Then we realised we liked each other for more than just sex. We kept in touch when we got home and he introduced me to Colin.'

'Does Colin know about your affair?'

'Colin knows everything,' Eddie said knowingly.

'And it doesn't bother him?'

'I think it did at first. They have an open relationship, but I can understand him being concerned when it looked like there was more to me and William than a casual fling.'

'Was there?'

'Friendship, nothing else. Colin came round to the idea soon enough... Right after he'd fucked me himself,' Eddie added with a laugh. 'What about Luke and Paul? Ever bumped nasties with them?'

'God, no,' he said, appalled at the idea. 'It would be like shagging my brothers. I don't think I'd be comfortable attaching sex to our relationship, this far on.'

'I thought it was obligatory for gay men to shag their friends.'

'No,' he was dumbfounded. 'Have you?'

'All but the truly ugly,' he winked, inching closer. 'Bodes well for tonight, don't you think? If we're going to become good friends, it's something we need to get out of the way first.'

Dale walked, wondering whether his growing sense of liberation was developed enough to allow sex and friendship to coexist. He'd been unable to stay on amicable terms with any of his ex-boyfriends.

'Have you ever slept with anyone you didn't stay friends with?'

Eddie laughed. 'Dozens. More often than not.'

'So why risk it? Why jeopardise friendship for the sake of a screw?'

'There is no risk. If the friendship doesn't survive through sex, then it's not worth having in the first place.'

'Interesting.'

'Want to put it to the test?'

'I thought we'd already decided that, *roommate*.'

'Why wait until tonight?'

Dale stopped walking. They were crossing over Elvet Bridge to the other side of the city. The crowds of Saturday shoppers surged around them. Dale looked at Eddie and their eyes rested on one another. Eddie indicated a narrow set of stone steps leading to a footpath along the river bank and he nodded in response.

They pushed through the surge of people, towards the steps, grateful to escape the crowds. The footpath stretched off in either direction, wide and open to the left, narrow with a bushy overhang to the right. Dale moved right.

'Wait,' said Eddie. He'd spotted the arches beneath the bridge and started walking towards them. Those further back, away from the river, were sheltered. 'I read in the guidebook that these were used to house prisoners at one point.'

Most of the larger arches had been fitted with doors and were used for storage, but they found a smaller recess, sheltered and dark, that could only be seen by someone walking directly in front of it.

Eddie's hands clutched Dale's sides, drawing him into the shadowy alcove. 'This should do nicely.' He moved his hands around Dale's waist, tracing the defined lines of his torso until he landed on his arse.

They kissed.

Dale's heart thudded faster. If they were caught, if they were arrested, his career would be over. There would be no room in any law firm for a solicitor with a record for lewd behaviour. But Eddie was nibbling on his ear lobe while his hands continued to knead and roam his arse. Dale's cock throbbed, pressing against the insistent bulge in Eddie's jeans. He didn't care about his career or his future. He was truly alive here and now and he knew what he wanted to do.

'Drop your pants,' he urged Eddie.

He looked around, back down the trail. They were alone.

Eddie undid his belt and tugged down the front of his jeans and his underpants, revealing a hard cock. His foreskin was withdrawn and tucked behind the crown. He stroked his organ proudly, licking his lips.

Dale descended, resting his weight on his toes, and looked at Eddie's cock. It was gorgeous, not massive but a decent size. His balls nestled within a nice bush of pubic hair. The skin of his scrotum was several shades darker than the rest of his body. Dale reacted on instinct: holding the balls, he guided Eddie's ripe, juicy dick into his mouth. He took him down to the root until his bushy pubes tickled his nose. The cock leapt inside his mouth, feeling even harder. Dale knew how to make him happy. He sucked up and down, twisting his head. He teased the little slit with the tip of his tongue, moving his mouth from side to side, and sucked him deep into his throat. He moved his hands round Eddie's back, kneading his arse and drawing him into his mouth.

Eddie gasped, 'Oh shit.' His cock hardened and Dale's mouth was filled with the scorching flavour of come. His body quivered, his hips bucked and squirt after squirt of strong-tasting spunk slid down Dale's throat, warming his stomach.

'S... sorry,' Eddie said breathlessly. 'I couldn't stop myself.'

'It's all right.' Dale stood up, unzipping his own jeans, and heaved out his dick. 'I'd love to fuck you but if you're not up to it, just blow me.'

A long trail of come dangled from the edge of Eddie's dick. He was still erect. He fumbled in his pockets, pulling out a small pack of rubbers and lube, which he handed to Dale. Eddie turned around and shoved his jeans and pants halfway down his thighs.

Dale heard voices above, passing on the bridge, but he ignored them and put on the condom. The voices faded until all he could hear was the watery inflection of the river. Eddie shoved his arse towards him. Dale looked down at the brown crack while slathering the lube over his cock. Eddie's arse was smooth, devoid of any hair. Dale fingered lube into the warm crack, finding the hole, tunnelling inside. Eddie groaned, spreading his cheeks wide. Dale withdrew. Edde's arsehole glistened in the shadowy light.

Urgently wanting him but still concerned about discovery, Dale shoved in with his dick. Eddie's anus was tight and opposed his cock. Dale pushed harder until the resistance was broken and his cock slipped into the silky passage. He fucked hard and fast, feeling the urgency increasing with each stroke.

'Yes,' Eddie hissed, grinding against him. 'Fuck me. Fuck me hard!'

Dale did fuck him hard, thrusting his hips. He hammered Eddie's arse with all the force he could, digging his hands into his waist. Eddie responded fiercely, his excitement growing, making the sex harder and faster. He took the brunt, gripping his thighs and clenching his arse muscles tight against Dale's cock when he thrust in, relaxing as he withdrew.

Sex that fast, that intense, couldn't last. Dale quickly felt the familiar tightening in his balls, a rush along his perineum, the outpouring from his cock into Eddie's arse. He squeezed Eddie's waist as he continued to come, but the intensity subsided. He slipped his right arm around him and held him close. Eddie had a hand on his own cock, jerking furiously.

Dale caressed his stomach, his pecs. 'Yes,' he purred enthusiastically. 'Go on.'

Eddie began breathing harder, desperately striving for a second orgasm, jerking his hips in an erratic rhythm. 'Oh,' he cried, suddenly there, 'I'm gonna…'

A shot of come came flying out of his cock and he yelled in relief. His body shook, his arse suddenly became tense. Eddie pumped his cock for another shot, and another and another.

Dale held the root of his own dick and slowly withdrew. The come-heavy tip of the condom remained inside Eddie's tight hole and needed a gentle tug to be released. Dale tied off the rubber and tossed it down a drain cover.

Fifteen minutes later they were sitting in Cafe Lush, a first-floor bar overlooking the river. They sat across from each other. Dale noticed with some delight that Eddie's face still bore the warm blush of sex. The cafe was full and it was only through luck that they'd managed to find a table by the window. They had both ordered beer but their thirst was so intense that they had already almost finished.

Dale caught the eye of the waitress, a good-looking woman in her thirties, and indicated two more bottles. She nodded.

'Nice place,' Eddie said.

'Yeah,' said Dale, 'there's a world of difference between Durham and Newbiggin Bay.' No sex shops, for a start, he added to himself.

'I haven't been to the bay for years,' Eddie admitted. 'How are you finding it?'

'It's been an interesting week.'

'Do you want to tell me about it?' Eddie asked, adding with a smile, 'Now that we're friends.'

There was a pause in which their eyes came together. Dale suddenly knew that Eddie meant just that; they were friends now. There was no question of anything more between them, Eddie wasn't interested in pursuing a relationship. This was it and it was something good.

The second round of beers arrived. Dale waited until the waitress had left before speaking. He told Eddie everything: about Sam and Charlie, the Cock Shop, The Chain, the night at XL and the cabaret.

He told him about his desire for Charlie and the shitty way he'd played with Sam's affections.

'It's a mess,' he admitted at the end. 'And then, as if life wasn't complicated enough, I just fucked my third man in a week. No offence.'

Eddie smiled. 'No offence taken. There's nothing complicated between us.'

'Thank you.' Dale drank his beer. After a while he said, 'I know the best thing would be for me to catch a train back to London on Monday morning. To forget about Sam and Charlie, and write the whole thing off to experience.'

'But you can't.'

'No. I know that's the right thing to do, but it's not what I want to do.'

'Bummer,' Eddie commented, tearing strips off his beer mat.

'Any advice? You mentioned you were involved with a married man. Have you ever fallen in love with one?'

'No... This is love then, you and Charlie?'

He chewed his lips. 'Yes. I love him.'

'You don't sound sure.'

'I'm not. I've been in love before and those feelings were nothing like what I'm feeling now. This is a thousand times bigger.'

'And these are the feelings you have for Charlie?'

'Yes.'

'Nothing for Sam?'

'Sam,' he sighed. 'Oh, God. I have no idea. I feel *something* but I don't know what. Could just be lust – I definitely fancy him.'

'You fancy me too. That's not enough.'

'Could be guilt.'

Eddie nodded. 'And you've every right to feel that.'

Dale scratched his head. 'You're not helping.'

'Sorry.'

'So...?'

'You want to know what I would do if I were you? I'd forget all about Charlie. He sounds like trouble, not just for you, but for everyone. Go to dinner with Sam, you owe the poor sod that much, then get the train home.' Eddie leaned back, both hands on the table. 'But that's not what you want to hear, is it?'

'No,' Dale sighed. 'It's not. What I want you to tell me... is how I can make Charlie love me.'

'Oh, Dale,' Eddie said softly. 'That's never going to happen.'

'You don't know that. I don't. I won't know unless I try. I think I should tell him how I feel.'

Eddie tutted slowly. 'I can't tell you what to do. I don't know Charlie or what you see in him, but he's married, Dale. He has a child. He has a gay lover too. I don't think a man like that will have much interest in what you have to offer.'

'Why not? I can make him happy.'

'Can you? He has three people in his life already and that's not enough to make him happy. How can you succeed where they haven't?'

'It's something I feel. When I'm with him, there's something between us, something strong and good.'

'Your cocks.'

'No,' he insisted. 'It's not just that. What happened between the two of us, just now by the river, that was sex. It was beautiful, incredible and very pleasurable. But it was just sex. There's no deep connection between us beyond the physical. It's not like that with Charlie. When I was inside him, I felt this incredible sense of belonging. He could feel it too, I know he could. There was nothing he wanted more than me – kids, wife, Max, nothing. He wanted me.'

Eddie looked stunned. For a moment he was speechless. The sound of the cafe seemed to grow in volume; the chatter of conversation, glasses chinking, Suzanne Vega on the stereo.

'What you describe –' he said, leaning forward '– it is just *sex*. When two men have incredible sex like you say you did, there's bound to be a connection. But that's all it is. Charlie knows that. You're just one more man to fuck a load out of him.'

'You're wrong.'

'Am I? What about Sam? Don't you think he feels a connection with you right now? You fucked him good and well the other day. He's probably still smiling about it. Sam probably thinks you are the most meaningful fuck he's had in a long time. But you're not, are you? You just told me, Sam was just another shag to you, just like me.'

Dale was tight-lipped. He stared at his bottle, twisting it around in his fingers. He didn't want to look at Eddie. He didn't want to hear what he had to say. Confiding in him had been a mistake – he couldn't grasp the depth of feeling running through Dale's blood at that moment.

'You were just another shag to Charlie,' Eddie said insistently. 'The sooner you accept that the better. Then you can stop fucking everyone else around.'

Eleven

UNDER THE INFLUENCE

Warm, soapy water enveloped him. Dale wallowed in the depth and length of the old-fashioned bathtub, straightening his legs and submerging his body until only his head remained above the water level. Steam rose from the surface, twisting to the ceiling like fingers of mist, hazing his vision, and escaping through the wide-open window. The sky was heavy with rain.

At the side of the bath stood a long-stemmed glass of Chardonnay, its sides cloudy with condensation. Dale reached over and took a sip, replacing the glass carefully. A portable radio was tuned to a local station, playing an Elton John record from a few years back. He softly hummed the tune.

Dale had been brooding since his conversation with Eddie that afternoon. He regretted opening his heart to him. Dale rarely confided his emotions, and it was a mistake to have trusted Eddie today. Eddie didn't understand, it was stupid of Dale to think he would. How could he? He'd never met Charlie. He couldn't comprehend the fascinating complexities of the man. Eddie didn't have a clue how charismatic and charming he was. He'd never held Charlie in his arms, or been inside him, or felt the warmth of his belly beneath his own. What did Eddie know about love? He was a man who made his living pretending to be other people, pretending to be someone he wasn't. All he knew about human nature or love he learned in the pages of a script, and no scriptwriter could capture in words a fraction of what Dale felt for Charlie.

He couldn't blame Eddie for what he didn't understand. Dale knew better than to take his opinion to heart. It wouldn't happen again. His feelings for Charlie, and how to deal with them, were something he would have work out for himself.

He sighed, stretching his neck beneath the water. Elton John was replaced with an old David Bowie record, 'Ashes To Ashes'. Dale checked his watch. He had another fifteen minutes or so before the others would want to use the bathroom to get ready. They were in the living room playing cards. After his conversation with Eddie, and the moody drive back to the cottage, Dale wanted time alone, time to unwind. Thoughts of Charlie continued to flow through his mind, arousing him, causing a fever that had nothing to do with the heat of the water.

He wondered what the object of his desire was doing now, tea time on Saturday. Dale assumed Charlie kept his weekends free for his family. Did he feel guilt for the time he spent with Max? Or his week nights at The Chain? After all the excess, did he see it as his duty to be with his family on Saturday and Sunday? Was he a good dad?

Why shouldn't he be? Just because he was a poor husband.

Dale had been giving some thought to Charlie's marriage and had come to a reasonable conclusion. The child, like the wife, was likely a mistake. An experiment, curiosity, maybe a twinge of lust – he wouldn't be the first gay man to sleep with a woman for those reasons. It didn't mean he was straight, or that he preferred women. How could he? He wasn't running round fucking dozens of girls on the side; it was hard cock he hungered for, not soft pussy. So it was fair to assume that the pregnancy was a mistake. Unlike most gay men faced with the same situation, Charlie had done the decent thing and married the girl. Maybe getting screwed by all those men at The Chain made the marriage bearable for him. But it wouldn't be enough in the long term. It couldn't be, not when he craved masculine love like he did.

He believed that Charlie's desire for other men was the glue that had held him to Max for so long. Max was his last tenuous link to the world he'd sacrificed.

Dale sighed, a watershed of emotions weighing on his heart. He had to act, think of some way to help. He couldn't go back to London without trying to prove to Charlie that he didn't have to be snared in such a life. There was no shame in divorce. Plenty of guys had been down the marriage route, it was a common enough mistake, even for men already conscious of their sexuality. He would be doing his wife a favour by leaving, giving her freedom – freedom to find a straight man who would love her in the way Charlie never could... In the way that Charlie loved Dale? Maybe that wasn't so far-fetched. The man felt some emotion for him, he was sure of it.

There was a tap at the bathroom door and Luke marched in without waiting for an answer. There was no lock.

'Hey,' Dale protested, covering himself beneath the water.

'Oh, come on,' Luke said, 'you haven't got anything I haven't seen already.'

'You haven't seen me,' he blushed.

'Dale, one soft willy looks much like any other and I've seen hundreds. Maybe even thousands. You don't get a tan like mine by being prudish. Paul and I go nude all the time. You're probably the only friend we have who hasn't seen us naked.'

'I'm in a bath in a country cottage,' he said, 'not sunning it in Ibiza.'

Unabashed, his friend sat on the closed toilet seat. 'I've been sent to get your opinion.'

'On what?'

'Plans for tonight. Do we stay in or go out?'

'What are the options?'

'Same place as last night, or we stay here and cook dinner ourselves. William found a market this afternoon and bought fresh supplies. We're well stocked with booze.'

'What do the others want to do?'

'No one's really bothered about getting dressed to go out. And the weather's so dull, one of us would have to drive.'

'Seems like a shame to go out when we've got this beautiful cottage all to ourselves. We can go to the pub any time.'

'Will you be okay staying in?' he asked cautiously.

Dale sat up, raising his shoulders above the water. 'Why not?'

Luke gave a little shrug. 'Just sensed some tension since we got back. What's going on with Eddie?'

'Nothing.' Dale reached for his wine and winced as a cold drop of condensation trickled down the stem to land in the hollow of his throat.

'I thought you liked him.'

'I do like him.'

'So what's the matter?'

'Nothing. We had a discussion, that's all, and he told me some things I didn't want to hear. We didn't have a fight. It's nothing. Honest.'

'So there won't be an atmosphere if we stay in?'

'Not from me, there won't.'

Satisfied, Luke stood up. He was almost at the door when he stopped and said, 'Is it something to do with that guy you like? The married guy?'

Dale's eyelids sank and he lowered himself below the surface. 'No more talk, okay? I'd like to forget about all that and enjoy myself. Just for tonight.'

Luke smiled, nodding. 'Okay. Get out of that water before you prune. We'll start dinner.'

Dale returned the smile and thanked him.

He allowed himself two more minutes, until the end of the current record – Beverly Craven, 'Love Scenes'. He hadn't heard that one in years. Emerging from the tub, he shook the water from his body, stepped onto a white bath mat and dried himself on a huge towel. His heart was beating fast from the heat.

He gazed at his face in the mirror, at the two-day growth on his chin. They might not be going anywhere special but he couldn't let it go until the morning; it was already beginning to itch. He filled the basin and lathered the lower half of his face. He watched himself carefully, keeping the water hot and drawing the razor from ear to chin with a steady hand. Finished, he rinsed the razor under the hot tap and washed the excess lather from his chin. Starting to feel better, he applied aftershave balm to his skin and soothed it into the pores with sweeping strokes.

Carrying the radio through to the bedroom, he stood it on the windowsill while he dressed. He put on clean underwear and socks, baggy cargo pants and a slim-fitting shirt with short sleeves. He towel-dried his short hair and smoothed it down with his fingers and a pinch of moulding wax. Spraying himself with a Clinique fragrance and finishing the glass of wine completed the transformation of body and mood. He was fit and ready to enjoy himself again.

Luke and Colin were busy in the kitchen, from where there issued the delicious odour of seared tuna steaks. Dale joined William, Paul and Eddie in the dining room, sitting beside Eddie.

'Feeling better?' his temporary roommate inquired.

'Much,' Dale smiled, holding eye contact as a gesture of good faith.

Eddie smiled warmly and refilled Dale's glass for him.

The room was warm and cosy. A real fire blazed in the hearth. Dale picked at a piece of garlic bread and joined the conversation, which was about bigotry in the workplace. They each had their own experiences to share. He found out William was a police officer, a desk sergeant, who'd been passed over for promotion three times and believed his openly gay status in the force was the main reason. Dale provided an insight into the laws regarding harassment and employment.

As the food was served, their mood lightened, aided by a steady supply of wine. They ate the seared tuna with mixed salad and wild rice, followed by frozen chocolate truffles. The temperature dipped as the fire died. William and Paul went outside for more wood and coal. Eddie had a wealth of theatrical anecdotes that kept them laughing over dinner, while William told some of the bluest jokes Dale had ever heard. Eventually they cleared the table and headed into the living room, which was smaller and warmer. William stoked the fire and added coal.

The drinking continued. William opened a bottle of Greek brandy and Luke started on Russian vodka. Paul rolled a fat joint and passed it round the room.

The combined heat of six bodies and a real fire soon grew unbearable, and they began shedding top layers of clothing. As Luke tugged his grey fleece over his head, his T-shirt rode up, revealing his flat, slightly hairy belly.

William wolf-whistled.

Luke flung aside the fleece and straightened down his T-shirt. 'Get a good eyeful, did you?' he asked brazenly.

'Seen it all before,' William said indifferently, pouring himself another brandy.

Luke necked his vodka and Red Bull. 'That's what I was saying to Dale earlier. He got all huffy when I walked into the bathroom.'

'I was in the bath at the time,' said Dale.

'So?'

'Have you heard of decency?'

'Ha, what's that?'

'Did you see anything?' Colin asked cheekily.

'Not a sausage,' Luke sniggered.

Dale sputtered, feeling vodka shoot up his nose.

'How about a drinking game?' suggested Paul. 'We could play strip poker if all we care about is seeing each other naked.'

'I don't need to lose a game of cards to show anyone my arse,' Luke said. 'I'll get naked this minute if you want to see.'

'Me too,' Colin chipped in.

Everyone laughed. Eddie, who was sitting in an armchair directly across from Dale, winked at him and then said, 'So, why don't you? If you're both so keen to get your kit off, go ahead. Give us a show.'

'Don't encourage them,' William groaned.

Dale saw the look that passed between Luke and Colin, the glint of mischief in their eyes. They nodded to each other and stood up.

'All right,' said Luke, crossing the room to stand beside his friend.

They slid their arms around each other's waists. 'If we're gonna do this, then we will make a show of it. A bloody good show. Excuse us while we confer.'

They left the room, holding each other close, and shut the door behind them.

'Any idea what they're up to?' Dale asked.

William and Paul shook their heads. 'God knows. We'll find out soon enough.'

Dale's heart started beating faster. 'I'm not sure I want to be part of this.'

Eddie got up and sat beside him, putting his arm along the back rest, around his shoulder. 'Don't be so sensitive. It's only a bit of fun. Just like today, at the river,' he added.

This whole week had been nothing but a pursuit of fun and, instead of clearing his mind as intended, it had left Dale more bewildered. He wasn't sure he could cope with the added complication of fucking his best friend. Did he really want to go that far?

'Just wait a while,' William said calmly. 'If you don't like what you see, you can ask them to stop – or go to bed. No one will force you to do anything you don't want. We're all friends. There's nothing to be scared of.'

Dale nodded, taking a long hit on the joint as it travelled his way.

Luke and Colin came back into the room with white towels wrapped around their waists and more towels stuffed under their arms. Colin flicked a switch beside the door, killing the bright lights. The room was now lit by three small table lamps and the incandescent flare from the hearth. Dale shivered, sinking right back into the soft cushions. He took another hit before handing the joint to Eddie.

Luke and Colin were similar in height and build. Their bodies were lean, hairy across the chest and below the navel. From the waist to the knee, they were hidden by the towels, but their calves were covered with thick brown hair. Their feet were bare. With similar haircuts and smouldering good looks, they were as much alike as brothers. With his enthusiasm for health and exercise, Colin had the more defined body of the two, a torso moulded into a perfect triangle. Luke had a simpler physique, with longer, less dramatic cuts of muscle. They moved into the centre of the room.

Clearing the floor, Paul joined Dale and Eddie on the sofa. William sat in the armchair by the fire, his bare feet propped on the coffee table.

Luke and Colin put down what they were holding and slid their arms around each other. They pressed together, grinding their pelvises, and started kissing, open-mouthed, full of desire. They were deeply into each other, their attraction very real and not just for show. Dale glanced nervously between William and Paul, but if either man was jealous, there was nothing in his manner or expression to show it.

Luke and Colin separated. Luke swept his hand across the knot in Colin's towel and the white apparel slipped from his waist with a soft hush. His cock jutted forward at an almost perfect ninety-degree angle from his groin. Dale's own cock began to swell at the sight. Colin's dick was beautiful, just short of seven inches, gloriously thick. He was circumcised with a big mushroom head; a tear of transparent fluid glistened in the tiny opening. His shaft was threaded with thick veins, throbbing just below the surface of its fine skin. Unlike most body-conscious men, he had a dense bush of pubic hair, curling above his cock in a wild thatch. His thighs were also covered in thick hair. Amid this spectacle of lush fur, his balls, shaved to perfection, were a startling sight.

Luke's fingers skittered along the line from Colin's waist to his groin, gently skimming the upper edge of his dick. Colin's cock leapt dramatically as Luke traced its sensitive underside.

Colin unfastened Luke's towel, tossing it to the floor. Luke's cock stood erect, jutting upwards more than forward. Dale stared with interest, feeling a shiver of guilty pleasure rocket up his body. Until this moment he couldn't remember looking at Luke with any kind of sexual interest. Had he ever been looking at him at all?

The two men kissed again, fondling each other with easy strokes.

Dale was hard, his dick wedged uncomfortably in his briefs, but he didn't dare move to adjust it. He scarcely dared to breathe.

The mood in the tiny living room was molten.

They got down on the floor, moving into a sixty-nine position without speaking. Colin lay on his back with Luke on his hands and knees above him. They pushed their cocks into zealous mouths, working over the heads, putting on a show as they gobbled the shafts.

William was the first to lean in for a better look, and the others didn't waste time following his lead.

'Go for it, lads,' William said.

From where he sat, Dale had a perfect view of Colin's head and Luke's backside. Colin had his arms around Luke's hips, palms resting on his buttocks. He kneaded the hairy globes as he sucked, squashing them tight, pulling them wide, giving Dale a stunning glimpse of Luke's honey-brown heaven. The orifice spread and distorted before rebounding to its flawless round beginnings. When Colin opened Luke wide, Dale caught sight of his soft pink insides.

Colin lifted his head from the floor, swallowing Luke's hard meat. His lips bulged around the swollen shaft. His hands continued to work over Luke's butt – his fingers were inside the crack, massaging the puckered hole. He wriggled his index finger inside, but Luke's anus was dry and he could only make it as far as the first knuckle. He released Luke's cock from his lips with a loud popping sound and moved to bring his face to Luke's arse instead, then flicked his tongue in and out of the crack. Guided by pleasure, Luke dipped his hips further, bringing his arsehole in effortless reach of Colin's ardent tongue.

Eddie leaned against Dale as they watched, sliding his hand into Dale's crotch, grasping the bulge. Dale squirmed, thrusting against his hand.

Locked in position, Colin and Luke abandoned their dicks and concentrated on their arses. Colin tilted his pelvis upwards, giving Luke the opportunity to lodge his face in the crack. Colin moaned, still licking Luke's hole. They devoured one another's arses, like starved men eating their first meal in weeks. Dale stared at Luke's hole and licked his lips, convinced the flavour was ingrained on his own taste buds. Colin continued with the juicy anus for a few more moments, before moving out of the crack, lifting his head to kiss the right cheek, then the left. He gave Luke's arse a slap, just hard enough to leave a red imprint on his skin.

'Let's show them what we have,' Colin said.

Luke climbed off him, his buttocks closing, the hole disappearing from view. Colin rolled over, rising to his knees, sitting back. His cock jutted between his hairy thighs like a lance, hard and dangerous, the head shiny with saliva and precome. Luke reached for one of the towels and unrolled the bundle. The contents hit the floor with a loud thud. The four spectators leaned forward for a better look.

Luke picked up the object. Dale recognised what it was; he had seen similar toys on sale at the Cock Shop. Filling Luke's hands, with an overspill at either end, was a huge, heavy-duty, double-ended dildo. It was thick and veiny, moulded in flesh-coloured rubber. Colin unrolled another towel, spilling dozens of condoms onto the floor, along with lube in both sachets and bottles. Dale spotted a couple of bottles of amyl nitrate, their seals unbroken. Colin and Luke looked at each other and smiled.

'You'll never take all that,' Eddie told them, massaging Dale's crotch.

'They will,' William and Paul replied in tandem.

Colin and Luke put on a show for their crowd, a ceremony of preparation. Colin took a bottle of lube, pumping a large glob into his double-gloved palm and working it over his fingers until they were slick and greasy. Luke turned around, bending over, showing his arse to his friend. Colin dipped his hand into the hairy crack, stuffing his lubed fingers into the opening, greasing Luke with a fluid, twisting wrist action. Luke let out a sound somewhere between a moan and sigh and arched his back. He was looking at William and smiling. When his arse was well lubricated, he traded positions with Colin, lubing his own gloved fingers and stuffing them up Colin's butt. He worked four fingers as far as the knuckle. Then they each removed one glove to reveal the second beneath, took the double-ended toy between them and worked it between their slippery hands, coating every inch of rubber in lube.

Dale felt blindly at his feet for his drink and took a deep draught.

'We need someone to help us,' Colin said.

William stood up and approached them. 'Get in position,' he said.

Colin and Luke got on their hands and knees, facing away from each other. Their feet were almost touching and a distance of around two feet separated their raised buttocks. Paul got off the sofa and knelt on the floor in front of Luke, stroked the side of his lover's face and kissed him.

William teased Colin's anus with his fingertips, opening him further before guiding the tapered head of the dildo into position. He pressed it into his hole. Colin exhaled, open-mouthed, offering no resistance. William fed the first five or six inches of rubber slowly into his rectum. He paused, stroking Colin's rump, before turning his attention towards Luke. He repeated the manoeuvre with the other hand, fingering him for a few strokes before guiding the toy inside.

'There you go.'

Colin and Luke craned their necks to look down their bodies. The dildo formed a bridge between them, running from one tunnel to the other. They pressed back, pushing from their hands, through their spines, closing the gap between them. The dildo disappeared, swallowed by their arses, inch by slow inch.

Dale was reminded of The Sex Cabaret, only this time it wasn't a troupe of professional performers he was watching. These were his friends; Luke, a man he had known for the best part of a decade.

They continued to close the distance between them, gently rocking their hips while inching backwards. Five inches remained, four, three. Sweat glistened on their naked bodies. Two inches remaining. One. The dildo vanished from sight. They were touching, butt to butt, their guts full of rubber. Dale could only imagine the pleasure they must be experiencing. William caressed them, running his palms down the curve of their backs.

They began to rock, inching forward until a small length of rubber could be glimpsed as a path from one anus to the other. With another hip roll, the image vanished.

Paul unfastened his pants, tugging out his cock. Luke reacted on instinct, covering the hard organ with his mouth, creating a tight seal with his lips.

In the warm, lamplit room, the remaining men took off their clothes. Dale got down on his knees in front of Luke, cock hovering before his face. Through half-lidded eyes, Luke perceived his presence. He released Paul's cock and took Dale's into his mouth. Dale groaned as he felt the warmth of his lips, followed quickly by the fiery heat of his whole mouth. Paul's arm slid around his shoulders and they kissed, open-mouthed, with tongues. Luke worked both their dicks with his mouth and hands, alternating between deep lunges and gentle sweeps of the head, before opening his jaw wide and cramming both hard cocks into his mouth. Dale and Paul lunged forward, still locked at the mouth, their cocks duelling for space inside Luke. Dale felt his dick grow harder.

Dale pulled out of Luke's mouth, allowing Paul unlimited access. His wet dick bobbed against his stomach as he felt around the floor for a condom. He wiped his cock, covered his shaft in rubber and lube and scurried round to kneel behind Paul. Paul did not resist when Dale started fingering lube into his tight hole – he moaned, spreading his knees wider and tipping his hips to allow him to benefit from both Paul's mouth and Dale's sticky fingers. Dale finger-fucked his pink ring into a state of juicy submission.

Colin and Luke remained united at the arse, while Eddie and Colin both lavished attention on William's fat cock with their lips and tongues.

Dale held Paul's arse open with both of his hands, looking at his inviting hole while edging his cock closer. He thrust inside, watching his cock disappear, in just the way the dildo had vanished inside Colin and Luke. Paul's head rolled back, twisting over his shoulder, searching for a kiss. Dale's mouth found his lips as he ground his cock inside. Paul worked his arse, clenching, caressing. Dale thrust, the impetus forcing Paul's body, shoving his cock down Luke's throat. Dale wrapped his arms around Paul's chest and rabbit-fucked him until he felt his arsehole tense. Paul let out a verbal stream of pleasure as he ejaculated, spurting his load down Luke's throat.

Dale pulled out of him and changed the condom. He slapped his dick around Luke's face, holding the head a tantalising distance from Luke's open lips. Dale pointed at his cock. 'I want you next.'

With Paul's assistance, Luke disengaged himself from Colin. One half of the dildo remained inside Colin's bowel – it hung from his hole like a stiff tail. Paul began to play with him, rotating the dildo, pushing more of it inside him.

Dale wrestled Luke to the floor, manoeuvring his old college friend onto his back. He lifted his legs, taking a moment to enjoy the view: the centre line, the brown halo, the glistening, puckered skin. Luke was wet and ready. Dale lay on top of him and entered easily. He hovered a second with just the head inside before driving the rest of his length into Luke's rectum.

'I've always wanted this,' Luke gasped, writhing on Dale's cock. 'Let me have it.'

They ground their bodies together, their limbs entwined, muscles tightening. Dale buried his head in Luke's shoulder and went for a full-on fuck. It seemed to last ages, and when Dale came close to orgasm he stopped, freezing until the moment passed. Three times he managed to delay himself.

As he rode Luke's arse, he felt hands all over his own backside, wet fingers poked at his sphincter. It was William. He lay over Dale's back, guiding his big animal cock into position. He shoved in. Dale gasped; it was big and he was tight. He breathed, relaxing. He allowed his body to be taken, following William's rhythm. The three men pumped and ground against one another. The sensation was mind-blowing – fucking and fucked at the same time.

William wrapped his arms around Dale's chest and pounded a hard fuck. Dale screamed. There was no way he could hold back his orgasm this time. 'I'm coming,' he gasped, 'nooowwww!', spewing a flood of come into Luke's arse. It started a chain reaction. First Luke, pumping hot milk into the space between their bellies, then William, unable to resist the tightening of Dale's arse, emptying his massive balls.

Through the fuck-crazed fog of his mind, Dale became aware of warm liquid falling on his body like rain. He opened his eyes in time to see Colin and Paul wanking out their spume over his tired, sweaty body.

Twelve

ENCORE

In the early hours of Sunday morning, with music pounding in his veins, Sam thought about returning to The Sex Cabaret. He was in the middle of a packed dance floor, surrounded by hot, excitable bodies, and wondering how to get away. Chaps was packed to the rafters like it was any Saturday. Even the VIP area, which Sam had visited earlier, had standing room only.

Sam was dancing with a lad from Southampton, who had ardently pursued him since they caught sight of each other in XL three hours earlier. The boy was cute, in his mid-twenties, blond and very tall. He was originally from the Northeast and still had the accent, but had moved south for work. Like two-thirds of the people here, he was only in town for the weekend, to get pissed and enjoy himself. On any other Saturday, Sam would have been gagging for him, but tonight he couldn't even remember the boy's name, which he had been told twice.

Sam was holding out for Dale. He'd promised to call on Sunday night when he returned from the cottage. Sam had reserved a table at Sakura Teppan-yaki on Monday. It was a Japanese restaurant and the finest place to dine in Newbiggin Bay. Maybe the relationship would end in nothing, but he had a feeling it was worth waiting to find out. Dale caused a stir deep in his core which Sam had not felt with any man since Martin, eight years ago. He trusted his intuition.

While he sweated it out beneath the neon lights with the boy from Southampton, Sam was thinking of a way to blow him out politely. He didn't want to hurt the boy's feelings, but there was no way he was taking him home. He didn't know what had possessed him to come here tonight, other than a desire to get out of the apartment. He was determined he would not spend the weekend brooding, waiting for Dale's call on Sunday night, which might not come.

In retrospect, going to the cinema would have been a better option, or getting out of town, maybe to visit relations. Chaps on Saturday was a meat market. It had been an insane idea to come here when he had no intention of pulling. But he wasn't ready to go home either, to his empty apartment and the empty bed that reminded him of Dale. He hadn't changed the sheets since sleeping with Dale; he could still smell the savoury scent of his sweat on the pillows, and his aftershave, ingrained in the fibres of the bedclothes.

Then he had the idea of going back to the cabaret. He could have a few drinks on his own and watch the show. No one would try to pick him up when there were so many generous mouths and arses available in the alcoves. If he got rid of this boy now, he could make it to the venue before two.

He danced with the boy a while longer, determined he would leave at the end of the record. No need to feel guilty, he maintained, there were plenty other men around; the boy would not be on his own for long. They danced, driven by the music, sweating with the heat generated by a mass of hard bodies.

He spotted a familiar face, not far from where they danced. It was Max. He had his hands on one of his boys, clasped around his waist. They were shirtless. The boy was about twenty, a junior version of Charlie who even had the same haircut. He leaned over and said something in Max's ear, laughing. Max nodded, not quite managing a smile. Then he turned and saw Sam. There was no acknowledgement, not even a nod. Max watched him and continued to dance.

Like a wave, a crush of bodies moved between them, a group of eight or nine men dancing together, sharing a round of poppers. They blocked Sam's view of Max.

Sam tapped his blond companion on the arm and pointed at his watch. 'I have to go,' he mouthed above the pulsating beat before pushing his way off the dance floor. The blond followed. Shit!

Over by the bar, the boy flung his arms around Sam's neck and kissed him. 'Where do you want to go? I'm staying at Xanadu. Or is your place nearer? I don't mind.'

This wouldn't be as easy as he planned. He gripped the boy's wrists and detached them from his neck. The boy's smile wavered.

'I can't... er...'

'It's James,' he said. 'My name is James.'

'Right. I'm sorry, James, but I have to go. Alone.'

James's face fell. 'I thought you liked me.'

'I do like you.' He hoped he sounded enthusiastic.

'So why are you ditching me?'

Sam decided to tell the truth, or half-truth. 'There's someone else. I thought I was ready to have fun without him but I'm not. If I was, I couldn't think of anyone I would rather spend the night with than you. But I'm not ready. Sorry... James.'

He pecked him on the cheek and left him standing by the bar.

It could have been worse.

He lit a cigarette and headed for the men's room before leaving. It was a clammy room with dark red tiles on the walls and floor. It had been decimated by the hordes. His feet splashed in piss and water. There was soggy toilet roll strewn across the floor and stuffed in the stainless steel washbasins, two of which were blocked and overflowing. The air was rank with various smells: piss, smoke, amyl nitrate, dope.

He stepped up to the urinals and took a piss. In the mirror that ran along the whole of the wall he saw the door to one of the stalls open. Max and his boy came out, conspicuously wiping their noses. The boy was all over the older man, pressing himself against his body. The physical effect of the drugs – coke, Sam surmised – was evident in their bulging groins.

Max caught sight of Sam in the mirror. He whispered something to the boy, who followed his gaze, staring at Sam, his eyes full of amusement, before going outside to leave them alone. Sam zipped up and turned around, his cigarette clamped between his lips.

Max stood with his arms at his sides, hands relaxed. With his T-shirt hanging from his waistband, his jeans dipped low on his hips. His hard torso – thick waist and mountainous pecs – was shiny and wet. His short blond hair was plastered to his brow and his expression was stony. 'I hoped I would see you tonight.'

'I'm leaving,' Sam said solidly, crossing to an unblocked sink to wash his hands.

Max turned and followed. 'With your chicken?'

'Alone.'

'Where's the guy you brought to The Chain this week?' His voice was emotionless and cold, like a machine.

'He's gone,' Sam said through his cigarette, drying his hands on paper towels. The waste bin was full, towels tumbling out onto the wet floor.

'For good?'

'No.' He folded his arms and challenged Max's blank stare. 'He'll be back tomorrow.'

'So who is he? New boyfriend?'

'Why does it matter to you? He's a man, not a boy, too old for *you*.'

Max sneered. 'I couldn't give a shit about that. He's the last man I'd want to fuck, before you. He's been sniffing round Charlie. I want to know what's going on.'

'Why don't you ask Charlie-boy? He'll know better than either of us.' Sam caught the briefest flicker of worry in Max's eyes. 'So Charlie's not letting on what happened,' he said, managing to sound more triumphant than he felt. 'Must be more serious than his usual fuck buddies. It sounds like he has something to hide, wouldn't you say?'

Max's lips twisted in another sneer. 'I haven't spoken to Charlie. This is just talk I've been hearing the last few days.'

'It's got nothing to do with me.' Sam moved for the door. Max sidestepped, barring his way. Sam stood still for a moment, then raised his head, looking straight into Max's cold eyes. 'Let me out.'

'Not until you tell me who your friend is and where I can find him.'

Sam was shaking inside but he managed to control himself. Max was a dangerous character. The rumours that he had murdered an ex-lover and his rival were nothing but hearsay, but his convictions for assault were authentic. He'd served time in prison. Sam was present in a bar called Instinct on the night Max smashed a bottle in the face of student who rejected his coke-fuelled advances. The boy needed over forty stitches to put his face back together.

If Max perceived Dale as a threat and thought Sam was concealing him, then they were both in physical danger.

'He's not here,' said Sam. 'I told you, he's gone.'

'But he'll be back on Sunday, you said.'

'He *might* be back. I don't know. He's on holiday. He may not stick around much longer.'

'We both know that's unlikely,' Max said coldly. 'He's coming back for Charlie, wouldn't you say?'

Sam drew the last breath out of his cigarette and dropped the butt into a puddle of piss. He was hiding his fear well. He inflated his chest and shrugged, blowing smoke in Max's face. 'We'll see. In my opinion you're over-emphasising Charlie's appeal.'

'I doubt your buddy sees it that way. Tell him I want to see him.'

'If he comes back.'

'Monday. On the pier at one o'clock.' He opened the door. Just as Sam was about to leave, Max added, 'Make sure he's there.'

The blond master of ceremonies, dressed in a white Roman tunic, stood alone on the spotlit stage, singing an English translation of the German cabaret favourite 'I Don't Know Who I Belong To' in a passable, if limited voice. The tables were all occupied. Sam leaned against an iron railing, down the left side of the club, drinking the house red. From where he stood he had an excellent view of the stage, as well looking directly across the room into one of the shadowy arches. He could not see what was happening in the dark, but he had a clear vision of the men entering and leaving the alcove.

He had calmed down after the confrontation. Max was worried. He obviously saw Dale as serious competition for Charlie. Sam wondered if his concern was justified. After spending time with Dale himself, he didn't consider Dale's attraction for Charlie to be as serious as he once thought. Dale was like most men when they first met Charlie – fascinated by his complexities. He wouldn't be the first man to think he was the remedy for his confusion, that he could make him happy when his wife, kid and Max had failed.

Charlie was a fleeting infatuation and Dale was already over him; Sam was positive.

The MC reached the end of his song. He took a bow, arse to the audience, showing he was naked under the tunic. He put both hands on his buttocks and opened them. The spotlight caught his tight pink rose before going out, plunging the stage into darkness. The coloured bulbs of the dance floor began to flash and a familiar track started to play, filling the floor quickly. There would be more cabaret later.

Sam didn't know if he was going to stay for the main show. Another few drinks and he might be ready to call it a night. He signalled a waiter, bare arsed in his leather chaps uniform, and asked for a refill.

He wondered what Dale was doing now. The idea of a country retreat was wonderful. He imagined what it would be like to spend time with Dale, the two of them alone in a cottage miles from anywhere; no clubs, no sex shops, no drags queens, no drugs, just themselves for entertainment. He could think of nothing better than walking by a river, hand in hand, lying on a checked blanket and fucking to the gentle sound of water. That would be bliss.

The waiter returned with his drink. He was strongly built, with chunky, footballer's thighs. Sam stuffed his money into one of the small silver balls and popped it up the boy's lubricated hole. The waiter thanked him and walked over to a table where another customer beckoned. Sam wondered how many of those money balls the boys could take up their arses before feeling the need to empty themselves. He figured an experienced hole could probably handle a good half dozen orbs before the weight and fullness became too much to bear.

He wandered the club, taking his drink. He caught the very distinct odour of marijuana on a table near the back. He followed the railing round, peering into the shadowy alcoves as he passed. He saw bodies pressed together, a flash of naked skin, roaming hands, a stooped figure, a bowed head. A man stood by one of the arched alcoves, holding a bottle of beer, one thumb tucked in his jeans, a bent knee pointing in Sam's direction. He was in his thirties, with a lean build and dark good looks. For a fraction of an instant he thought it was Dale, that he'd cancelled his trip. But it wasn't him. The face was too sharp, the eyes too cold. The man did not smile, but from the manner in which he stared, there was no mistaking his intention. Eyeballing Sam, he gave an almost imperceptible nod towards the darkness behind him.

Sam shook his head and kept walking, past a bank of videos screening an American porn movie. It was the kind that starred massively endowed, perfectly maintained men who were just as likely to provoke a sense of inadequacy in the viewer as arousal. The muscular, fatless physiques they portrayed as the norm were nigh on impossible to obtain for an average man with a full-time job and a social life that revolved around food and alcohol.

Next to the video screens were posted photographs of one of these porn gods. Russell Clay was a British model with hunky good looks, reminiscent of a young Richard Gere. He made a name for himself in the mid-1990s, starring in over fifty porn movies for various American studios. He returned to England to write a memoir of his career in porn, as well touring Europe with a one-man show based on his book. The poster proclaimed that the show was coming to Newbiggin Bay for two weeks over the summer. Russell would be performing nightly at the Gala theatre opposite the pier, followed by a second, exclusive show each night as part of The Sex Cabaret. Sam made a mental note to contact Russell when he arrived in town. Hopefully he'd be interested in an autograph session at the Cock Shop. Sam sold enough of his merchandise: books, CDs, posters, videos, DVDs and a dildo modelled on his infamous ten-inch cock.

Sam wandered into a small lounge area at the rear of the club, quieter than the main room. About fifteen men sat around on leather sofas, talking, drinking, kissing. A Russell Clay porno played on a widescreen television sunk into the wall.

A couple sat close together on one of the sofas. Sam asked if they minded him sitting down for a while.

'Not at all,' they answered, shuffling up to make room.

He thanked them and sat, setting his wine on the low, glass-topped table. He yawned and stretched, thinking he would call it a night very soon.

''Scuse me mate,' one of the men asked in a Scottish accent. 'When does the show get going?'

'Around four,' he said. 'It goes on for about an hour and half.'

They were both the same age, early thirties, clean shaven. They had identical hairstyles, short and neat, like a couple of boys smartened by their mothers for a Sunday visit, not a single hair out of place. Their clothes were trendy and expensive. It would be fair to assume that even their underpants and socks bore designer labels. If they weren't so obviously a couple, Sam could have mistaken them for brothers, they were so alike.

'So what's it like?' the second man asked. He had less of an accent than the first and a slimmer build.

'Worth waiting for,' he said. 'You won't have seen anything like it.'

'Is it anything like the sex show at Manumission?'

Sam laughed. 'Manumission would get a PG rating compared to the show here.'

'It had better be good,' the first man said. 'We came all this way just for this.'

'You won't be disappointed,' Sam assured.

'I'm Taylor,' the first man said, extending his hand. 'This is Doug.'

'Hi.' Sam introduced himself and shook hands with the Scottish couple.

Taylor's shirt was open halfway down the chest, showing a strong neck and a tuft of black hair. Despite his preppy image there was a raw masculinity about him. Sam could best imagine him naked, shorn of fashion, allowing his hairy body to run wild, to fuck like an animal.

Doug had softer features, his eyes were wider, his lips fuller. There was no hair showing through the open neck of his shirt. Sam would be very surprised if they did not conform to top and bottom stereotypes.

If given a choice, he knew which one of them he would go to bed with.

They were good company, friendly and warm. They listened with interest when he spoke about his shop and promised to visit before leaving the bay on Monday.

A waiter came into the lounge, collecting empty glasses on a tray. His hard cock swayed through the room before him, tied with a leather strap, pointing west. Sam, Taylor and Doug watched him move around the room, loading his tray. They watched his arse, the way that it spread when he bent over the tables, so they could steal glimpses of his naked hole.

'Look at his thighs,' Doug whispered.

The boy bent over again and Sam saw what he meant: a trail of semen dribbled lazily down the back of his right leg. Sam caught his breath.

'Damn!' Taylor exhaled. He called the waiter over.

'What are you doing?' Doug whispered.

'You'll see,' he murmured.

Sam waited.

The boy's cock bobbed up and down as he approached, holding his tray at shoulder height. 'Can I get you any drinks, gentlemen?'

Sam recognised him. His name was Billy. He came out on the scene when he was just sixteen. He wouldn't be more than eighteen now. The last he'd seen, Billy was working behind the bar at Luscious Lipstick. He wondered whether waiting on tables at The Sex Cabaret was a more lucrative career for a worldly eighteen-year-old than pulling pints in a drag revue.

Taylor pulled a note out of his wallet and flashed it to Billy, before picking one of the silver orbs out of a bowl and stuffing the money inside. 'You can have this,' he said.

Billy pouted. 'What do I have to do for it? I'm not rent.'

'I don't want to fuck you,' Taylor grinned. 'Just turn around and you can have it.'

Billy considered the offer, he was a smart boy, he knew nothing was for free, especially in a place like this. After a moment's thought he set the tray he was carrying down on the coffee table. He turned around and assumed the position for payment, hands on his thighs, arse poised for acceptance. The trail of semen stretched from just below his right buttock to above the back of his knee. It was wet and obviously still fresh, though it had lost its white hue and become transparent.

'Come a little closer,' Taylor directed.

Billy backed up, edging his arse nearer to him. From his position at the other end of the sofa, Sam could see everything: Billy's flared buttocks, the smooth line down the middle, his shell-pink hole, his cock and balls, strapped in leather, pointing down between his thighs.

Taylor held the waiter's hips, lowered his head and trailed his tongue slowly up the back of that right thigh, washing over the river of come, devouring it. He continued into the crack, caressing the anus with a couple of wide strokes before pressing the silver orb into the hole and pushing it inside with his fingers. Then he sat back, licking his lips.

Billy said nothing as he straightened, collected his tray and exited the lounge.

Sam smiled and lit another cigarette. It was time for one more wander before leaving the club. 'It's been nice meeting you,' he told the Scottish couple.

'You too,' Taylor said. 'We'll see you on Monday before we leave.'

Sam walked back into the main room, ordering tequila to warm him for the walk home. On stage, two strippers were down to G-strings, oiling each other beneath the spotlights. Uninterested, he didn't pay the act much attention. A sight further down the room seized his attention instead. It was Max.

How did that bastard get tickets for this place? It was infuriating that Sam couldn't go anywhere without seeing him. Max with sitting with his coked-up Charlie clone, three tables away from the stage. There was another boy at their table, naked, staring at Max in adoration.

It was James, the boy Sam had abandoned at Chaps earlier in the evening. Sam sneered. So the poor boy had found a replacement to dote on. It was little comfort to know that Max had been James's second choice – not that it would be up to the boy to make the choice. Max wouldn't have wasted any time before seducing him.

'Why do I care?' he asked himself.

Sam downed his tequila and left the club.

Under the open sky, the night was just starting to get light, changing from dark to ash grey. Sam walked home rather than wait for a taxi. He stuffed his hands in his pockets and inhaled, gratefully filling his lungs with clean air after the polluted atmosphere of Chaps and The Sex Cabaret. He wondered, not for the first time, what he was doing. He was an integral part of a gay community for which he was rapidly losing empathy. Men like Max were poison. He shuddered, thinking of the things Max would do to the boy James. Sam should never have left him. The boy wasn't asking for much, a fast wank in his hotel room, maybe a blow job – safe fun. Now what would happen to him? He would certainly be drugged – whether he accepted Max's narcotics voluntarily or had them slipped into his drink was irrelevant. He wouldn't know what he was doing when Max took him home. Sam had heard the stories.

Ketamine was Max's drug of choice for making the boys do what he wanted. Sam overheard him with a lad one night in XL, a tourist who couldn't have been more than nineteen.

'Take this,' Max said, handing him a pill.

'What is it?' the boy asked.

'Never mind,' he snapped. 'Just take it!'

Dirty bastard!

There was a cafe on the promenade that stayed opened twenty-four hours. Sam went inside, gratefully breaking up his journey. It was a mild morning, but in a short-sleeved cotton shirt, he felt the cold. He ordered hot chocolate and toast and sat on a stool at the bar in front of the window. The early editions of the Sunday papers were in. He glanced through the tabloids, at headlines full of scandal; kiss-and-tell tales of footballers and soap stars he had never heard of. He pushed the papers away, uninterested. His encounters with Max had left him with a cloying sense of sleaze, he had no desire to exacerbate his uneasiness by reading about other people's boozed-up mistakes.

He held his cup in both hands, warming his fingers. He blew on the hot chocolate before drinking. A couple of women sat at a table behind him, in quiet conversation while enjoying fried breakfasts. Another man dozed at a table on his own, a half-finished cup of tea in front of him.

Sam stared out of the window, wishing Dale was with him. Dale could be the only man in the world who understood his growing antipathy for the life he had drifted into. Dale wasn't part of this world, he was a tourist here. He knew that there was more to life than fucking nameless, faceless strangers week after week. Sam didn't know when it had happened, but somewhere, without him even noticing, the fun had gone out of enjoying himself.

The Cock Shop was business. The one-night-stands he had each week and the sessions he attended at The Chain were habit, preferable to being on his own in a beautiful but empty apartment. How many times had he fucked Charlie, a man he couldn't stand? Thirty? Eighty?

It was a ludicrous state to be in.

He drank his chocolate with a determination that things had to change. He would start today, tonight, when he spoke to Dale.

When Dale fucked him on Thursday it was the first time Sam had truly enjoyed sex in ages, and at twenty-eight years old, with countless sexual partners behind him, that meant more to him than anything else he could think of.

Everything would be different now. He finished his drink and headed home, finally smiling.

Thirteen

EDDIE

The guests at Raby Cottage had agreed they wanted to sleep late on Sunday and might go for lunch in the afternoon to the pub, where food was served all day.

Dale woke up early and couldn't get back to sleep. There was an agitated, tingling sensation all through his body, particularly in his stomach and the centre of his chest. It was a restless excitement. During the night he'd formed a plan. He was returning to Newbiggin Bay on a mission: his aim, to confront Charlie and persuade him that they had a chance of being happy together.

He got out of bed, easing from Eddie's warm embrace, and took his bag to the bathroom, where he showered and dressed. In the kitchen, he poured orange juice and boiled the water for coffee. While waiting for the kettle he went round the ground floor, opening all the curtains. In the living room he found the evidence of what had happened last night.

The coffee table had been pushed against the wall, creating an open space in the middle of the floor, which was strewn with condom wrappers, tissues, used towels, poppers, lube and Colin's double-ended dildo. The air reeked of sex; the indisputable scent of amyl nitrate, rubber and arse. After opening the curtains, Dale hunted for the key to the window locks, eventually discovering it in a pot above the fireplace. He opened the windows wide to air the room, and began clearing up the debris of their orgy.

He carried the dildo up to the bathroom where he washed it in hot, soapy water, admiring its weight and the attention that had been paid to small details – there were even piss holes channelled in the cock

179

heads. He remembered the sight of Luke and Colin, how surprised he'd been that they were able to take the lengthy piece of rubber between them. He wondered if there would be any embarrassment when the others woke up, but dismissed the idea. Why would they feel embarrassed about what had happened? They had done it all before; Dale was the orgy virgin, and he was not ashamed.

He dried the dildo and wrapped it in one of the used towels. He left it on the floor outside Colin and William's room.

He ate a breakfast of coffee, toast and cereal at the kitchen table, enjoying the quiet, while he thought about his future. If he achieved what he wanted in the next few days, his life could be very different. He saw himself with Charlie, back in London, dining at his favourite restaurants, going for walks in the park near his flat. With their dual incomes they'd be able to afford a better place to live, maybe even a house with a garden.

Dale wasn't stupid, he knew he could not expect Charlie to turn his back on promiscuity, but there was no reason that they couldn't make it work for them. Sleeping with other men could be another thing for them to share. Other couples did it, like Luke and Paul, William and Colin; they made it work – Dale and Charlie could too.

Sexual fidelity was unrealistic, he realised that now. It was human nature to desire sex with other men. Better to deal with it openly than have secrets. That would be the difference with this relationship, he wouldn't impose any expectations on Charlie, there would be honesty from the start.

He was getting ahead of himself, planning too far in the future. The most important consideration was how to handle the next few days, to decide exactly how he was going to make Charlie see the way ahead. He was bound to be reticent. He'd stuck by the wife and kid for so long; they would be Dale's greatest obstacle. Max was not a problem; persuading Charlie that he was better off without him would be the easiest factor in all of this.

He had an idea, something that would prove to Charlie

upfront how serious he was about him.

Eddie came into the kitchen. He was washed and dressed. He poured a mug of coffee and set about making toast. He looked rested and well. 'Morning,' he chirped, sitting across the table.

'Morning,' Dale greeted. 'Any of the others up yet?'

Eddie shook his head. 'No sign of life from either bedroom. I doubt we'll see the boys before midday.'

'What a waste of the day.'

'How are you feeling?' Eddie asked over the rim of his mug. 'Any regrets about last night?'

'None.'

His mouth rose. 'That's a relief.'

'For me too. I'm constantly surprising myself at the minute.'

'You really got into it, didn't you? The look in your eyes when William started fucking you was just incredible. It was like you were on another planet.'

Dale agreed. 'I feel like I've only been living half a life. This last week has been a revelation, even this weekend. Only on Friday I told you I believed in finding one man to love for a lifetime.'

'You've changed your mind since then?'

'No, just redefined the notion. What last night has taught me, more than anything, is that you don't have to love one man to the exclusion of other partners. Sex and love *can* be divided. I never believed that before, I thought it was just an excuse to be unfaithful. I've been so naive all these years.'

'I'm a fatalist,' Eddie said.

'What does that mean?'

'That there's a time in your life for everything to happen, to meet someone, to fall in love, separate, find someone else. It's all predetermined and will happen when it's mean to happen. This is your time to expand and grow. Don't discredit everything you've done before, because it is still relevant, just accept what's happening now.'

Dale brooded. 'What about those things you said yesterday? About staying away from Charlie and not wrecking his family? If fate proclaims that he's meant to be with me, his family will get hurt whatever we do.'

'You still have choices. You can't use fate as an excuse for hurting those people.' He took a bite of toast, washing it down with coffee. 'I'm not going to tell you what to do. It's your life and your decision, just think about it beforehand. You have to be absolutely certain that you're doing the right thing.'

'I've never been more certain of anything.'

After breakfast, with no indication that the others were ready to surface, Dale and Eddie went for a walk across the moor. They headed down the incline away from the cottage. Watched by a small flock of sheep, they climbed over a fence and descended the bank until they came to the river at the bottom of the valley. It was a grey but dry morning. They wore their jackets but it was not that cold. Although they were walking downhill, the exertion of the exercise began to tell. Soon they were panting.

'Enough,' Eddie announced, dropping to the grass. 'I need a rest.'

Dale joined him, laying back on the grassy slope and taking in the valley around him: the hills, the river, the plants and flowers, the grazing sheep. He closed his eyes and breathed deeply.

Eddie reached for him, rolling on the grass to lie across his chest. He kissed Dale's mouth. Dale laughed, 'What's that for?'

'Because I wanted to. You're taking yourself off the market, aren't you? I have to grab my chances while I can.'

Dale's hands crept around the small of Eddie's back, resting in the curve of his spine. He kissed him back, softly at first, just touching his lips, then more ardently. Eddie tugged a small packet out of his back pocket and pressed it into Dale's palm – condoms and lubricant.

'You planned this,' Dale teased.

'It could be the last chance I get,' Eddie said, reaching for the fly of Dale's jeans.

He pulled jeans and briefs down together, Dale raising his hips from the ground to aid him. Eddie got them down as far as his calves and trailed his fingers over Dale's legs, up the inside of his thighs. He lowered his head, pressing kisses on his body, avoiding his cock, circling the area instead, kissing his thighs, hips, abdomen, navel, everywhere but his cock. Dale sighed, putting his hands behind his head and surrendering to Eddie's mouth. The sensations almost maddened him. His blood seemed to flow faster, he could hear it in his ears, inside his head, burning through his arteries.

A shiver ran through his whole body when Eddie finally pressed his soft, warm lips against the tip of his cock. 'Oh God,' Dale groaned, when Eddie took more of him in his mouth. The sensations were electric.

Eddie sucked greedily, twisting his head from side to side. He didn't swallow the whole shaft but concentrated all his effort on the most sensitive area around the head. He flattened his tongue to graze the underside of the slit, then curled it to caress it. He fondled Dale's scrotum with one hand, rolling his balls between his fingers, then cupping the whole sac in his palm, tugging downwards. Dale jerked, pressing up onto his elbows, allowing Eddie to nourish his tender organs.

'Oh, you'd better stop a while,' he gasped. 'I can't stand much more.'

Eddie sat back, open-mouthed. They reached for each other, freeing themselves of their clothing, which they spread out on the ground as a makeshift blanket. They lay down, caressing each other, naked in the open air. Dale delighted in the contrast between the warm body beside him and the morning breeze on his skin.

They wrestled on the hillside, their eagerness flourishing. They twisted and crawled, getting out of breath, until they found themselves lying on their sides, head to toe in a sixty-nine position. Dale could feel the blood rushing to his head as he lay pointing downhill. He reached for Eddie's appetising cock, wanting it in his mouth. He studied it a moment, its contours and veins, the thick, rounded head which was sticky even before he sucked it. He moved his lips over the glossy tip, sampling the dewy fluid. He poked his tongue around the head, under the foreskin, and heard Eddie moan. He put the cock in his mouth, careful with his teeth, feeling it quiver and tremble as he took it deeper, the head pressing against his palate.

Eddie had his head between Dale's thighs, sucking again. He caressed Dale's balls and moved around to hold his arse, squashing and grinding his buttocks. Dale spread his thighs and increased his tempo, ducking up and down Eddie's shaft. Eddie's warning was gagged by Dale's cock. He shuddered, filling Dale's mouth with a jet of extremely salty fluid which he swallowed, nuzzling the shaft with his tongue until the orgasm stopped.

'Sorry,' Eddie gasped afterwards.

'It's all right,' he assured.

'You can still fuck me,' Eddie said.

Dale pressed his cheek against Eddie's thigh, noting he was still hard, which was a good sign. 'I'd rather you fucked me.'

Eddie sat up, looking at him. 'Are you sure?'

Dale nodded, squeezing Eddie's cock. 'I'm a changed man.'

They separated. Dale lay back on the blanket of clothing, while Eddie prepared himself. He wiped his cock before rolling on a condom. He applied lube to the surface of the rubber. Dale raised his knees and tilted his hips, opening his pelvis. Eddie lubricated his hole, pushing a finger inside.

'You're quite tight,' he said.

'I'll be okay,' Dale said.

Dale drew up his knees, hooking his elbows around his thighs, exposing himself. Eddie pressed the head of his cock against the tiny opening and pushed. It was true, Dale was very tight. He pulled his knees in tighter and focused on his hole, willing it to relax. Last night, sedated with wine and poppers, he'd let William into his arse easily. Now he was sober, it took more of an effort. He was determined to take it. Being fucked by Eddie was a symbolic gesture for his future, proving versatility and open-mindedness.

Eddie thrust gently. Dale bore down, opening his arse, the head was nearly there. Just a little further, open a little wider. Eddie gave one last thrust and he was there. With the head inside, the rest of the shaft followed effortlessly.

'Oh, yes,' Dale sighed, clasping the cock to his core. The sensation was incredible and his pleasure only increased when Eddie began to move. Eddie leaned over him, digging his knees into the slope, and began to move back and forth inside him. Dale gazed at his eyes, wordlessly urging him to go further, thrusting up at him.

On the warm hillside they clung to each other. Eddie moved his cock in and out and side to side, reaming every inch of Dale's arsehole. Dale gripped his shoulders, buried his head against his neck, and surrendered to the unequivocal passion of a good fuck. Only now he wasn't fucking, he was truly fucked.

Eddie supported the weight of them both, preventing a slide down the hill. He pushed his hands into the earth and dug in his knees while thrusting. Dale writhed beneath him, twisted his head from side to side, clenched his arse. Eddie would have come by now, Dale knew, but he'd already come once and could hold out for a long and intense ride.

But then he pulled out, leaving Dale gaping and hungry. Eddie lay on his back and held his cock straight up. 'Ride it,' he said.

Dale swung a leg over his body and lowered himself back on. Glad when he felt the fullness inside. He steadied himself on Eddie's stomach and rode him, lifting his arse to the top of the pole and sliding slowly down. His own cock tapped against his stomach with the motion, spattering dots of precome over his skin. He rose onto his toes and came down harder and faster. His heart battered his rib cage, sweat stung his eyes until Eddie was a blurred vision beneath him. He found it harder and harder to breathe.

Eddie jerked rigid and twisted his face. Dale felt his cock grow even harder inside; he was coming. He grabbed his own cock, jerking off as he rode – it was a rollercoaster, edging nearer and nearer to the fall. He screamed, throwing back his head, covering Eddie with a tide of milky fluid.

When it was over they lay together, naked, enjoying the gentle breeze on their skin. Dale could barely move, it felt as if a fire smouldered in his arse, the embers slowly going out. He lay on his back with his legs parted, knees raised, allowing nature's breath to cool his core.

'We should think about getting back,' Eddie said, reluctantly.

'Let's just think for a little while longer,' Dale drawled.

He could easily have lain there all day. His thoughts drifted from his present state, prematurely returning to Newbiggin Bay. He thought about Charlie, about making love to him in the sunlight, on a hill like this one, or a beach. Wherever it was, it would be special, an experience unique to themselves.

How soon would it be before he could make that fantasy a reality? It would take a while; there were many factors in their way before they could be free. As well as the other people involved, Charlie's business was based in the bay, and he wouldn't close it down until he was certain of Dale. Dale toyed with the idea of moving north himself – it would be easy for a lawyer with his qualifications and experience to relocate. But he knew that would not work. The answer was not to remove the obstacles in Newbiggin Bay but to remove Charlie from the obstacle course. Get him away from Max, and his wife, and the men at The Chain. He needed to start his new life from scratch.

Dale and Eddie stood up and retrieved their grass- and semen-stained clothes from the ground. Eddie laughed, holding up his shirt which was streaked with mud. He put on his jeans and shoes, tucked the shirt in his back pocket, and they walked slowly back to the cottage.

The others were up, having breakfast in the kitchen, still in their nightwear, looking bleary – except for Colin, who was contorted in a yoga position. Dale and Eddie said good morning before going upstairs to change their clothes and pack for the journey home.

Dale sat on the edge of the bed in clean underpants, folding his dirty clothes into a separate pile. Eddie unzipped his bag and began a similar process.

'Fancy a smoke?' he said, waving a ready-rolled joint. 'It's my last one. I don't feel like taking it home with me.'

Dale considered for a moment. 'All right,' he agreed, 'why not?'

'Good man.' Eddie opened the leaded window wide and sat cross-legged on the bed with an ashtray and lighter. Finished with his laundry, Dale shuffled back and adopted a similar pose, while Eddie lit the joint, took a couple of tokes and passed it his way. Dale did not smoke cigarettes. Inhaling a joint without choking was a skill he mastered in college.

'I always enjoy travelling,' Eddie said softly, 'but I look forward to going home just as much, if not more. When I get back tonight, I'm going to stick my feet up, open a bottle of wine, and vegetate in front of the telly. There's nowhere better than your own living room.'

'That sounds good,' Dale said.

'I might even hire a movie.'

'Something good?'

'No, something really cheesy and crap. The more brainless the better.'

They laughed easily. 'Do you live alone?'

'I share with a lad called Justin, another actor. It's like living alone because we hardly ever see each other. He's in Chester right now, in a play.'

'I hate living alone,' Dale sighed. 'Sleeping in an empty bed, cooking a meal for one and spinning it out over two nights.'

'Yeah, but there's watching what you want on tv, playing your own music, going to bed when you feel like it, only doing housework when you can be bothered or you know someone is coming round.'

He laughed. 'I have a cleaning lady.'

'That's even better. Does she do your ironing?'

'Yes.'

'You've got it made. Why would you want to share that with anyone? If you can afford to live alone, you'd be mad to do anything else.'

'I want to share my life,' he said. 'I like having someone there when I get home. Someone to talk to, to eat dinner with, to sit on the sofa together watching crappy movies.'

'Is that how you see it playing out with your married man?'

'Possibly,' Dale said. The joint and the sex had put him in a mellow mood and he wasn't going to spoil it by arguing with Eddie.

'I wonder how many other men and women there are out there, in love with married men, hoping for the exact same thing.'

They loaded the cars at three o'clock and checked round the cottage for anything they might have forgotten before locking up.

'Do we need to drop off the keys?' Dale asked.

Luke shook his head and shoved the bundle of keys through the letter box. 'The caretaker has his own copies. He said he'll call round for this set tomorrow.'

'You mean he could have walked in on us at any time?' Colin quipped. 'He could have stabbed us in our beds, or worse.'

'I think he'd have had a bigger shock than us if he came nosing around.'

'He could have joined us. The more the merrier.'

'I doubt it.'

'Was he shag-worthy?' Colin asked.

'As a buffalo.'

They hugged each other goodbye with the customary assurances to stay in touch, to not leave it so long before getting together again. Dale and Eddie exchanged phone numbers and e-mail addresses, knowing it was unlikely that either of them would keep their promise to seek the other out. Dale promised to see him in his forthcoming play even though he rarely checked the local press for such productions.

They parted with a brotherly embrace and a kiss on the cheek.

For a moment, as the weak sun glared across the glass of the departing car, Dale caught a glimpse of Eddie's face, square jawed, smiling softly... then he was gone.

Another opportunity had passed him by. Had he made a mistake, letting Eddie slip so easily from his life? His old self of just a week ago would not have allowed it to end like this. He would already be composing a text message to Eddie, thanking him for a wonderful weekend, ensuring he knew how much it had meant, arranging to see him again, maybe next week, or next month, but some time very soon. But his new self allowed Eddie to go unchallenged, unchecked and unwanted.

They drove back to the bay at a leisurely pace, stopping en route to visit the Angel of the North, a colossal statue standing on a hill outside Gateshead. Constructed from copper-coloured steel, twenty metres tall, with a wing span wider than a jet, it was the largest sculpture in Britain, according to the guys. Paul asked an American tourist to take their photograph while they posed by its feet.

After stopping again for ice cream, it was almost seven when they arrived home.

'How about going for a drink or two in town,' Luke suggested, 'to finish the weekend on a high?'

'Good idea,' said Dale, carrying his bags in from the car. 'I have a phone call to make first. I won't be long.'

He went up to the spare bedroom and closed the door, before getting out his mobile and retrieving Sam's card from his wallet. He kicked off his shoes and watched himself in the mirror while slowly dialling the number. He was nervous; resolute about what he had to do, but still knowing it was wrong. Sam answered after two rings. Had he been waiting by the phone?

'Hi,' Dale said, cheerily. 'It's me.'

'Hi,' Sam replied, just as breezy. 'I thought it might be. Did you have a good time?'

'Yes,' he said, 'it was good.' He stared at his reflection while he spoke, watching the act unfold. He was smiling a fake smile, even though Sam could not see.

'Good.'

'How was your weekend? Did you have fun too?'

'It wasn't bad,' he said. 'But nothing special either. I was missing good company.' A pause. 'All the best men seemed to have left town.'

Dale struggled for an answer, uncomfortable with the compliment. 'I'm sure there were plenty of cute local guys around. There seems to be a never-ending supply.'

'Local guys have lost their appeal.'

Dale stopped smiling. 'You're... er, embarrassing me.'

'Sorry. Did you come to a decision?'

'Decision?'

'About when to go home?'

'Oh. Nothing definite yet. I was planing to stay around a few more days.'

'Excellent. I provisionally booked us a table for tomorrow night. I hope that's okay. It's a fabulous restaurant.'

'Thanks, that sounds great.'

'It is. I've booked a table for eight o'clock, but meet me in XL at seven, we can have a couple of drinks first. I got you a present too.'

'You have?'

'It's nothing special. Just a CD, the Kylie track you said you liked.'

'Thanks,' he said, 'but I already have it. I was... wondering about The Chain. If you were going to the meeting this week.'

There was a long pause before Sam answered. 'Do you want to go?'

Dale tried to make his interest sound casual. 'Well, it is my last week. I might never get the opportunity to do something like this again. It would be a shame to miss the chance while I have it.'

'Okay.' The note of optimism had gone from his voice. 'The next meeting is Tuesday.'

'It's hard to believe it's been less than a week since the last meeting. So much has happened.'

'Listen,' Sam cautioned. 'I wasn't going to tell you this, but if you're planing to go to The Chain you should be warned.'

Dale's fist tightened around the phone.

'I saw Max last night,' Sam told him. 'He asked to see you. He wants to meet you tomorrow afternoon.'

'What does he want?'

'I don't know but it has something to do with Charlie. Dale, they are a seriously fucked-up pair. I don't think you should go. The man is dangerous. He's hurt people before, even done time. If he sees you as a threat, he won't think twice about hurting you.'

Dale turned away from his reflection. 'When and where?'

'Don't go,' Sam retorted.

'Tell me,' he insisted.

Sam sighed. 'He wants to see you on the pier at one o'clock.'

'I'll be there,' he said with determination.

Fourteen

IN DENIAL

On Monday morning, the weather turned worse. A raw wind blew in from the North Sea, stirring a leaden sky. Though tourists were still evident around the bay, they avoided the promenade, favouring the shelter of the town centre and the rows of shops running parallel to the exposed sea front.

Dale spent the morning rattling around the house, nervously drinking cup after cup of tea. He tried to read, but gave up after five failed attempts on the same paragraph. The television was tuned to BBC *News 24* but he paid no attention to the bulletins. Finally, at midday, he left the house and began the walk into town.

He wore a sweatshirt and fleece beneath his waist-length coat and had borrowed a Burberry scarf from Luke. Still the wind cut through him. He stopped at a coffee shop, holding the paper cup in both hands to thaw the chill in his fingers. He couldn't decided whether the shiver in his stomach was due to the cold or the expectation of meeting Max. He bought a chocolate biscuit and ate it straight away, hoping the sugar would give his energy level a boost.

He walked down to the promenade, passing the Strand and the Cock Shop. Sam had called three times already but Dale wasn't answering his phone. He deleted Sam's text messages unread. He didn't want to consider the romantic meal Sam had planned for this evening, or what would happen afterwards. But Dale was resolute about what he had to do; he had to keep favour with Sam until tomorrow night – even if that meant fucking him again. What a delectable, yet hateful, duty that would be. Best not think about it until necessary.

Dale stuffed his hands in his pockets and hurried along the promenade, towards the pier. Without the protection of the buildings, the wind increased in strength and the cold was bitter.

He walked out onto the pier. The planks beneath his feet were ancient and grey, in need of paint. The tide was high, a sluggish brown swell that rushed under the boards.

There was no sign of Max. Dale checked his watch, wondering if he had he made a mistake about where they were supposed to meet. No, there was only one pier in the bay. This was it. But he was early by a good ten minutes. He looked around and saw a couple walking along the front, clinging to each other and laughing as they bowed their heads into the wind. The boy, as much as Dale could see, was cute. Another man was walking his dogs, three mongrels on leashes, though one of them looked like it could pass for a German Shepherd.

There was a series of kiosks and amusement huts along the pier. Most hadn't bothered opening, but he found a small van selling hot dogs and burgers, the seller huddling behind his counter. He bought a cup of tea to keep warm while waiting.

It began to drizzle with rain.

He would give Max the time it took to finish his tea, then he was leaving.

A few minutes later, as Dale was on the verge of giving up, he saw a large figure walk along the promenade and turn onto the pier. Even from a distance, the broad shoulders and white blond hair were unmistakable. He swayed as he walked with his hands at his side. His short blond hair whipped about his forehead and the cold brought a ruddy colour to his face.

'You're still here, then?' he said as he approached.

He did not stop when they drew level, but kept on walking, further out onto the pier. Dale cautiously kept pace with him.

'I was going to give you a few more minutes,' Dale said, sounding calmer than he felt.

'I meant you're still in town.' Max looked straight ahead as he spoke. 'That pussy-wipe Sam said you might not being coming back.'

'I'm staying the week.'

Max sneered. 'Then I don't know if you're brave or stupid.'

'I'm not scared of you.'

They had come to the end of the empty kiosks and the end of the pier. They stopped. Dale felt the wind claw more insistently at his body, as the boards vibrated with the strength of water below. It occurred to him that he had every reason to be afraid of Max. Why had he asked to meet on this desolate pier? He would have known the weather forecast in advance. Did he intend throwing Dale over the side? Even the strongest of swimmers would be lost to the sea in conditions like this, battered by the tide against the support structure. He glanced towards the railing at the edge. It was above waist height, but Max had the strength to heave him over the side if he wanted to.

Max turned to look at him. His expression was unfathomable until he smiled. His eyes were as cold as the sea that surrounded them.

'People around here think I'm a cunt because lads like Charlie can't wait to drop their pants for me and open their sweet arses. You must have a big opinion of yourself,' Max said knowingly, 'if you think you can compete with me.'

'I know my worth,' he shot back. 'And next to you, I'm a king.'

'A king, well, well. Your kingdom must be worth a lot if you think Charlie's gonna drop everything important in his life for the sake of being with you.'

'I haven't asked him to.'

'Not yet, you haven't, but you're going to, aren't you, Dale? What else did you come back for? It can't be for our glorious weather.'

'You sound frightened,' he said triumphantly. 'Are you afraid Charlie will say yes? *Why else would you be here?*'

Max looked him up and down. 'Have you any idea the number of guys who have fucked Charlie? Not just at The Chain. There are other orgies. Charlie goes cottaging too, and cruising; he must have the most popular Gaydar profile in the whole of the Northeast, maybe even the whole country. I can't begin to count the dicks that boy's had in him – and I've seen him take some meat. He's had thousands and I've seen them all.' He paused, then added, 'Except you. You fucked him last week, *without me*. Not that I'm bothered – he told me what happened. It's not quite a first, but he hasn't been fucked by many other men when I wasn't there to watch. So what I want to know is, what's so special about you?'

'Don't you know? I thought he told you everything.'

'I'm asking *you*,' he said firmly.

Dale held onto the railing, looking across the turbulent sea. 'I'm not just interested in fucking him,' he shouted above the wind. 'That's the difference.'

'You did fuck him. There's no difference.'

'Clearly there is! Why else are we having this conversation?' His eyes flashed. 'You're worried sick. Charlie sees something in me that none of those other men had, including you.'

'What's that?'

'Love.'

Max laughed loudly. 'Love. What a fucking drip you are. You haven't got the first idea what makes that boy tick. Love is what has kept him with me for eight years. I'm not scared of him leaving me for a runt like you. If you think hearts and flowers will win him over, you're in for a shock. Do yourself a favour and fuck off back to London, before Charlie rips your sappy heart into a million fucking pieces.'

'I'm not going anywhere. Not until he knows there's a choice.'

'He's made his choice: Julie and me.'

'Julie?' So that was her name.

'*His wife*. Surely you know about her.'

'That he married her *after* he met you, yes I know that. They've got a kid, so what? Loads of men make that mistake, he doesn't have to spend his life making up for it.'

'A mistake,' he said slowly, his words almost lost to the wind. 'Such a *huge* mistake, he's making it again.'

'What?'

Max grinned triumphantly. 'Didn't you know? Julie's pregnant again, five months gone.'

Dale stared at him. Was he lying? Was this nothing more than fight talk? Max was desperate, his tactics were transparent. 'I want to talk to him. He can tell me himself if he doesn't want me.'

'He doesn't want you.'

'He can tell me himself,' Dale repeated.

'You're wasting your time.'

'It's mine to waste,' he said firmly. He clenched his jaw so tightly, he could feel the side of his face pulsing. He wasn't about to give up – if he wanted Charlie, he had to fight.

'If I tell Charlie not to see you,' Max drawled, 'he won't. You'll never see him again.'

'You really are scared of losing him.'

Max shook his head. 'I'll make it easy for you then. You can see him today.'

His pulse quickened. 'When?'

'After I fuck you,' Max said indifferently.

They stared at each other. 'No,' Dale said at last.

Max shrugged, stuffing his hands in his pockets. 'Fair enough. You've proved my point; you're not man enough for my boy. Now fuck off.' He turned away from the railing and began walking back down the pier.

Dale panicked and reacted on instinct. 'Wait,' he shouted. Max stopped but did not turn round. Shaking, Dale walked towards him. 'You'll let me see him afterwards?'

Max turned slowly. 'If you're so keen to have your heart broken.'

He shivered. 'All right.'

Max's smiled widened and he came closer. He reached out, running his hand up the side of Dale's face, which was cold and wet with sea spume. He wrapped his huge paw around Dale's head and pulled him forward to kiss him. Dale opened his mouth, feeling the roughness of Max's unshaven skin against his face. Max forced his tongue into his mouth, filling him. Dale tried to show some kind of willingness, but when he lifted his hands to the big man's chest, Max swatted them away. The pressure on the back of his head remained firm.

Then Max released him, breaking the mouth lock. He put his hands on Dale's shoulders and forced him to the wooden floor. The sea boomed in the gaps between the planks. From his position, Dale's eyes were level with Max's worn and bulging crotch. Guessing that the big man wanted him to suck him, Dale reached for his fly. Max's batted his fingers aside. Dale looked up at his grinning face. 'What do you want?'

Max pointed at his feet. 'Lick my boots.'

He was about to protest when he hesitated. He thought about Charlie and nodded, lowering his head. Part of him revolted. This was something new. He ran his closed lips over the surface of Max's left boot. The black leather was old and cracked. Tentatively he opened his mouth and flicked his tongue around the toe, tasting work dust. He searched his brain. Had Sam ever mentioned what Max did for a living? Wasn't he a roofer? So this was the taste of someone's attic. He kissed a trail over the boot, following the curve of the toe, brushing his lips across the stitching on the sides.

He looked up at Max, who was staring at him, and caught the outline of his dick, straining against his jeans. 'Keep your fucking eyes down,' Max snarled.

Thinking only of his prize, Dale washed the dusty hide with his mouth, sweeping his tongue all over the surface of the left, moving onto the right, not stopping until both black boots shone as though newly polished.

Max prodded him with a toe and Dale lost his balance, thudding hard on his arse. Max laughed at him. 'Stand up,' he said.

Dale struggled to his feet. 'You cunt!'

Max's hand came out of his pocket. Dale heard a sudden click and saw a flash of steel. The bastard had a knife. The five-inch blade glimmered in the dull afternoon light.

'What are you doing?' Dale asked, genuinely afraid.

'You know what I'm doing. I'm going to fuck you.'

'You don't need a knife.'

Max pointed to the side railing with his blade. 'Over there,' he directed.

Dale hesitated. He was turned on, sure, but surely Max wouldn't be mad enough to use the knife? But what about all those rumours? Max had already proved his capacity for violence.

'Scared?' he taunted.

'No,' Dale lied.

'I thought you wanted to prove your worth.'

Dale was terrified, but he was fucked if he'd let Max see it. He moved towards the railing and gripped it tight, taking a rigid stance. If Max planned on throwing him over the side, he was not going to make it easy for him. But the look in Max's eyes told Dale that he could see through the pretension, that the fear was visible. He sensed that, in some perverted way, Max respected him for it.

He waited.

He felt a tugging at the back of his jeans and heard a tearing sound. Cold wind whipped around his buttocks. Max had slit the backside of his jeans right down the seam. He rived open the two sides of denim before slipping the cold blade down Dale's underpants. With a rapid flick of the wrist, the backside of his briefs was split in two. Despite the cold, Dale's face burned red hot.

Max laughed at his blistering humiliation.

His hands were on Dale's arse, brusquely squeezing and spreading, squashing his butt like a piece of fruit. He dug his fingers into the muscle. The cold sea wind caused goose bumps to raise on Dale's skin and when Max slapped his arse with a flat, open hand, the pain was sharp and shocking. He slapped Dale again and again, laughing devilishly with every stroke. Dale gritted his teeth and bore it.

He waited – while Max unfastened his jeans. Max's cock was pierced, and he removed the piercing before rolling a condom on his cock and lubing himself – anticipating the final humiliation. Max's thick fingers slid between Dale's icy arse cheeks, coating the hole with lube.

'Are you ready for your daddy?' he said, his voice low in Dale's ear. The head of his cock was nudging his anus. '*This* is why Charlie will never leave me.'

Max slid his cock deep into Dale's arse.

Dale's cry of pain was snatched by the wind. His knuckles whitened around the rail as a searing ache shot through his insides. Max's cock throbbed deep in his lower bowel. Max pushed, forcing it deeper, sending hot vibrations through his guts. He pulled back, dragging his cock head slowly through the tight opening, then slamming back inside, pushing Dale's chest against the rail, forcing the breath out of him.

Max slid a hand around his waist, to his groin. Dale burned with shame when Max found him hard. Max grabbed his balls tightly, pulling the sac away from his body, twisting. His cock throbbed and dribbled.

'What would Charlie think if he could see you now?' Max said, emphasising each word with a hard thrust. 'Not much of a saviour, are you? You're nothing but a squishy pussy. One of daddy's bitches!'

'*Fuck you!*' he spat

'No, bitch. I'm fucking you.' He held his waist with both hands and began to screw his hole with a strong, steady rhythm, the flesh of Dale's arse jiggling with every thrust.

Dale concentrated on the pain, blotting out Max's words. He breathed deeply, the cold air seared his lungs. It didn't matter, he told himself. It would be over soon, then he would see Charlie.

He realised, horrified, the pain was not as great as it once was. The big cock tearing through his rectum was as enjoyable, no pleasurable, as it was painful. He fought against the pleasure, unwilling to surrender to it. Unwilling to enjoy what Max was doing to him.

He won't make me come, he said to himself, repeating it, like a chant, in his head. *He won't make me come.*

Max teased him, tickling his sphincter with short strokes, just pushing his cock head in and out. Dale groaned dismally; the sensations in his warm hole were exquisite. He could feel the hardness grazing his chute. He was unable to resist it, his arsehole had never felt so good.

'*You cocksucking motherfucker!*' he swore.

Encouraged by the outburst, Max ploughed his arse in a steady rhythm. He swatted his buttocks and Dale could feel the red hand prints burning his cold white flesh.

'You like it now,' Max taunted. 'I can feel your little pussy melting like honey. Come on bitch, ride your daddy's cock.'

He couldn't keep his body from responding. A small part of his mind still wanted to resist, but his body admitted defeat. His hole was chewing Max's cock, responding to his thrusts. Angrily, he shoved his hips back at him. Max fucked him harder, jabbing his prostate with his blunt cock head, causing Dale's dick to leak a sticky river of precome. Despite the cold, their faces glowed, damp with sweat and rain and sea water.

Dale's thighs were weakening, they ached with the effort it took to resist. He felt the big piece of meat stiffen inside his body, swelling to fill his juicy chute. It was almost time. Max was grunting like a boar, plunging in his meat at an erratic pace. Dale raged, gripping the rail. His arse was electric, communicating pleasure to his entire body, his balls ached and his cock went into spasms. He came hard, squirting and trembling, blowing his load over the side of the pier into the furious tide. Max gave a roar, slamming deeper into his arse, and shot a powerful load into his guts. His fat tool pulsed and pounded inside the warm cavity, until every drop of semen had been exhausted.

Max pulled out, tossing the rubber over the edge, wiping his greasy hands on Dale's buttocks. Dale's hole closed slowly, dribbling liquid lube down the back of his thigh. He stood, pulling up his tattered clothes, holding his split jeans across his arse, wondering how he could get back to Luke's like this.

He stared at Max, who had pushed the piercing back into place before stuffing his slimy cock back in his jeans and buttoning up. 'I knew you were a pussy,' he gloated.

'I want to see Charlie,' he insisted.

'I'm not sure Charlie will want to see you, not after what his daddy's done.'

'Now!' he shouted, holding onto his dignity as well as his pants.

Max sneered.

'If you don't get him for me, I'll search through every name in the phone book until I find him. There can't be too many carpenters listed as Adrian Foster.' He did not fail to notice the change that came over Max's face, the flicker of uncertainty. 'Yes, I know his real name. Now, you'd better get him for me, now! Or I'll do it my way and make a hell of a fuss about it.'

'Keep your knickers on,' Max jeered. He zippered up his coat. 'I'll call him. You wait here. If he's not here in an hour, he doesn't want to see you.'

'I don't trust you.'

'Tough. I'll speak to him. It's not my fault if he doesn't want to see you.'

He stalked down the pier without looking back. Dale shuddered with the cold and tried to shelter from the wind, ducking behind one of the closed kiosks. His clothes were a mess – however he tried to arrange his jeans, it was impossible to conserve his modesty. His arse was icy cold. He rubbed his cheeks to warm them. Then he remembered he was wearing two layers underneath his jacket. Moving quickly, he shrugged off his coat and the fleece beneath it. Even with the shelter of the kiosks, the wind bit through him. He hurried back into his jacket and tied the fleece around his waist. He didn't feel any warmer but at least his bare arse was covered.

He walked down to the hot dog stand for another cup of tea and waited at the entrance to the pier. Max could not be trusted. The chances of him sending Charlie down to meet him were minute. Still, he would wait the hour, however cold it got. He wiped his nose on his sleeve and lingered.

'Ahem.'

He jumped, spinning around.

It was Charlie. Dale's heart flipped at the sight of him. He was wearing a navy jacket, the collar turned up to his throat, his uniform cargo pants and work boots. Dark stubble coloured the lower half of his face and his sideburns needed trimming. There was a tired look about his steely eyes but he was still the most beautiful creature Dale had ever seen. He was compelled by an urge to grab him, to squeeze him tight and pledge eternal love. He resisted.

'I don't have much time,' Charlie said. 'I'm on a job. Mind if we eat while we talk?' He nodded to a cafe across the street. 'You look like you need thawing out.'

The heat in the cafe was a joyous relief. Charlie ordered the special: fish and chips, mushy peas, bread, butter and tea. Dale ordered hot chocolate, too nervous to eat. They took a table next to a radiator.

'What happened to your jeans?' Charlie asked, sitting opposite him, stuffing chips in his mouth with his fingers while drenching his plate in salt, vinegar and tomato ketchup.

'Max got handy with his knife.'

Charlie paused. 'Max fucked you?'

He reddened. 'I didn't have a choice. It was the only way he would let me see you again.'

'What's going on?'

'What did Max tell you?'

'He didn't tell me anything. Just to meet you here within the hour. I wondered what he was playing at, he's been acting funny all week. I think he's pissed off that we got together last week.'

'Did you tell him about that?'

Charlie shook his head, forking through his cod fillet, checking for bones. He took a bite and chewed. 'But he knows. He's got spies all over this place.'

So Max was lying – Charlie hadn't confessed.

'Why didn't you say anything?'

Charlie considered this for a moment. 'I don't know. To keep the peace, probably. He doesn't like it when I fuck other guys without his consent.'

'Without consent.' Dale shook his head. 'Has it happened before?'

'Only once,' Charlie said. 'Max lost it, big time. Made a right mess of the other guy. I was worried the same thing would happen to you, that's why I didn't tell him.'

'Well, he knows.'

'Did he try to hurt you?'

'He fucked me, cut up my clothes.'

Charlie chewed slowly, swallowed. 'Consider that a warning – you won't get another.'

'Doesn't it bother you? That he's so violent. So controlling.'

'He'd never hurt me. As long as we're careful, he won't hurt you either. You're leaving soon, aren't you?'

Dale looked at him. 'End of the week.'

'Good.'

'Do you want to see the back of me?'

Charlie smiled. 'I don't want to see your pretty face rearranged. It's better that you leave.'

Dale started. *He has no idea how strongly I feel for him. He thinks I'm just another casual fuck, who wants to use him and move on.*

'You'll be safe enough at The Chain,' Charlie continued. 'Max won't touch you there, he values his membership too much to risk getting kicked out. But you don't want to hang round too long. If you see him in one of the bars or a club, keep out of his way.'

Dale wanted to tell him everything, to pour out his heart and beg Charlie to leave with him. But he saw in that moment that words would not be enough. Charlie would think he was insane if he opened his mouth now and spewed out his vision of happy-ever-after. At best he would not take the declaration of love seriously, at worst he would be shocked, maybe frightened, even revolted. Through the confusion in his mind, Dale saw that Charlie was a man who responded to action, not words.

'Will you be at The Chain tomorrow?' he asked.

His eyes lit up. 'I wouldn't miss it. They've been planning this one for weeks. Eighty-six hard cocks in one room. I can't wait. They're gonna ruin my arse.'

Dale froze. 'Eighty-six men. You're not seriously thinking of having them all?'

'Are you kidding?' he said eagerly. 'Thirty-seven is my record for a single session. Tomorrow night, I'm gonna blow that away. Make sure you get there early, if you want a shot. My hole will be nothing but a worthless wreck by the time all those cocks have gone through me.'

Fifteen

HISTORY

Max Grant lived alone in a three-storey townhouse on a long Victorian terrace. The house was in a dilapidated state when he put in his offer for it, six years ago. It was home to a widowed school teacher, whose upkeep of the house receded in the years following her husband's death. Her children put the family home on the market to pay for the old woman's keep in a so-so nursing home. Due to its neglected condition, Max got the place for a fraction of its true value.

Six years later, it was not recognisable as the same house. He was responsible for most of the renovations himself, calling in favours from friends in the building trade. The house had been gutted; it had been rewired; new windows had been fitted, as well as a new kitchen and bathrooms, built-in wardrobes and brand new floors. On the ground level was a large hall with a grand staircase, a large living room, dining room, breakfast room and kitchen, as well as access to the cellar, where he stored his tools. There were three bedrooms and a bathroom on the first floor. On the second floor, he had knocked down the walls between two smaller rooms to create a more open space, which he used as a home gym, equipped with weights, treadmill, exercise bike and punchbag. There was also a second bathroom on this level.

Max stood pummelling the punchbag, which hung from the ceiling. He was naked from the waist up, huge globules of sweat rolling off his bare skin. He worked out six days a week, two strenuous sessions per day. He'd always been a large man. Body building was a hobby he acquired on his first term in prison, when there was little else to occupy the time. It was a constant progression. Even when the officers denied him time in the gym, he never let his fitness slip, but did press-ups and crunches in his cell. Eventually the hobby became an obsession. The space for a gym of his own was his primary reason for buying the house.

He finished with the bag, breathless, and grabbed a towel from the weights bench, wiping his brow and torso. Working out was a great stress reliever, a way to loosen the tension in his mind and body, but tonight it wasn't working. He was as tense now as when he began.

He swore, grabbing a bottle of water and guzzling the contents in one go. Then he heard a noise downstairs. The front door.

'Finally,' he muttered, draping the towel over his huge shoulders and heading for the door.

Charlie met him on the landing of the first floor. He was still wearing his work clothes. They hurried together and embraced passionately.

Charlie tried to pull back from Max's tight grip. 'Careful,' he said. 'You're crushing me.'

'Where have you been so long?' Max asked, irked by the cold shoulder. He stepped back, watching Charlie's face for signs of guilt, half afraid of what he could have been doing.

'At work,' he said, heading for the bathroom.

Max followed him, turning on the lights. It was a large tiled room with concealed lighting. A vast white bathtub dominated the space, with a separate shower, washbasin and toilet.

Charlie opened a cupboard and took out a thick towel. He perched on the bath to remove his work boots and socks.

'I thought you would have called,' Max said, still watching him.

'There wasn't time, I had a job to finish.'

'What happened with Dale?' he asked, sitting on the closed toilet seat, watching Charlie strip. He never tired of looking at his body. Keeping fit seemed effortless for Charlie, he didn't work out at all. He claimed his work was exercise enough. Maybe that was true, if you took into account all the fucking he did. Charlie couldn't just fuck for England – he could fuck for the world, maybe the whole damned universe.

Charlie shrugged off his plaid work shirt and the black vest he wore beneath, dropping them in a heap at his feet. Max watched, amazed by his effortlessly flat gut, split down the centre by a lush trail of black fur, which widened over his abdomen into a thick, glossy bush around his cock. His muscular forearms were thatched with the same silky hair, while tattoos curved around his generous biceps. Max had gone with him to the tattoo parlour each time Charlie wanted a new design inked into his skin. The tribal band on his right shoulder was the first, five years ago, followed by the Celtic cross on his left bicep. The black panther design on the small of his back was the most recent and, at eight inches in length, the most painful, he said.

'Are you going to tell me, or aren't you?' Max persisted.

Charlie gazed back, wearing only his blue boxers. 'There's nothing to tell. I don't know why you were so adamant I meet him.'

'He didn't tell you he loved you?'

His eyes narrowed. 'Loved me?' He laughed. 'God, no. Is that what you think?'

'That's what he said to me.'

'He didn't say a thing. Dale doesn't love me, Max. He's winding you up.' Charlie slipped down his boxers and turned to the shower, reaching inside to turn on the water. His weighty buttocks swayed with the movement. Max grew hard, wanting to be inside them.

'He was very convincing.'

Charlie held his fingers beneath the spray, waiting for the water to heat. 'Why are you worried about Dale? He's a tourist, he'll be gone in a few days. We'll still be here.'

Max nodded. 'You're right. Still... the man pisses me off. And it wouldn't be the first time you'd left me.'

A cloud passed over Charlie's face. 'Don't be like this. I'm here now, aren't I?' He stepped into the shower and closed the door.

Max sat still, his jaw set.

Half an hour later they were lying on top of the bed, naked and clean. Charlie lay on his stomach, drinking vodka from a well-iced glass. Max lay beside him, on his back, one arm propped behind his head, the other caressing the curve of Charlie's spine, stroking the panther tattoo. His anxiety was unseated, Max couldn't dismiss the threat Dale personified. He didn't trust Charlie when he said nothing had happened.

'Why didn't you tell me he fucked you last week?' he asked, finally broaching the subject.

'I don't ask you about the boys you fuck when I'm not around.'

Max pulled back from him. 'It's not the same. You know it isn't.'

'What are you saying?' Charlie turned away form him. 'That they mean nothing?'

'Next to you they mean nothing. What else am I supposed to do? If I saw more of you I wouldn't need the other boys.'

'Not even little Henry?' Charlie taunted. 'My own little clone.'

'Why do you do this to me? Why are you acting like this?'

He rolled over slowly, stretching. 'I don't know,' he said. 'What else are we supposed to do?' He dipped his fingers in his drink, scooping out a piece of ice. He brought the ice to his lips and traced the outline of his mouth. Max watched as he moved it over his jaw, down his throat, leaving a glittering trail of water on his skin. He touched the cube to his left nipple, circling until it hardened, moved over to the right. He gasped with pleasure, arching his back.

'What are you doing?' Max murmured.

Charlie groaned, biting his lower lip as he moved the ice lower down his body. Goose bumps sprang across his skin, the hairs on his belly stood erect. Charlie opened his legs wide, moved his hand down. He gasped, tilting his pelvis upwards, trailing the ice along the line beneath his balls, towards his anus.

Max sat up, watching, still tense, but unable to resist his young lover's game.

Charlie widened his thighs, and pulled his knees into his chest, exposing his arse. He held the ice cube directly above his anus. Max gazed in wonder as a drop of water began to hang from the edge of the cube, seemingly suspended there for ages before finally falling on the orifice below.

'Oh God,' Charlie groaned. His arsehole clamped shut as the cold water spattered its puckered rim. A second drop fell on the target, another direct hit. He exhaled slowly. He brought the ice down to touch his hole, shuddering with the cold sensations. The ice melted slowly with the heat of his skin, blunting the edges. He pressed against the hole, pushing the frozen cube inside himself, crying as the cold penetrated his core.

'Do you want me?' he drawled.

'Yes,' Max said breathlessly. He wanted him so badly he would do anything. Fuck, he would die for this boy.

'Tell me.'

'I want you more than I've ever wanted you. I want your hot fucking hole on my face. I want to taste you. I want to drink from your cunt.'

Charlie's eyes flashed with excitement. He pushed himself up from the bed, to straddle Max's chest. He crawled up his body, smearing precome over his smooth chest as he brought his pelvis closer to his face. Max's heart was pounding. Charlie rose onto his knees and lowered his arse over Max's mouth. The mouth was open, ready for him.

Max could smell the scent of soap, together with the natural odour of Charlie's arse. He felt the first trickle of water fall on his lips and moved his head to catch it fully in his open mouth. The ice, melted by the heat of Charlie's arse, dribbled from his hole like warm rain, and he sighed and squirmed as it thawed inside his core. His hairy balls fell across Max's nose, obstructing his breath, and he breathed through his mouth as he drank.

Charlie was intoxicating, more potent than undiluted vodka. Max reached for those hips, pulling that arse lower, bringing the hole to his mouth. He sucked the water from Charlie's hole like he would suck the juice from an orange, but it tasted better than any fruit.

'I want you inside me,' Charlie said huskily.

Max would live inside him if he could. He rolled out from under

Charlie, pushing the younger man into position on his back. He scrabbled with his left hand in the bedside drawer, locating condoms and lubricating jelly, while massaging Charlie's balls with the right. He tugged on the hairy sac, squeezing the contents, making the prone man moan and widen his legs. He let go and gave the exposed arsehole a couple of sharp, stinging slaps. Charlie moaned enthusiastically.

Max was hungry for that hole, to sink into its depths. He rubbered his dick in a hurry, giving it a good coat of lube. He knelt between Charlie's open thighs, got his cock into position, and looked into his eyes while sticking his cock straight into him. A look of pure ecstasy flew across Charlie's face as Max filled him with meat. They savoured the sensations for a moment, like sex connoisseurs. Max grabbed his ankles, holding them high and wide, and began to shove back and forth. Charlie rolled his head around the pillow, his eyes shut tight, his lips curled back from his teeth.

Max couldn't stop, he was driven by a deep, primal force. He thrust, letting go of Charlie's ankles to knead his hairy pecs, leaning over to kiss his brow, his cheeks, his lips. He screwed his cock deep into his greedy hole and all the time Charlie begged for it harder, deeper, faster. He lifted his hips from the bed, chasing Max's cock each time he withdrew.

'Come on,' he growled, pushing with his entire body, crazed with cock. 'Fuck me harder, you bastard! *Fuck me harder!'*

The bedroom echoed with the desperate sound of their slapping skin. Max gripped his arse, digging his fingers into the muscle, and pounded his body. Giving him everything he demanded, everything and more. It didn't matter what he wanted. He could have it all, body, spirit soul, the whole fucking world if he wanted it. The only thing Max cared about was being part of him.

Max Grant had lived all his life in Newbiggin Bay. His mother was an idiot of a woman called Joy, who had a succession of temporary jobs in the town. She worked in the amusement arcades and funfairs during the prosperous summer season, through the autumn and winter she eked out a living in the bingo halls. She just about got by from year to year, living on her own, screwing her way through the endless parade of horny tourists and chancers who came to the bay each summer. She'd once told Max that his dad was a solider on leave, who took her to the cinema on her night off from the Pier Lounge. He'd promised to come back and marry her, she said, when his next tour of duty was complete.

Another time, when she was pissed on cider and black, the story went that his dad was a gypsy who worked the donkey rides along the beach during the summer of 1962. Then he was a professional boxer competing in a national tournament.

The reality was that Joy didn't have a clue who his father was, he could have been any one of a dozen horny bastards who fucked her that summer. When he was growing up, she seemed to curb her sluttish ways. Max needed a daddy and there were always plenty of them around, but they never lasted long. Looking back on his childhood, Max didn't blame any of them for pissing off – Joy was moron and it was a wonder any of them lasted as long as they did.

As a kid he was strong and healthy but extremely withdrawn. He didn't have any friends. He was feared by the other kids at school for his proficiency with his fists. One day, a bully, two years older than him, tried to steal his football scarf. Max battered his face to a gory mash. No one picked on him after that.

When he was around thirteen, his body began to change. He became even stronger. His moods changed too and he was filled with strange desires. Desires for other men. Joy's boyfriend at that time was a butcher called Hank, a brick shithouse of a man. One night Max got up to use the toilet around midnight and caught Hank taking a piss with the door open. His eyes widened at the sight of the naked body, his shoulders, his back, his arse. He was fascinated by the dark hair that covered Hank's buttocks, and when the man turned around he saw more of it, on his belly and all around his chubby cock. Max's own body had only just started to develop in this way.

From then on he used to lie awake on the nights Hank stayed over, to listen for him going to the bathroom. Max would stumble out of bed, feigning tiredness, and wait outside the door, hoping to catch sight of his naked arse again. He found a pair of Hank's underpants under Joy's bed one day. They were white, with a worn elastic waist, and yellow stains around the crotch. Max stuffed them down his own pants, smuggling them back to his room. He used to rub them round his face when he wanked, inhaling the spirit of Hank's cock and arse, pressing his tongue against the old piss stains.

Hank caught him at it one day, sitting on the edge of the bed with his pants over his head, beating his angry rod. Max thought the house was empty, he didn't know his stupid slut of a mother had given Hank a key. The butcher was furious, calling him all kinds of names, like pervert and faggot. He shoved a balled fist into the teenager's stomach. Max was consumed by a rage of his own. Blood boiled in his veins. He didn't understand the things that Hank was saying but he reacted on instinct. He half-killed the butcher that afternoon with his own hands.

Joy was flaming but within a fortnight she had a new man.

The names that Hank had called him tormented Max. He tried to erase the poison from his mind by fucking as many girls as possible. The bay was teeming with sluts, younger mock-ups of his mother, and he had them all. His sexual appetite was insatiable, some weekends he would screw three or four sluts in a single afternoon, but he was never satisfied. When he was fifteen, one bitch said she was expecting and claimed it was his, she wanted him to marry her when they were old enough. Max told her to fuck off. Whether the baby was his or not, she didn't have it in the end.

He left school and began an apprenticeship with a local firm of builders. The other men were wary of him, and the joking behaviour and ribbing they doled out to all the new recruits didn't last for more than a week with Max. He enjoyed the work and after a variety of training, began to specialise in roofing.

The secret attraction he harboured for other men continued, fuelled by the raw masculinity that surrounded him every day.

His first experience with another man didn't come until he was twenty-three. He was working in Newcastle, where large-scale renovation work was taking place on a series of listed buildings. He went out on his own one Saturday night, having heard of a place down by the river – they called it The Gardens – where men would go to meet. It was a desolate place, pitch black and overhung with branches. The man, as much as he could see in the darkness, wasn't much to look at. He was skinny and a good few years older than Max. But when he dropped to the floor and wedged Max's cock into his mouth, he sucked him with more skill than all the bay sluts put together. He gave Max the most exquisite orgasm he'd ever known.

Afterwards the man asked for five quid.

Max beat the skinny runt unconscious and left him bleeding in the shadows. He checked the local news and papers for weeks afterwards but the beating appeared to go unreported. It took the best part of a year before he went near a man again. Later he became involved with a guy called Simon, ten years his senior. Simon was into submission and role-play. He was the first man, or woman, to allow Max to fuck them in the arse. Simon introduced Max to a world beyond copping off with strangers in shady areas or a quick tumble in the sack. Simon even had a makeshift playroom set up in the spare bedroom of his flat, equipped with a sling, dildos, lube, gloves, whips, nipple clamps, videos, books, magazines, poppers and coke. He had a small network of friends, both dominant and submissive, who came round to play in the room. What Max liked best of all was to fuck Simon and three or four of his friends, one right after the other. He liked them in the sling, which he could adjust to bring their hungry arseholes in line with his cock. They couldn't get enough of him.

Simon also introduced him to the bay's gay scene. He knew it existed, but hadn't had the nerve to check it out, not when it was on his doorstep, where people knew him. Through the scene he met other men and discovered he had a preference for younger guys. Simon wasn't getting any younger and their relationship tailed off, though Max still didn't mind fucking him and his buddies when they invited him round. Max developed a taste for men in their late teens and early twenties, guys who were experienced and willing to do all the things he asked them to. He developed a small stable of compliant, delectable bottoms.

When one of his boys left him for a rival top, Max was incensed. He beat the pair of them to a bloody pulp. This time the crime did not go unreported and Max found himself serving a two-year sentence in Durham prison.

Joy died of bowel cancer while he was inside.

He was thirty-two when he got out. With his improved, muscular physique, the bottoms were as hungry for him as ever. He returned to the roofing trade and resumed his life in the same mould as before, only now he had body building to relieve some of that pent-up rage.

Max was thirty-four, working on a new housing estate three miles out of Newbiggin Bay and putting money by to start out on his own, when he met Adrian Foster.

'Call me Charlie,' said the twenty-year-old carpenter on the day they met. He was sitting on the concrete floor, inside the shell of a new house, eating sandwiches out of an old ice cream tub.

'Why? The other men call you Adrian. Isn't that your name?'

'It is,' the boy said, looking directly at him. 'But I want you to call me Charlie.'

Max knew he'd found his newest conquest. Sitting against the bare brick wall in his work pants and vest, legs spread, showing an impressively bulging crotch, Charlie oozed a kind of sex that Max alone understood. There was no speculation about Charlie's sexuality on the site, none of the usual derogatory fag comments. As far as the other men were concerned, Charlie was straight. They had no reason to doubt the young recruit, he was all man.

But Max knew. He knew instinctively. He saw the boy watching him over his newspaper while they sat on their breaks. He saw his eyes following his cock bulge when he walked across the site. He saw Charlie watching him from the roof of an adjacent house, while he worked shirtless, his gym-built muscles glistening in the sweltering August heat.

At the end of his second week, Max offered him a ride back to town. The lad accepted with a smile, hitching up his baggy work pants as he climbed into the passenger seat of Max's van. He had the most sensual brown eyes, full of desire and a hunger for experience. Max wanted him so badly that he was scared to make his move.

He dropped Charlie off in town, close to his home. 'See you on Monday,' he said gruffly, waiting for him to get out. He couldn't be certain, but a cloud of confusion and disappointment seemed to pass across Charlie's brow as he grabbed his backpack from the floor and got out. He thanked Max without looking back.

Max watched him walk down the street and turn the corner. He couldn't stand to see him go. He locked the van and followed, sticking close to the vehicles parked along the side of the road for cover. He needn't have worried, Charlie didn't turn around.

Max followed him to the promenade. When Charlie descended the steps to the beach and disappeared into the shadows beneath the pier, Max knew he'd been right about him. He followed.

Charlie was on his knees in the sand. Three men formed a circle around him, their cocks hard and exposed. He worked them over with his mouth and hands. Max hung back, hiding behind one of the broad support beams, watching as the young carpenter was fucked by each of the three strangers. They were rough; slapping, spitting, slamming him with total abandon, filling his mouth and arse. They were a poor-looking bunch, fat and mean, but he begged them for more.

Each man shot his load and walked away without saying a word. The last man zipped up his dick and strode off across the beach.

Charlie stayed on his hands and knees in the sand, his trousers rucked around his ankles. Max hung back and saw him stand up slowly, coughing, spitting a mixture of saliva and sperm into the sand. He pulled on his clothes. As he walked back towards the steps, Max appeared from behind the pillar, seizing his arm.

Charlie halted. If he was surprised to see one of his site buddies in this notorious cruising ground, it did not register on his face.

Max took him back to his house that night and fucked him with more force and vigour than the three other men combined. Charlie was tireless – though sore and bruised, he screamed and groaned, always begging Max for more. Max bound his arms and legs with cord, stuffed a gag in his mouth and fucked him with the biggest and meanest dildo in his collection. When he finally removed the damp and sweaty rag from Charlie's mouth, the first word he said was 'More'.

Max was enraptured, hypnotised by him. None of his other boys could compare; Charlie took it harder and went further than any boy he had met. Despite Max's dominant position in their sex life, it was he who was the slave and Charlie the master. Max loved him. He told Charlie that he was going to finish with his other lads, he didn't need any of them when he had him.

'Don't be silly,' Charlie said. 'You'll need them when I'm married.'

Max was devastated. They'd been involved with each other for over a year and this was the first he'd heard of a girlfriend or engagement.

'We're fine as we are,' Charlie said to him one night in bed. 'We'll still be able to see each other after I'm married, just not as often. You'll be glad of your other lads then.'

'Why are you doing this?'

'I want a family, Max. I want kids. You give me a lot but you can't give me that. This way I get the best of everything. We all do.'

He asked Max to be his best man. Against his better judgement, he accepted. He even found himself growing to like Julie. As a wedding present, he paid for their Caribbean honeymoon.

Although outwardly he appeared happy, Max was falling apart.

The loss of his great love to a woman devastated him. He sought solace in narcotics and sex. One Saturday night in XL, sozzled on E and coke, having been awake for two days, he tried to entice a pretty young chicken into the toilets for a quick fuck. The boy refused. Infuriated, Max smashed his glass into the boy's face, grinding the broken pieces into his skin.

He served another three years in Durham prison.

Charlie came to visit him every month. Their relationship picked up as if nothing had happened when Max was released. Julie was expecting by then. When little Andy was born, Max became his godfather.

He wondered if Charlie had any idea how much it hurt to do these things for him. But there was no question of saying no to him. He'd do anything his favourite boy wanted because he was the only man he'd ever loved.

They were lying in each other's arms, naked, beneath the covers. It was dark outside. The room was lit by two lamps, on either side of the bed. Charlie dozed after they had sex. Max lay awake, holding him, thinking about their relationship. It seemed like that was all he ever did. He lay there for more than half an hour, sifting through their history.

Charlie took a deep breath. He was awake. Max squeezed closer.

'What time is it?' Charlie asked sleepily.

'It's after nine,' he replied. 'Nearly ten.'

'Shit,' he sighed, moving out of Max's arms, sitting up and stretching. 'I have to get home. Julie's pissed off about all the time I spend away from home.'

'This is the first night I've seen you in a week,' Max said.

Charlie turned, looking in his eyes, switching on his smile. 'We've got The Chain tomorrow, remember. I can't stay out late two nights running, she'll go nuts.'

Max reached for him. 'Give me five more minutes, just to cuddle. I have to share you with eighty other men tomorrow.'

Charlie beamed. 'I know. Isn't it exciting? I probably won't be able to sleep tonight.'

Max looked at him, overwhelmed by a heavy lump in the centre of his chest. I'll never be enough for him, he thought, nothing will. Charlie always wanted more. It was enough that he had to share him with the regular Chain men, but now he would have to compete with eighty. With any of his other lads, the prospect of seeing him screwed and banged by a room full of horny bastards would be the ultimate sexual thrill. But Charlie wanting this so badly broke his already burdened heart.

Charlie ignored his plea for a few more moments of intimacy. He pulled away and got out of bed, reaching for his clothes.

'I don't want you to spoil anything,' he said, stepping into his pants.

'What do you mean?' Max asked.

Charlie looked at him. 'I think you know. There's a good chance Dale will be there tomorrow. He'll probably want to join the line. I don't want you to do anything to stop him. Pretend like he isn't even there. Just let him have what he wants and that will be the end of it.'

'I think you're underestimating the way he feels.'

'But I'm not underestimating you,' he said firmly. 'Don't do anything stupid, Max. I couldn't stand it if you went back to prison. Dale isn't worth it. He's just one more cock going in my arse, one of many. If you put it in those terms, it doesn't seem so bad.'

Max had to laugh.

'That's better,' Charlie said, the edge dipping out of his voice. 'You know I'm right. You don't want to get banged up again for the sake of him. He means nothing.' He came around the side of the bed and sat down beside him, finally hugging him. 'What would I do if my daddy went back to jail, eh? You know I'd be no good without you here to look after me.'

Max hugged him back, gratefully. He was entirely at his mercy.

Sixteen

TOO FAR

The last customer of the day bought the current issue of *Indulge* magazine and two bottles of poppers. When the man had left the shop, Sam reached beneath the counter and flicked off the window lights. There were fifteen minutes left before the shop was officially due to close, but he'd had enough. It had been a long day already and it was nowhere near over. He quickly counted the day's takings and locked the money in the safe at the back of the shop.

In the tiny bathroom at the back of the stockroom, he stripped off his clothes and washed as thoroughly as he could at the small basin. He brushed his teeth and gargled with mouthwash before putting on deodorant. He played with his cock, teasing it into a state of semi-stiffness, and fastened a leather strap around the base of his balls. He put on the clean change of clothes he'd brought with him that morning – white jockstrap, worn jeans, tight blue tank top – and pulled on clean socks and boots. He ran a touch of wax through his short blond hair and applied a squirt of Lacoste to either side of his neck.

Outwardly, he was ready to go. Internally, he was not so prepared.

Monday night's dinner with Dale had not gone well. Sam knew as soon as they met that there was something weighing on Dale's mind. He was distant from the start, greeting Sam with a lacklustre hug and an air kiss that fell wide of the face. He hadn't made any effort with his appearance, his hair was a mess and he needed a shave. His clothes bore the creases of where they'd been folded in his suitcase.

Making conversation was a real effort. Sam even had to drag the details of his weekend in Durham out of him. Dale answered in monosyllables, conceding only when pressed that he had had a nice time.

Guessing that Dale's mood owed something to his confrontation with Max that afternoon, Sam asked what had happened. He wouldn't be drawn, only admitting that Max had not hurt him.

Instead of the romantic evening Sam had been looking forward to, the night was a huge effort. They went their separate ways at ten o'clock.

Sam was confused and hurt. When he last saw Dale on Thursday, everything had seemed perfect, leaving him hopeful that they had a chance. He earnestly believed Dale's infatuation with Charlie was over. How stupid he had been. Dale wasn't over Charlie; he was more obsessed than ever. It occurred to Sam that Dale might have been using him as a device to get to his true object of desire, but he dismissed the idea as being too insulting to consider.

He was tired and he'd had all day in the shop to think. He wasn't going to make the same mistakes as Dale, flirting with obsession and disaster. If Dale wanted to fuck up his head because of a heartless fraud like Charlie, then he could do it on his own. Sam had decided; he was cutting his ties. He would take Dale to The Chain tonight to find his precious Charlie, and that was it. Sam had been hurt enough, he'd wasted too much time and emotion. Now he was going to get over it.

Dale was waiting on the street when Sam left the shop.

'Hi,' he said, cheerfully.

'Hi,' Sam said, fiddling with the lock. He stuck a cigarette between his lips, lighting up, before turning to look at Dale. He stared.

The man who stood before him now was the opposite of his date twenty hours previously. He was clean shaven and rested. He wore a frayed pair of jeans, worn at the crotch, ripped on both knees. The top button did not fasten and displayed an inch of pubic hair. He also wore a black leather biker jacket, unzipped. Beneath it he was wearing a chain-mail vest, which fell short of his navel, exposing a taut midriff and more pubic hair. Heavy black construction boots completed his appearance. He looked more like a West Hollywood hustler than a well-heeled lawyer. There was a wanton darkness in his eyes that had not been there before; he exuded sex.

'New image?' Sam asked.

'Just trying something out,' he said. 'I wanted to look the part tonight.'

'Mission accomplished,' Sam said tartly.

His car was parked in its usual spot. He noticed Dale flinch on sliding into the passenger seat.

'Are you wearing the butt plug again?' he asked.

'No.' Dale fastened his seat belt. 'Have you got that Kylie track I like? To get us in the mood.'

Sam turned on the engine and pressed a button to start the third CD in the player. Strains of Indie Kylie filled the car as he put it in gear and drove off. He opened the window, chucking out his cigarette stub. The previous day's storm had passed over and it was a warm balmy night in the bay. Sam took the road out of town. Dale drummed his fingers to the music.

'Nervous?' Sam asked.

'A little bit,' he replied, looking straight ahead. 'This is all still new to me. There's so much to learn. Do you know what's meant to happen tonight?'

'What always happens: a group of men fuck their brains out.'

'What's so special about tonight? Why are the other groups uniting?'

'It's what they do. It happens all the time, like an exchange visit. We'll go to their Chain meeting in a month or so. Tonight's the first time we've had three groups together, usually it's just two.'

'What's the biggest session you've had before now?'

'I don't know,' he shrugged. 'Forty-five, maybe fifty men. I remember the Christmas party was a busy one last year.'

Dale gave this some thought. 'Charlie said he'd had thirty-seven men fuck him one night.'

Sam gripped the wheel and tried to keep the edge from his voice when he spoke. 'I remember. That was last Christmas. They stuffed him like a turkey.'

'He says he wants everyone to fuck him tonight, all eighty-six.' Dale sounded nervous as he said this.

'Then he's in for a disappointment,' Sam said. 'He'll have to make do with eighty-five because I'm not touching him.'

'It's insane,' Dale interjected. 'He'll be raw for weeks if he goes through with this.'

'He knows what he's doing,' he said disdainfully.

'I don't think he does. Max has put him up to it, I'm sure he has.'

'If Max has put him up to it, it's because it's what he wants. Charlie isn't a pawn here, he knows exactly what he's doing.'

'I'm going to try and stop him.'

'Aw, shit, Dale. Why are you doing this to yourself? Let's just go home. Whatever you say won't make a shit's worth of difference. I don't even think Max has any control of him. He's going to do what he always does and please himself. I don't think you want to see. This could be an image that will haunt you forever.'

'No,' Dale insisted. 'Keep going. I can change his mind. I know I can.'

Dale understood Sam's reservations but he had faith it wasn't too late to change Charlie's mind and divert him from this extreme course. He had been running the scenario through his mind like a film on a constant loop and he couldn't stand back impotently and allow it to be played for real. Charlie didn't want to be part of this. He was doing this for attention, it was a cry for help; it seemed that Dale alone could hear him.

Dale was nervous, both excited and afraid.

They reached the dirt road to the old farm. Up ahead there were vehicles parked all round the buildings, on the verges, and all down both sides of the road. Sam found a place to park a hundred yards back from the farm.

'It's a hell of a turnout,' he said, shutting off the engine.

Dale got out of the car and stretched. His stomach growled.

Sam looked at him across the roof and smiled weakly. 'Don't expect a miracle, okay.'

They walked down the road. Despite his fear, Dale couldn't help feeling excited. It was a similar feeling to the way he felt the first time he ever kissed another man – thrilling. He was about to take the biggest risk of his life here tonight but he knew it was worth it.

Sam led the way round the side of the building to the door. He knocked, four times slow, twice fast. It opened slowly, just a few inches.

'Julian Glover,' he said in a clear voice. The door swung wider and they went inside.

Big Harry was in attendance at the door, just like the time before. He was as mean looking as Dale remembered. Dale and Sam smiled curtly and stepped around him, into the stall where they could leave their clothes. Every available space was covered in folded trousers and T-shirts. Dale hung his leather jacket on a hanger with three other coats. He could feel Sam's eyes on his back.

'What's the password all about?' Dale asked. 'It's not the same as before.'

'No,' Sam said, removing his tank top and folding it neatly. 'It's changed each time, e-mailed out to members on the afternoon of the meet.'

'So what does it mean? Is it always a name? What's the significance?'

Sam laughed. 'They're the names of actors who appeared in episodes of *The Avengers*. Julian Glover was in the show more than once. Last week it was Edward de Souza, the time before that Michael Latimer.'

'I see,' said Dale, failing to get the significance.

Sam stripped down to a jockstrap and put his boots back on. He looked good with a nice bulge filling the cup of his jock. For a fleeting moment, amid the chaos in his mind, Dale wondered whether he had chosen correctly. He quickly cast away the thought; now was not the time to wonder. He'd decided on a plan of action and he intended to stick with it.

He followed Sam to the door, stealing an illicit glance at his exposed backside.

The smell inside the main room assailed him first: dust, sweat, poppers and the unmistakable scent of come. The interior of the barn was decked out more elaborately than on his previous visit. Illuminated by the fluorescent ceiling lights, bales of hay had been arranged around the room, covered in blankets, in batches of varying size. The bales were teeming with the bodies of men, some naked, others dressed in fetish wear; leather, rubber, denim. Everywhere he looked he saw a wealth of bare flesh. Music was pumping into the barn via unseen speakers, the volume loud but not loud enough to cover up the moans, grunts, sighs and swearing of the pack of rutting beasts. A whip cracked continuously out of sight, each stroke followed by a desperate cry, 'Thank you, Sir!' *Crack*!

A naked man hung from the ceiling, suspended by his ankles, his face blissful but scarlet. His wrists were bound to his waist and you could hear sounds of pleasure even though his mouth was stuffed with rags. Two other men beat his swollen cock with short canes. His hard rod leapt each time it was struck. Sweat poured over the bound man's torso as he dangled.

'Let's get a drink,' Sam said, nodding to the temporary bar, further down the room.

As they made their way to it, a bald man came crawling towards them on his hands and knees. It wasn't just his head that was bare, his entire body had been shaved clean of hair. The effect of his pink body was startling. He stopped at their feet, looking out at them with wide, expectant eyes. 'Suck your cock, Sir?'

They smiled and shook their heads, stepping over him.

Dale's eyes searched the crowded barn for Charlie or Max. He scoured each bale and bench, looked into the gloom of the furthest corner. He could not see either of them. It was early, he reassured himself.

They passed a bare mattress with six men gathered around it. Dale paused, keen to see what they were looking at. Three naked bodies writhed across the mattress. One man lay on his back with the other two piled on top of him. It took him a moment to realise what was so unusual about the scene; the guys on the top and bottom both had their cocks wedged up the arse of the middle man. He'd seen similar sights before in porn movies and at The Sex Cabaret, but this was different. This was no half-hearted attempt to get two cocks into one hole just for the sake of it. These men were really going for it. The two tops rammed their dicks into the middle guy's arsehole, giving it to him hard. Dale watched the face of the middle man, a handsome young guy with a fine build who looked Spanish. 'Yes, yes,' he hissed as they ravished his arse.

As Dale watched, the cock of the man on top slipped free. They all paused for a moment. Dale could clearly see the bottom guy's squishy pink hole. The top man rammed his dick home and they continued to pound his arse, heaving and swearing without mercy.

'Shit,' Dale gasped, aroused and appalled.

He stepped away from the scene.

In a sling, suspended from the ceiling, lay a slight brunet boy in his early twenties. An older black man plunged the gloved fingers of his right hand into the boy's anus. The boy's buttocks and arse crack were smeared with white Crisco lube. The man sank two, three, four fingers into the well-greased hole.

'Fill me,' the boy demanded.

The black man's whole hand sank into the boy's arse. The boy gripped the chains suspending the sling and began to rock gently on the engulfed fist. He threw back his head and screamed for more.

Further along, three men where gathered round a kneeling blond. They took turns directing piss at his suntanned body. The blond closed his eyes and turned his face towards the amber-coloured stream.

Dale's eyes continued to look for Charlie, unable to find him in this decadent crowd. They reached the bar and ordered the only drink available, beer.

'See Charlie anywhere?' he asked Sam.

The Cock Shop owner shook his head.

'I'm going to look around,' Dale said, not waiting for a reply.

He toured the barn, stepping over and around prone, writhing bodies. Everywhere he looked, he saw dicks: in mouths, arses and hands. Partners were exchanged. There was every kind of body type assembled there: fat, thin, hairy, bald, teenagers, geriatrics, disabled, gym studs, athletes, swimmers, footballers and quite average 'normal' guys.

His eyes wandered. He noticed the Spanish lad still had two cocks deep in his arse but the fistee was climbing down from the sling while a fifty-odd-year-old clone waited to take his place.

The scene tonight went way beyond anything he had seen the week before.

He quickened his pace, frantically searching for Charlie, praying it wasn't already too late. Turning the corner, round the side of a twelve-foot pile of bales, he found him.

Charlie lay on his front, splay-legged across a single bale of hay, surrounded by three grinning strangers. Charlie was naked expect for his work boots and a pair of small white briefs. The seat of his briefs had been split, revealing his delicious brown hole. Someone had taken a marker pen and scrawled across the remaining white cotton 'FUCK THIS' with an arrow pointing to his anus. He was blissfully unaware of Dale's presence.

One of the men had his fingers in Charlie's arse, twisting his hand, delving in and out.

'Come on, man,' Charlie said, wriggling his butt. 'I'm counting on you guys to loosen me up for later. Get my hole open.'

The man who fingered him thrust deeper. Charlie arched his back, flexing the panther tattoo. The other two men busied themselves with a string of balls. The silver spheres were roughly the size of a golf ball and there were five of them on a thick black string, approximately three inches apart. They lubed up each of the silver balls. Dale watched as they began inserting the string into Charlie's arse. The first ball entered. 'Yes!' he cried. One of the men pushed a second ball into his rectum, then a third. Charlie moaned and begged them for the rest. A fourth ball disappeared into his greasy brown hole. One remained.

'Can you take the last one?' one man teased, running his hand over Charlie's arse.

'Yes,' he growled like an animal. 'I want them all. Come on, shove that bastard in me.'

One of the men pushed the last silver ball against his hole. Slowly it disappeared, following its companions into his well-stuffed cavity. A small length of black string dangled from his anus like a tail. The three men leaned over him, stroking his bare skin, kissing him.

Dale felt a surge of jealousy. He cleared his throat and said, 'Charlie.'

Charlie paused, turned, and saw him for the first time. He smiled. 'Could you give us a few minutes alone,' he said to his companions. Reluctantly they rose, looking Dale up and down as they pushed past. He stared back, refusing to be intimidated.

Charlie sat, straddling the bale, and then stood up, brushing strands of straw from his body. There was an excitable tint to his skin, a rosy flush that coloured his face and extended across his chest and shoulders. 'Dale,' he said, taking in his appearance, 'you look amazing. I never had you pegged as a fetish dresser. It suits you.'

'I did it for you.'

'I like it.' Charlie smiled sweetly. 'I spoke to Max. You don't have to worry, he promised to leave you alone tonight.'

'Where is he?'

He shrugged. 'He's around here someplace. He'll find me when he wants me.'

'I want you,' Dale said. He'd waited long enough to say those words.

'You're in luck then, tonight's the big night. The whole world can have me if they want me.' He tossed his head, laughing.

'That's not what I mean,' he said urgently. '*I really want you.*'

Charlie took a step away from him and began brushing down a blanket, pretending he hadn't heard. Dale rushed forward, seizing his arm. 'You don't understand what I'm saying.'

Charlie looked at him. When he spoke his voice was soft and calm. 'I don't think *you* understand what you're saying. You don't know anything about me.'

'I know enough.'

'I'm not for you. This is what? The third, maybe fourth time we've met.'

'That doesn't matter. I'm in love with you.'

His smile faded. '*You're in love with me*? Get real, Dale.'

'I am real,' he insisted. 'I've never felt more real about anyone in my life. Let me show you just what you mean to me.'

Dale turned around, slowly raising his chain vest to reveal the black panther tattoo on his back.

Charlie gasped.

The artwork was painfully fresh, less than four hours old. The skin tissue was raised and swollen, droplets of blood sparkling on top of the black ink. It was an exact replica of the tattoo on Charlie's back.

Charlie stared. 'What? Why have you done this?'

'It's the same as yours,' he said. 'To show you how far I'm prepared to go for you. I can make you so happy, Charlie. I know you're not happy now, with all this.'

'You sound sure of yourself.'

'I'm sure of you,' he said. '*Of us*.'

'There is no us.'

'But there can be. I've got a good job and a nice apartment – it's small but it will do for now. We could get something better later on. You'll love it in London, there's so much to do, bars and clubs. You'll be in your element.'

Charlie stared. 'You're suggesting I move in with you? That I leave my family and my business for you?'

'I can always move here, of course, but London would be better. It would be a fresh start for you, away from Max. You'd have no problem starting your business again down south.'

'And what about my family? You're forgetting I've got one son and another due.'

'If your family mean so much, then what are you doing here?'

Charlie's face darkened. 'Get out of my way,' he said. 'I've heard enough.'

'Sorry, I didn't mean that the way it came out.'

'I'm not interested.'

The words did not have any effect on Dale, he grabbed Charlie by both arms. 'Please. I mean every word. I love you. Max doesn't care about you, you're just a possession. He's using you for his own kicks. This thing tonight, it's insane. You don't have to let all these men fuck you just to please him.'

Charlie stiffened. 'This was my idea,' he said slowly, as though trying to get a message through to a child. 'When I first brought it up, Max tried to talk me out of it. He didn't push it because he knows how much this means to me. He knows me that well, he understands me. Clearly you don't.'

'But why? You don't have to –'

'I don't have to do anything I don't want. Every dick that's ever gone up my arse has gone there because *I* wanted it to. I've never done anything I didn't want to. My marriage, my son, the baby on the way, Max, my affairs. I want it all, Dale, and I have it all. You couldn't keep me happy for more than a few hours. I'm not interested in your life or your apartment or London. The only thing I care about is your cock, and I've already had that.' He shook his arms free. 'If you still want a piece of me, you can stand in line. There's a room full of men here who are going to fuck my hole to a mushy pulp.'

'You can't want this,' Dale gasped. 'What are you trying to prove?'

Charlie studied him for a long moment. 'That I can do anything I want,' he said simply. 'You're way out of your depth,' he added. 'Go home.'

'Don't do it,' Dale said desperately.

'Goodbye.' Charlie stepped around him. He strode around the bales of hay, full of self-assurance, giving Dale a tantalising glimpse of his meaty rump through his torn briefs.

Desolate, Dale watched him turn the corner. It was over.

He sank onto one of the bales, overwhelmed by a sensation of emptiness. He felt a twinge of pain all through his back from the raw tattoo, but this pain was nothing next to what he was feeling in his heart. He wanted to scream, but the emotion stuck in his throat. He sat forward, putting his head in his hands.

He'd blown it. Charlie didn't want him. He never had. This whole fucking affair had been a one-sided romance in his head. Had Charlie even given him a thought beyond their brief coupling in the spare room at Luke's place? Or the butt plug session in Sam's storeroom? All Dale meant to him was sex. One more cock for his insatiable hole. Dale had thought about nothing else all week but loving him. *What a fucking idiot.* His limbs trembled. He felt that he was going to be sick. He had to get out.

He rose to his feet.

'It hurts, doesn't it?'

Startled, he looked up. Max was standing in front of him, wearing black leather trousers and boots, his huge arms folded across a bare chest.

'Don't gloat over me,' Dale said angrily.

'Who's gloating?' Max asked. Dale thought he saw a trace of compassion in his emotionless eyes. 'I know exactly how you feel. After eight years I'm almost accustomed to the pain.'

Dale looked at him. For the first time ever he felt an understanding for his tormentor. 'Why do you put up with it?'

'Because I truly love him,' he said slowly. 'I've been in love with Charlie from the day we met, much like you are now. But my love is realistic. I know I can't change him so I haven't tried. You have to love him as he is or not at all. You've underestimated my feelings from the start. Do you think I want to see him fucked by these losers? It breaks my fucking heart. But he always gets what he wants.'

Dale shook his head. 'How can you stand it?'

Max laughed. 'I've had longer to get used to the way he works.'

'I don't understand him. Why is nothing ever enough?'

Max shrugged. 'I have to admire his spirit. Why should he settle for less than what he wants just because everyone else does?'

'For the sake of other people: you, his wife, his kids.'

Max scoffed. 'You didn't care what happened to us, yesterday.'

'I know,' Dale said. 'I'm ashamed of the way I've behaved. I'm sorry. Does she know?'

'Julie? Yes, she knew what Charlie was like before she married him.'

'So why do it?'

'Julie's like me, she has the stamina for him.'

Dale shook his head. 'I'll never understand it. I couldn't live with anyone on those terms. If you make a commitment, it should be just that. Maybe the sex is not so important, but the commitment to each other is.'

'He's still married to her, isn't he? How much more committed could he be?'

'But what about this?'

'What? The Chain? Three or fours nights a month. If I'm lucky, I get to see him two or three times too. The rest of the time he's either at work or with Julie and the boy. He doesn't spend his weekends in the pub, she doesn't lose him to football and he doesn't gamble. When Charlie's not here or with me, he's with his family. Julie and the boy are lucky to have a man like him around.'

'Funny idea of luck.'

'I wish I'd been so lucky and had a father a fraction as loving and caring as that boy is.'

Dale shook his head. 'No. I refuse to believe this. If he was such a good dad and a happy husband, he wouldn't need to fuck around the way he does. You can't make me see it otherwise.'

'Fair enough. What are you going to do now?'

'There's nothing I can do. He doesn't want to know me and I don't want to watch this sick spectacle. I'm going home. I'll probably catch the train to London tomorrow.'

Max nodded. 'Wise. I wish we'd known each other under better circumstances. Maybe this wouldn't have been so strained.'

'See you around,' he said, moving to go.

'Hang on a minute.' Max stepped sideways, blocking his exit. 'Charlie told me about the tattoo. Can I see?'

He gave a weary laugh. 'God, the tattoo. Of the all the stupid things...' He turned his back to Max, raising the hem of his vest to display the skin art.

'Nice,' said Max. 'They did a good job.'

'Just as well, now I have to live with it.'

Max grabbed his arms. Dale felt cold metal against his wrists. It happened too fast. His wrists were bound behind his back in handcuffs.

'What the fuck are you doing?' he shouted, pulling at the cuffs. 'Let me out of these.' He twisted and tugged, trying desperately to get free but at the same time aroused.

Max came up fast behind him and slipped something over his head.

'Hey –' Dale's interjection gave Max the opportunity to slip a sturdy rubber gag into his mouth and tie it tight behind his head. A phallic length of rubber filled Dale's mouth.

Max turned him round. Face to face, they eyeballed each other. 'I didn't plan this,' he insisted. 'Charlie always gets what he wants. If you've learned nothing else this week, you should know that much by now.'

Max turned him round and, holding him by the seat of his jeans, quick-marched Dale out of the small alcove. He struggled to remain upright as his feet skimmed the floor. Max marched him over to the middle of the barn where Charlie was hanging on his back in a sling. Half a dozen bales of hay had been stacked beside the sling to form a viewing platform. A couple of younger men were blowing an old black guy on top of it. They scattered as Max approached and he dumped Dale unceremoniously onto the stack. A crowd had gathered around the sling.

Dale's eye level was in line with Charlie's ready arse. While a naked man slowly withdrew the string of metal balls from his rectum, Charlie watched Dale and gasped as each ball was extracted. Two remained. 'I reserved you the best seat in the house,' he called to Dale, 'so you won't miss a thing.'

His sphincter stretched, widened, and another silver ball popped free. Charlie groaned.

'One left,' said the man.

'Pull it out,' he insisted, his eyes shining brightly.

The man made a big show of it, slowly tugging at the string until Charlie's arsehole bulged, offering a glimpse of metal. He tugged harder, exposing more metal. The hole expanded. The audience cheered encouragement until, with a final yank, the ball popped free. Dale stared at Charlie's hole through the tear in his underpants – it looked loose and wet, ready for anything.

Max held Dale's head in a gloved hand, forcing him to watch. A line had already begun to form, condom wrappers were torn, lube applied. The first man to step up to the sling was Big Harry, the colossal doorman. He was naked, apart from his boots. He had a massive piece of meat, topped with a blunt mushroom head.

'Come on, Harry,' Charlie said. 'Get this party started.'

As Big Harry stepped into place, his huge, hairy arse obscured Dale's view of Charlie. It was obvious from the forward thrust of Big Harry's buttocks and Charlie's cry of 'Oh yes!' that he had entered. There were cheers of encouragement from round the barn.

'Fuck him, Harry!'

'Give the bastard what he wants!'

The beary man's hips began to hump, long and deep thrusts that caused his fat arse to wobble. His body, from his neck to his ankles, was covered in hair. Dale could smell his sweaty scent from his position on the hay bale.

'Come on, you fucker,' Charlie moaned, 'fuck me. I can take it harder than that. Fuck me, you big bastard!'

Big Harry's hips increased their speed as he built up a more intense rhythm. He grunted and groaned to a very noisy orgasm. When Big Harry pulled out, Dale caught slight of Charlie's hole before the second guy entered. Although it clamped shut when Harry withdrew, it was starting to be stretched.

The line moved slowly, with Max counting up the numbers in Dale's ear. Charlie would not allow anyone to withdraw until they shot their load. Some men came quickly, moments after entering his loose ring, others took their time, hammering his chute for ten to twenty minutes. One guy had already come twice that night, but Charlie wouldn't let him quit until he orgasmed inside his arse. 'Don't think about faking it,' he growled. 'I can always tell.'

He moaned and swore with enthusiasm all through the ordeal, like a professional porn star. Dale watched with a morbid fascination, like a witness at the scene of a car crash, horrified but unable to look away. He thought about the boy he'd come to love over the course of this last week. It was difficult associating that image with the troubled figure he saw now.

'Thirty-two,' Max said. '… Thirty-eight… Forty-seven…'

Charlie was tireless. When the count reached fifty, two of the men lifted him down from the sling and sat him in the lap of a paraplegic guy in a wheelchair. They held Charlie under the arms and thighs and lifted his arse up and down the man's cock until the man groaned and blew a load. Tired of the sling, Charlie lay across the hay bale in front of Dale and the next man mounted him from behind. Saturated with sweat, Charlie looked at Dale and smiled as number sixty, a teenage blond, entered him. He's mad, Dale thought, seeing the crazy glaze in his eyes.

Dale squirmed against the handcuffs. How many hours had passed now?

It went on. Seventy, seventy-one, seventy-two. They were every shape, every age, some were handsome, many were ugly, they all used him ruthlessly. Dale was glad Charlie was facing him now, because although the crazed expression on that face worried him, he did not want to imagine the horrible state of his arsehole. How much damage had been done? Would his ring ever close again? Was he the only man here who cared?

It was too much. This wasn't sex, it was bedlam. No one could enjoy this.

He looked at Charlie's face again. His beauty was distorted by the strain. He bared his teeth like a sick dog, his brow furrowed and the sounds that escaped his throat sounded increasingly like pain more than pleasure. Tears mingled with the sweat that poured down his face.

Dale couldn't stand it any longer. He pulled away from Max, scrambling over the side of the bale. Max grabbed him. Dale reacted instinctually, headbutting the other man. Max stumbled backwards, more from surprise than pain, falling against the man in the wheelchair.

Dale lurched across the floor, shouldering his way through the crowd of spectators. Max followed.

'Stop him,' he shouted, but the men were more interested in watching the climax of Charlie's bizarre endurance test than arresting the wayward slave.

Max reached for him, just missing. Dale kept running. He almost lost his balance on a wet section of the concrete floor, but managed to stay upright. He scanned the route ahead, avoiding obstacles. He had no idea where he was going. His situation was hopeless, he couldn't open doors or call for help, but he refused to quit.

Max rushed him. Dale swerved to avoid him, too late. They collided and went crashing to the hard floor. The impact jarred through his body. Dale tried to get to his feet, but Max had him in a tight lock. He crawled on top of Dale, his weight forcing the breath from him.

'Where do you think you're going?' he taunted, his breath hot against Dale's face. 'You can't go before the end of the show, not when you're the guest at the top of the bill.'

'No way!' He tried to shout but the words were incomprehensible.

'Come on,' Max said, hauling him to his feet. 'Time to get ready for your big finale.'

Dale tried to struggle but Max was stronger. Without the element of surprise he had no chance of escaping him. He was also feeling dizzy from the fall.

Suddenly a fist lashed out and caught Max full in the face. Stunned, he released his hold on Dale.

Sam stood before them, fully dressed, his hands balled into fists. He stared Max down. Dale stumbled towards him, gratefully. Max made a move to follow.

'Forget it,' Sam said, stepping between them.

'Or what?' Max laughed. 'You'll hit me with your handbag?'

'I'll have you thrown out. They've been wanting an excuse to bar you from The Chain for a long time now. You see, Max, you're not as popular as you think you are and most of these guys depend on me for their paraphernalia. I think they'll value my membership more than yours. Then what will happen to your little bitch when he can't get his regular round of dick? He might just run off and find a new daddy who can give him what he wants.'

Max looked like he was about to pounce. He clenched his fists and stared straight into Sam's eyes. Behind them, Charlie's cries of passion had transcended into a frenzied scream: 'Fuccccckkkk mmmeeeee!'

'You deserve each other,' Sam spat. He turned to Dale and led him to the doors, unfastening the gag.

Dale spat out the rubber and breathed gratefully through his mouth. He turned to look behind. Max stood where he was, watching them leave. He did not attempt to follow. Further down the barn, Dale caught his last glimpse of Charlie, still bent over the hay bale, his head thrown back in a scream while the eighty-third participant ground his dick into his arse.

Seventeen

BREAKING THE CHAIN

Sam found a key on a hook behind Big Harry's counter that opened the handcuffs. 'These things are pretty standard,' he explained. 'One key usually fits all.'

Dale nodded, rubbing his red wrists, expecting they would bruise by the morning. 'Thanks,' he sighed.

Sam ducked into the cloakroom, returning moments later with Dale's leather jacket. 'Put this on,' he said. 'I'll take you home.'

As they stepped out into the clear night, Dale breathed deeply, clearing the scent of sex from his nostrils; the scent of The Chain. 'I feel numb,' he said expressionlessly.

Sam put his arm around Dale's shoulder and led the way through the darkness to his car. They didn't pass anybody else. Once inside, he opened all the windows, turned off the stereo and executed a three-point turn in the dirt road to drive away from The Chain.

'I'm never going back to that place,' he said, shooting a sideways glance at Dale. 'It's the end for both of us.'

Dale nodded, his eyes drooping with fatigue.

'Are you all right?' Sam asked softly.

He shrugged. 'I have no idea. Thank you for getting me out of there. I couldn't have gone through with the thing they wanted of me. How could I fuck him after all those guys? What do you think will happen?' Despite everything, he was still worried about Charlie.

'I don't know. He'll be sore. He might need a doctor. His arse was pretty swollen, the last I saw of it. I don't know, maybe it can heal on its own. I'm sure he'll be okay. Charlie knows more about this than we do. Once the high wears off, he'll know how to look after himself.'

'Can I stay at your place tonight?' he asked slowly. 'It's fine if you say no. I've treated you despicably. I just... I don't want to be alone. Not after this.'

'Stay as long as you like.'

A supermarket wagon passed them on the other side of the road, loaded with the first delivery of the day. Dale checked his watch. It was almost five, later than he thought. They had been at The Chain for over eight hours. How much longer would the session continue? He wondered how Charlie would react when he learned they had left and he would be denied his magical total of eighty-six dicks. What difference would it make? It would never be enough for him – next time he'd want eighty-seven, then ninety, one hundred, two hundred. The total would only ever rise. Dale had come to realise the most fundamental difference between Charlie and himself. There was no such thing as enough for Charlie, he could never have too much or go too far. Dale knew when to stop. Charlie would never stop.

After seven days, Dale was calling time on his infatuation.

They drove the rest of the way in silence. Sam directed his car into the underground park beneath his apartment building and they took the lift up to his floor. The violet fingers of dawn were streaking across the sky and the view from the living-room window was magnificent.

Dale went to the bathroom and removed his fetish costume. He stood under the steaming shower for a good ten minutes, washing his hair, trying to eradicate the grime of the last seven days from his pores. He dried himself vigorously and went back into the living room with a large white towel wrapped around his waist.

Sam was sitting on the balcony, his bare feet propped against the railing, smoking a cigarette. He smiled softly as Dale came out to join him.

'This is gorgeous,' he said, inhaling the salty air, oblivious to the cold.

Sam murmured his agreement.

'You should get some sleep,' Dale said. 'You'll be wrecked for work.'

'I'm not going in today,' he said, cigarette smoke curling around his face.

'No?'

'No.'

'What are you going to do?'

'Today? Absolutely nothing. I'm going to sleep late, ignore the telephone and forget all about the Cock Shop. I'll play my set at XL tonight, but the shop stays shut.'

'And then what?'

'You mean tomorrow? The future?'

'Yes?'

He put out his cigarette and gazed at the rising sun. 'I'm going to hire a manager. I've sold as many dildos and butt plugs as I can stand, for now anyway. As soon as I find a man for the job, I'm gonna take a holiday. And when I come back... I'm going to pursue the music, get into DJ-ing full time. I'll travel if I have to. It's about time I got what I wanted for a change.'

'I thought you wanted to settle down and grow old gracefully.'

'Right,' Sam scoffed. 'What would be the point in that? I'm bored enough with this place as it is. Settling down here would drive me mad. I thought, for a few mad days, that you were the answer, that we could give each other what was missing in our lives.'

Dale contemplated what he was saying. 'In theory, we should make a great couple... but in reality...'

'We'd suck.' Sam laughed. 'I see that now. You were my Charlie – a nice idea while it lasted. So what about you? You're not going home to resume your chicken-chasing ways, are you?'

'Not a chance. Boys are off the agenda.'

'I know what you need,' Sam said. 'A daddy.'

They both laughed.

'I'll never forget you,' Dale said, reaching over to stroke the side of Sam's face. 'In a few years I reckon I might look back on this time and curse myself for the choice I've made. Things could be different in another place and time.'

'I know,' Sam nodded. In the natural light of the morning he looked young, fresh faced. 'I'd like to do one thing before you go.'

Dale brushed his fingers over the growth of blond stubble on his cheek. 'Mmm?'

'I want to make love. Like we did last week. Just the two us, in bed, without dildos or poppers or cock rings. Just us.'

He stood up, smiling, holding out his hand. Dale rose, allowing himself to be led to the bedroom. They began kissing at the door. Sam slid his hands to Dale's waist and loosened the knot in his towel. The white towel slipped silently from his clean body. His cock leaned up between them. While they kissed, Sam dipped one hand to the shaft, curling his fingers round its girth, tracking the veins like a blind man with Braille. He gently fingered the fold of skin over the tip, easing it back to release the head. His other hand moved over Dale's arse, cupping the left buttock.

'Take off your clothes,' Dale said, hooking his fingers under Sam's tank top, slowly peeling it off his torso. Sam raised his arms to take it all the way off. Dale seemed to realise for the first time how beautiful a body Sam had. He'd been obsessed with Charlie to the exclusion of this treasure that was beneath his nose the whole time. His hands roamed over furry blond pecs, caressing the sweeping curves. 'Gorgeous,' he murmured, running his tongue along Sam's lush bottom lip.

He unbuckled his belt, pulled down the zipper, and eased his jeans down his thighs. As he realised Sam was still wearing his jockstrap, Dale's hands moved straight to his exposed arse, grasping the fuzzy cheeks. He kneaded and squeezed, dipping his fingers in the hot cleft. He pulled him closer, thrusting his tongue deep into his mouth.

They moved towards the bed. Dale knelt on the floor and pulled Sam's jeans down the rest of the way. Sam sat on the edge of the bed and Dale crawled between his open knees, gripping his thighs. He ran his tongue up his leg, inhaling the musky scent of his jock. He buried his nose into the white cotton, inhaling the smell. Sam raised his hips and slipped the jock down his thighs. 'I want to be as naked as a baby,' he explained as Dale removed the jock the rest of the way.

Sam was wearing a leather cockstrap underneath. He reached under his balls and loosened the stud fastening. His balls sagged lower with the release. His cock stayed just as hard. Dale leaned closer and Sam rubbed his cock across his face. Dale closed his eyes, savouring the heat. He felt a wetness as the tip brushed against his lips. His tongue darted out to taste its sticky trail. He nuzzled Sam's ball sac, pressing his mouth into the loose folds of skin. Sam groaned, dropping back on his elbows, raising his hips. Dale rolled his tongue across the hairy skin. He took the right nut into his mouth and sucked, very gently, then swapped it for the left. When the entire sac was wet, Dale crammed both balls into his mouth.

'Oh, God,' Sam gasped, his knees jerking involuntarily. He lifted his bare feet onto Dale's shoulders and edged his arse forward.

Dale abandoned Sam's nuts, dropping into his arse, sliding his tongue along the rich seam towards his pink pucker. He tickled the rim with his tongue, swirling, poking gently, getting the hole deliciously moist. Sam's anus was beautifully drawn, tight and pink, it couldn't have looked more different to the ruined pulpy mush that was now Charlie's snatch. Dale pushed his tongue into the dark centre, tasting the manly sweat of that crack.

He climbed onto the bed and they lay down side by side, head to groin. Dale sucked Sam's meat into his mouth, swallowing the shaft inch by inch. The organ flexed once it was wedged deep in his throat. He felt Sam's lips work their way down his own dick, forming a tight seal around the shaft, moving back and forth. He grabbed Sam's arse, pulling his cock deeper into his mouth.

Sam spat out Dale's dick. 'I want this in my arse,' he whispered.

Dale wriggled round into position. Sam put the condom on for him, lubing up his dick with long, loving strokes, then lay on his back, stuffing a pillow beneath his hips, wrapping his legs around Dale's torso. Dale lay over him, guiding his cock into position. He held himself at the root until his head had passed the resistance of Sam's sphincter. He held Sam with both hands and pushed in the remainder of the way until his balls pressed against that arse. Sam smiled, looking deep into his eyes. 'Beautiful,' he mouthed.

Dale began to move his hips, just a fraction to begin with, slowly increasing the tempo. Sam wrapped his limbs tight around Dale's frame and opened his body entirely to him, mouth and arse. Dale drove into him, grinding his dick into the offered hole. His hands roamed over Sam's body, gripping the back of his thighs, cupping his arse. Sam opened wider. Their bodies glowed. Sweat trickled down both of their faces, Dale licked a film of perspiration from Sam's upper lip. They groaned gentle encouragement at each other.

Their moderate lovemaking became more intense. Their bodies, consumed with each other, thrashed across the bed. Dale dug his hands into the covers and the mattress creaked loudly beneath them. 'I want you to come while I'm fucking you,' he groaned.

Sam nodded, wide eyed. He grabbed his dick and started pulling, taking his palm over the head. He began panting desperately. His face twisted, baring strong white teeth. 'Aaaaaaarrrrghhhhh! Yeeeeesssssss!' Dale felt the blast strike his stomach, hot and strong. Sam cried in ecstasy, blasting his load across his belly and chest. Dale leaned over him, trapping Sam's cock between their bellies, smearing his come over their skin. Sam's arse tightened and Dale started coming quickly. He roared as his load began pulsing out, filling the condom inside Sam's arse. Gripping him tight, Dale buried his head into Sam's shoulder as his cock continued spurting in the tight confinement of that hole.

He pushed back onto his elbows when it ended, still inside him. They looked at each other, grinning. Sam lifted his head and Dale kissed him deeply.

The Newbiggin Bay railway station is small with only two platforms. It is situated on a hill above the town, with an astounding vista of the Northeast coast. For the delayed traveller, the station offers little entertainment or amusement. On Friday morning Dale sat with Sam on a small red bench on platform two, awaiting the late arrival of the eleven-thirty train to King's Cross. Although it was another mild day, the high location of the station brought a cold wind whistling along the platform. They drank so-so cups of coffee from the vending machine beside the cigarette kiosk to keep warm.

There were twenty or so other passengers waiting for the southbound train, killing time with newspapers and magazines.

Dale's bags were on the ground beside the bench. He'd said goodbye to Luke and Paul over breakfast that morning, amid much hugging and kissing.

Luke promised to visit him later in the year. 'We were thinking of coming down to London for Paul's birthday,' he said.

'You'd better come and stay with me,' Dale warned.

'Promise,' Luke said, hugging his college friend again. 'I feel guilty that I haven't been able to spend more time with you this week. We've left you to fend for yourself. It's not right.'

'I survived,' Dale assured him. 'If I hadn't had so much time on my own I would never have learned half of what I did.' He thanked them for letting him stay. 'It didn't seem like it to begin with, but this trip has been exactly what I needed. I feel like I'm going home a changed man.'

Now Sam was telling him about the Cock Shop; he'd promoted his assistant Stuart to temporary manager until a permanent replacement could be found.

'How much time are you planning to take off?'

'I might never go back,' Sam said, sounding like he was serious. 'I've made a list of all the things I want to do before I'm thirty and I intend to take my time working through it. The Cock Shop will have to survive without me.'

'What do you have on your list?'

'Loads of silly things: go on holiday, read more books, play more gigs, start learning another language. It all adds up to one thing – fun.'

'That sounds like a good list. It's a pity I'm thirty-three, I could have done with something similar myself.'

'So make a list for your thirty-fourth or thirty-fifth. It's never too late to enjoy yourself.' They both laughed. Sam bowed his head, looking at the track. 'Charlie's okay,' he said, brushing imaginary dust from his jeans. 'Physically, at least.'

'Have you seen him?'

'No, I heard from a friend of a friend from The Chain. He called me last night. I didn't know whether to tell you or not.'

'I made a fool of myself,' Dale sighed. 'I can't pretend it didn't happen.'

Sam went on. 'There was a fight on Tuesday, after we left. Max went berserk. He smashed the place up and started laying into the guys who were there. A few people got hurt, some bones were broken. They say he hit Charlie.'

'Shit!'

'It didn't last long,' Sam explained. 'Max is a hard bastard but there are worse. He picked a fight with Big Harry and ended up in hospital. Some of the other guys took Charlie home.'

'And he's all right?'

'As all right as he'll ever be. I don't think he'll be down for long. Max is barred from The Chain, so we'll have to wait and see what happens there.'

'Or rather, we won't,' Dale said.

Sam grinned. 'Some people don't change. Unlike us.'

An announcement came over the speakers that the train would arrive in a few minutes. Dale felt a jolt of emotion in his chest, knowing that this might be the last he'd ever see of Sam. 'If I come back to visit,' he said, standing up and gathering his bags together, 'you might not be here.'

'No,' Sam said. 'It's highly likely I won't. But you can always ask around – XL, Cock Shop, someone will know where to find me.'

Dale nodded. There was a moment of silence in which their eyes came together. Dale dropped his bags and opened his arms. They embraced tightly. Dale felt a strange urge to cry but held the emotion in check. People were watching them but he didn't care.

When they separated, Sam reached inside his jacket and handed Dale a gift-wrapped box, about six inches long. 'Memento from the Cock Shop,' he smiled. 'Open it on the train.'

Dale smiled warmly and slipped it into his pocket. 'I will miss you,' he said, sincerely meaning it.

The train pulled into the station. Sam helped him carry his bags onto the carriage. Then suddenly it all seemed like such a hurry. The stationmaster blew his whistle. Sam jumped back down onto the platform, closing the door.

Dale pushed down the small window, leaning out. 'Thanks for everything. I hope this isn't the last I'll see of you. Good luck with everything you do.'

The train began to pull away.

'Goodbye.' Sam waved solemnly. He said something else, but his words were overpowered by the noise of the departing engine.

'Take care of yourself,' Dale shouted back. He stood at the window waving until the train turned a bend and Sam and Newbiggin were stolen from sight. He took a deep breath, closing the window.

Dale consulted his ticket and carried his bags down the carriage to his seat number. Thankfully, the carriage was only half full and he had a double seat and table to himself. He contemplated the journey home and remembered something Eddie had said to him earlier in the week, about how good it was to go home. He appreciated the sentiment more now than he had then. He was returning home on his own, but with a sense of optimism he had not felt in years.

He remembered Sam's parting gift and took it out of his pocket. There was a note attached. In a mature hand Sam had written: *Something to remember until that other time and place.*

Dale smiled softly and unwrapped the present. Inside he found a medium-sized black rubber butt plug and a sachet of lube. He looked down the carriage to the far end where a vacant sign was illuminated above the toilets. Thinking of the three-hour journey ahead, he slipped out of his seat with Sam's present tucked under his arm, and headed for the narrow stall.